# A LEGEND of STARFIRE

Also by Marissa Burt

*Storybound*

*Story's End*

*A Sliver of Stardust*

# MARISSA BURT

# A LEGEND of STARFIRE

**HARPER**

*An Imprint of HarperCollinsPublishers*

A Legend of Starfire

Copyright © 2016 by Marissa Burt

All rights reserved. Printed in the United States of America.
No part of this book may be used or reproduced in any manner
whatsoever without written permission except in the case of
brief quotations embodied in critical articles and reviews. For
information address HarperCollins Children's Books, a division of
HarperCollins Publishers, 195 Broadway, New York, NY 10007.
www.harpercollinschildrens.com

Library of Congress Control Number: 2016939552
ISBN 978-0-06-229158-5

Typography by Alison Klapthor
16 17 18 19 20   CG/RRDH   10 9 8 7 6 5 4 3 2 1

First Edition

*For the captives*

# ONE

*Oh where, oh where has my magic gone?*
*Oh where, oh where can it be?*
*When the dust won't spin,*
*And the stars won't sing,*
*Oh where, oh where can it be?*

Wren Matthews held the pile of stardust in her palm. Sweat beaded on her forehead as she willed it to do something . . . anything. Her fingers wouldn't cooperate, and their trembling threatened to humiliate her in front of all the other Fiddler apprentices. Boys and girls—most of them older than Wren—filled the stone benches that ringed the Crooked House's amphitheater, and every single one of them was staring at Wren.

Wren rarely wished that she were an ordinary girl,

someone who couldn't see stardust or work magic, but lately she had been daydreaming about what that would be like. If she wasn't an Alchemist, she would be at home in her room, working on a chart of the con- stellations or watching one of her favorite sci-fi shows. There would be no Crooked House full of Fiddlers who could see and manipulate the magic of stardust. No apprentice lessons to teach her to use stardust rhymes. No failures at falcon riding. And none of the strange events of the last few months would have hap- pened. There would be no nightmares where the evil Fiddler Boggen tried to manipulate her. No discovery that Boggen and his allies had colonized another planet and were now trying to return to Earth. No betrayal by her good friend Jack, who had been secretly work- ing to help Boggen. No adventures. No Fiddlers. No falcons. No stardust. No magic.

But Wren was an apprentice Fiddler, and all of those things had happened. And other, unforeseen things were still happening. No matter how hard she tried to hide it, her ability to use the magical stardust was becoming unpredictable.

The little pile of dust in her hand flared up in a flash of rainbow colors, and for one hopeful moment

Wren thought she might actually succeed in working the magic. Then the stardust turned a sickly purple and fell in on itself with a rush, returning to a stagnant pile. Wren took a deep breath and started over for the third time, trying to ignore the whispers between the apprentices nearest her.

"Wren killed Boggen," murmured a boy in the front row.

"I don't believe it," said an older girl who had probably never noticed Wren's existence before the rumors had started flying. "That girl defeated the evilest Magician in centuries? Doubtful."

"*And* she kept him from returning to Earth." The boy's voice grew animated. "Didn't you hear what happened at the gateway? How she saved Jack's life?"

"So she claims." The older girl snorted. "No one has seen Jack in weeks. He's been shut up in the infirmary. How are we to know that Wren didn't make the whole thing up?"

Wren's ears burned hot, and a puff of stardust escaped from her fingers. She could hardly blame the girl for doubting her. Based on how Wren had been performing in her apprentice lessons, it was a wonder that anyone believed she could even work magic with the stardust, let alone her story about the gateway.

"But she's a Weather Changer." The boy probably thought he was far enough away to be discreet, or maybe he simply didn't care if Wren overheard.

Wren gritted her teeth. She would be happy if she never heard the phrase *Weather Changer* again. Being one had brought her nothing but trouble. At first, she could hardly touch the stardust without bringing on a thunderstorm or warping into a dream world where she saw things she didn't understand. But that had all been before the gateway. What had happened there had changed everything, and now Wren was lucky to feel anything at all from the stardust.

She tried again, adding another pinch of stardust, her face growing even hotter as she spilled nearly half of it on the ground. She heard the older girl's scornful laughter mixed in among other voices.

"Not a problem, not a problem, Wren, dear. Take your time." Fiddler Elsa swooped toward Wren, her narrow face crimped with a pleasant expression that looked strangely out of place. The Mistress of Apprentices wasn't known for her smiles, but she had done little else since Wren's return: smile and have extra food sent to Wren's room, smile and give her lighter apprentice work duties, and smile some more. Since Boggen, who was responsible for the deaths of many of Elsa's loved ones, had finally been defeated, Elsa seemed determined to replace her infamous angry demeanor with cheerfulness. One good thing about this turn of events was that Elsa's apprentice Jill was no longer miserable. "Elsa's like a completely different person," Jill had said recently. "I think hearing about Boggen's death has worked its own magic on her." Wren could see her friend out of the corner of her eye. Jill was sitting on the edge of her seat, giving Wren a sympathetic look.

Elsa laid a hand on Wren's shoulder. Her words came out stiffly, like she was controlling each syllable. "May I help?"

"I've got it," Wren said hastily, dodging what she supposed Elsa meant to be a motherly pat. Wren began the rhyme again, whispering the words and tracing the pattern in the air. Embarrassment over her failure and dislike for Elsa warred within her. Why were they all sitting here anyway? What was the point of group apprentice lessons when the world as they knew it might be changed forever? Wren wanted to drop the stardust and jump on a seat and shout it out: "Space travel, you guys! We can freaking fly through outer space, and we're sitting here learning how to light a fire with stardust? *We have matches for that!*"

But she swallowed it all down and instead tried to focus on the stardust rhyme. As she did so, the tiniest breeze drifted in from the cavern's open balcony. A small spark flashed in Wren's hand, and her heart quickened. Perhaps the rhyme was going to work after all.

The stardust flared to life, but with it came the searing memory of the fight at the gateway. Of the sick, tainted rhyme that nearly killed Jack and did away with Boggen. Of Jack's lifeless body on the floor, and the moment when Wren had to funnel all her stardust into his body to jolt him back to life. The memories came like flashes, and when they had passed, Wren stood in the middle of the auditorium, empty-handed, her stardust settling at her feet.

"I'll do it." Simon leaped out of his seat in the front row, scooped up some of the lost stardust, and shaped it expertly into the formation needed to work the magic. Wren was torn between relief that Simon was taking over and irritation at his interference. Simon was her best friend, but it hadn't always been that way. Back in their former life, before Wren and Simon knew about the stardust, before they had learned they could work magic, before Fiddler Mary had recruited them to come join the other Fiddlers at the Crooked House, she and Simon had been rivals in every science competition eleven-year-old homeschooled kids could enter. Even now, after they had been through so much together, Wren was still irked that he was trying to tell her what to do.

"Breathe, Wren. Just breathe," Simon whispered before transferring the stardust into her palms. Wren repositioned herself, flexing her wrists in a circle. She had learned that these small physical movements helped control her emotional response to the stardust and the resulting dramatic changes in the weather. "Do you want me to work the whole rhyme? Maybe you should rest," Simon whispered again.

Wren glared at him and said through clenched teeth, "I've got it." As happy as she was to have someone who she knew wholeheartedly believed in her, Simon's unsolicited advice could be really annoying. What made it worse was that all the gossip and pointing fingers didn't seem to bother him at all. He got his fair share, of course, once everyone had learned how Simon had courageously risked his own life to help Wren thwart Boggen, but every time someone whispered about him, Simon remained unruffled, like a serene pond of water. Wren wished she had a cup of water handy to dump over his red head. Maybe that would get a rise out of him.

A blast of cold wind blew in from outside, and Wren caught herself just in time. She was letting the magic get the best of her again. That was what was so tricky about being a Weather Changer—it took whatever small feelings were there inside her and magnified them out of control. Wren might be annoyed with Simon, but she didn't really want to douse him. She tucked her hair hard behind her ears, pulling on the ends a little to rein herself in, and willed herself to focus. Maybe it was a good sign that her emotions were affecting the weather. Maybe the stardust would actually respond this time. Wren took the glowing stardust from Simon. He gave her a reassuring nod before stepping back to give her space, but Wren didn't need any more of Simon's encouragement. She had already regained control, shutting down the memories and feelings as though she were capturing them in a little box with a lid that snapped shut. She had seen firsthand what happened when Jack hadn't respected the power of stardust, and she, for one, would never let it catch her unawares again.

"Notice how Wren channels the stardust's energy," Elsa was saying, that painful-looking grin still plastered on her face. She pointed to the air in front of Wren, where Wren had worked the stardust into a tight funnel. "Excellent," Elsa breathed.

Wren felt a little bead of sweat run down her forehead. It most definitely wasn't excellent. Wren would be lucky if she could keep the stardust swirling long enough to say the rhyme. And apparently, she wasn't the only one who knew it.

"Rubbish." Baxter's voice boomed from the entranceway. "That's the shoddiest attempt at a fire-starting rhyme I've seen in my entire life."

For the second time that lesson, Wren lost most of the stardust, as Baxter came over and snatched it from her palm. He directed a calm-as-ever Simon toward his empty seat. "Come now, Elsa," he said. "Apprentices teaching apprentices? That isn't quite the thing. Besides, Fiddler Mary has requested that Wren come before the Council." A hushed whisper ran around the class, and Wren's whole body went rigid. Being called before the Fiddler Council was the last kind of attention she needed. She had met with the Council often after her return, for of course they wanted to hear every detail of what had happened at the gateway, but it had been at least a month since she had spoken with them all together. *Why do they want to see me now?*

Elsa managed a frigid nod in Baxter's direction, as though she had planned this interruption all along. "Ah, Fiddler Baxter. We'll be happy for you to share your expertise with us." She turned to Wren with an even frostier expression. "Run along, then. You don't want to keep *them* waiting." She beckoned Jill to follow. "Go with her in case the Council has a message for me." Wren could tell by the way Elsa forced out the words that she was angry. Any more talk of the Fiddler Council would likely set her off. Now that Mary had taken back her rightful place on the Council, Elsa had been edged out. Wren almost felt sorry for her.

Wren rubbed the sleeve of her apprentice cloak over her forehead as she and Jill made their way out of the amphitheater. The back of her head continued to burn with the heat of dozens of apprentices' gazes even once she was far out of view. "Are you okay?" Concern was evident in Jill's voice, but Wren tried to ignore it. She hadn't told her friend about her trouble with the fickle stardust, but surely Jill had noticed. Now the fact that

Wren was keeping something from her sat awkward and heavy between them. Iridescent blue waves glimmered as they walked across the weathered wooden bridge over the Opal Sea that flowed through the main cavern of the Crooked House. Wren wanted nothing more than for the entire day to be over so she could escape back to the solitude of her room.

"I'm fine," Wren said, and then forced a laugh. "If you call having an audience wherever you go 'fine.'" Curious faces were turning to watch her and Jill as they made their way through the Crooked House. Over the past few months, Fiddlers had been arriving from around the globe, and the abandoned wings of the Crooked House were hurriedly being cleaned and polished and restored.

Fiddlers who had spent years tucked away in laboratories now congregated in open spaces that echoed with heated conversations. Wren ducked her head as she passed one such group, hoping to avoid notice. The ones allied with Cole and Mary and the rest of the Council were easy to spot. They would come up to Wren or shake her hand or congratulate her on a job well done.

And then there were the others. The ones who

looked at Wren suspiciously and seemed to think the reemergence of the Magician threat was her fault. For many years they had believed that Boggen and all their other Magician enemies had been destroyed at the end of the Fiddler Civil War, but recent events had proven otherwise, and now they had the threat of a whole colony of Magicians to deal with. She understood how this might be hard for them to accept, but not how they could blame her, as though her traveling to the gateway had somehow created the problem rather than simply revealed the truth. These Alchemists were the militant ones, the Fiddlers whose conversations were punctuated with conspiracy theories and plans to go to Nod and finish the Civil War once and for all. As Wren drew near the stone stairs that led down to the Council's meeting chamber, she could see such a group of Fiddlers, clustered around the kiosks that stood outside the oldest laboratories, men and women whose voices dropped as she drew near, their cool stares quickening her pace. *Definitely the unfriendly type.*

Baxter had told her to ignore them. But then Baxter was the only grown-up who seemed to tell her anything. He had practically taken over Mary's old job as Wren and Simon's tutor. Liza was too busy tending to

Jack, and Mary was endlessly occupied with Council business. Business that was about to involve Wren.

"—this is my last afternoon here, can you believe it?"

Wren gathered her thoughts. Jill had been saying something, something Wren should have been paying attention to. Her friend's expectant look turned into a frown accompanied by the awkwardness that was becoming all too common between them.

"Last afternoon?" Wren echoed. "You were saying . . . ?"

"I get to leave this place!" Jill nearly skipped down the stone stairs.

*Of course!* Wren had been so preoccupied with her own problems that she had forgotten her friend was leaving the Crooked House. Jill had taken advantage of Elsa's newfound kindness and persuaded her to let Jill experience some of the outside world. An internship of sorts. At Wren's house. Wren's parents had loved the idea of having a Fiddler foreign exchange student, and now Wren almost envied Jill, who was about to embark on her big adventure of settling in to Wren's old room and sitting in the kitchen eating pizza with Wren's parents and doing the hundred daily things Wren used to do while checking in on Pippen Hill, which had been abandoned now that Mary, Baxter, and Liza were all needed at the Crooked House.

"I know you'll have a great time," Wren said. "My parents are so excited for you to visit." Wren thought of the last day she had seen her parents. Her dad had given her a tight hug, telling her not to work too hard on her studies. "Your subconscious has a lot to deal with, Little Bird," her dad had told her in what he probably meant to be a reassuring voice. "Give yourself some time." What Wren thought he meant was that *his* subconscious had a lot to deal with. Her dad and mom had stayed at the Crooked House the first few weeks while Wren recovered from her encounter with Boggen, sitting stiffly whenever anyone entered Wren's sickroom, and gaping openly at the empty air when Fiddlers used stardust. They couldn't see it, but they knew now what Wren was. It was a lot to wrap their minds around. It had been Mary who had finally encouraged them to go home. She explained how unusual it was to have non-Fiddlers at the Crooked House, that in fact it went against Fiddler law, and perhaps Wren would best be able to recover if she occupied herself with her studies.

Wren's mom had been all hovering and anxious. "Are you sure you don't want us to stay?" she asked about a million times on their final day in the Crooked House. Wren was absolutely positive she couldn't sit through another tortured stare-fest with her parents. She supposed she could handle the whispers and looks from everyone else in the Crooked House, but not from them. And suspending her studies was out of the question. Wren wouldn't even entertain the thought, and neither would her parents. Wren was proud of them for that. So with a promise to visit home at Christmastime, she had said good-bye to them, but now she wondered if she hadn't been too quick to send them away.

"Did I tell you that Simon gave me one of his notebooks to bring with me?" Jill said. "He told me to record all of my first impressions. Said it would make for an interesting cultural study."

"That sounds like Simon," Wren said with a laugh.

The staircase ended, depositing Wren in a chilly stone hallway framed by arched ceilings that led toward an imposing wood door at the end. Another apprentice Fiddler was seated behind a table, looking importantly at his clipboard.

"Does the Council have any messages for Fiddler Elsa?" Jill asked, though both she and Wren knew what the answer would be.

The apprentice shook his head and then peered over his clipboard at them. "Wren Matthews? You're wanted inside." He held out a hand to forestall Jill. "Only Wren Matthews."

Jill gave Wren a quick hug. "In case I don't see you before I go."

"Two weeks will go by before you know it," Wren said in return. While she would miss her friend, she wouldn't miss having to hide her magic problems from someone close to her. Soon Jill was skipping back up the stairs and Wren was left to make the long walk down the hall to the intimidating door alone. When she reached it, Wren hesitated, overcome by a foreboding sense that once she walked through that door, things would never be the same again. But before she could compose her thoughts, she heard a familiar rustle, and the gentlest sound of unearthly music—of hollow wind and whispered song—a sound she hadn't heard since right before the gateway. *Wren,* a voice said. *Enter.* And the heavy door swung open all on its own.

# TWO

*Along came a spider*
*And crawled up beside her*
*And frightened the poor girl away.*

Inside the Council Chamber, the members of the Fiddler Council were seated at an ancient-looking round table. Beyond them, one of the Crooked House's wide-open balconies stretched out into the clear afternoon sky. Silhouetted against the cerulean blue were the tall winged silhouettes of the Ashes. In the daylight, their feathers looked like a rainbow of shadows, blacks and grays layering up to the domed ceiling of the room.

*Wren.* The voices of the Ashes reverberated inside her chest. *Welcome.*

Beyond the Ashes, birds wheeled and circled above the balcony.

"You're here!" Wren gasped, feeling the same warmth and sense of well-being she had felt the last time she had seen the Ashes.

"Of course we're here," Mary said, giving Wren a confused look. "Have a seat, please." She gestured to the open space near Cole, whose ever-present falcon was shifting on his shoulder.

*The Council members do not see us,* the Ashes told Wren. *Only you and the other Dreamer. Do not tell them what you see.*

Cole gave Wren a knowing look as his falcon settled in to roost.

"The Weather Changer finally joins us," Fiddler William said. "Perhaps now we can get to the business at hand?" He stroked his neatly trimmed white beard with long fingers and watched Wren as though she were a dessert he would like to gobble up. Baxter had told her that William claimed to be fascinated with Weather Changers and had been begging the Council to let him observe Wren. She hated to imagine what it would be like to be his research project.

Next to William sat Astrid. She was the official Fiddler record keeper. She said little but recorded every important decision in the thick square book that dominated the surface of the table. Astrid flipped a page over and sat with her pen poised, ready to write down all the details.

William took out a pocket watch and studied it with a sigh. "Might we hurry things along? I have important research to tend to."

Cole gave him a level look. "No research is more important than this." He looked respectfully at the Ashes then, but to the others it must have appeared that he was gazing out onto the balcony.

Wren heard only the sound of rustling feathers, but it seemed as though Cole was somehow dialoguing with the mysterious creatures. She wondered if he was hearing that warm voice reverberating inside, and if perhaps the Ashes spoke to each of them as individuals.

The conversation apparently finished, Cole leaned forward intently, the falcon perched on his shoulder responding to his sudden movement with an impatient squawk. "The Ashes have visited me with a dire warning. Jack's attempt to force open the gateway has proved harmful not only to himself. The entire gateway is now corrupted." He ran his palm over the falcon. "The same taint that nearly killed Jack is spreading through the galaxy. If we don't act quickly, the corruption will soon reach Earth's stardust as well."

Wren thought of how the sickly bruise-colored stardust had pierced Jack in that awful moment at the gateway. She remembered the force of it, the way it seemed to suck the very life out of her friend. "What will happen if it does?"

"We don't want to find out," Cole said calmly. "The Ashes warn us that the corrupted stardust has long afflicted the colony on Nod, nearly destroying life on the planet." Cole went on to describe the way in which the vegetation had been scoured and the animal life damaged, but his words faded to a muted rhythm.

*Wren.* The Ashes were speaking to her, and she felt as if the feathers on their wings were a thousand eyes penetrating to the very depths of her soul. *You must cleanse the stardust.*

*Me?* Wren thought. *What can I do?* She felt a wave of desolation as she considered how she could barely manage a stardust rhyme during her apprentice lessons, let alone stop something that had the power to damage an entire planet. *I'm sorry, Ashes, but you've got the wrong person,* she thought as her cheeks flushed with the shame of failure. *I can barely get the stardust to work anymore.*

*This task requires not stardust, but starfire.* The words echoed forebodingly in her mind. *Weather Changers alone can wield starfire.* The words fell like a stone sending ripples through water, and as the Ashes spoke, Wren realized that this was why Boggen had wanted her in the first place. This was why he'd wanted a Weather Changer on Nod.

*But how will I know what to do?* Wren thought.

*The Crooked Man will reveal all in due time.* The feathered rustling of the Ashes faded with these words, and Wren knew that their conversation was nearly at an end.

*Who is the Crooked Man?* she thought. *And where can I find him?* But only the barest whisper of fluttering wings answered her.

"I can't do this," she said, aloud this time, and the other members of the Fiddler Council stopped midconversation. Even Astrid paused her meticulous note-taking to study Wren silently. When Wren glanced back over to the balcony, she saw that the Ashes were gone.

"Ha!" William barked. "The Weather Changer balks." He looked triumphantly at Cole and Mary. "I told you we should have kept this information from her. In my experience, subjects of research respond best when they know as little information as possible."

Mary waved away William's words with an annoyed expression. "Wren is as capable as any full Fiddler. Besides, interstellar travel is not something we could keep from her for long."

Wren looked from Fiddler to Fiddler. "Interstellar travel? You mean . . . ?"

Cole placed a large, intricately cut golden gem on the table in front of him. "The Ashes delivered the gateway key to me. With their help we will cleanse the taint."

Wren stared at the beautiful key, which seemed to shimmer with a light all its own. She hadn't seen it since it had fallen from Jack's hands into outer space.

"We leave for the gateway before dawn," Cole continued. "Gather clothes for the journey and any other supplies you want to bring." The urgency in Cole's voice made Wren feel like leaping up and obeying immediately.

"And while we may be telling you about our quest," Mary said, "you must keep it a secret from everyone else. The Crooked House is already riddled with division between those who want to make peaceful contact with the colony on Nod and those who want to pick up right where the Civil War left off. Hearing about a trip to the gateway would be like a spark on a pile of dry grass. The whole thing will go up in flames."

Wren nodded slowly. She could see Mary's point. She could only guess what the Fiddlers who whispered that she was somehow in league with the Magicians would do if they found out she was traveling once again to the gateway between Earth and Nod. A thought struck her. "But we won't be opening it." She looked worriedly between Mary and Cole. "Right?"

"No. Not in the foreseeable future, at least. Right now, we need a Weather Changer to cleanse it before Nod's corruption spreads to Earth," Mary said, sharing an uneasy look with Cole. "There are troubled days ahead, I'm afraid, but we won't consider opening the gateway until we've reached a peaceful decision as a Council and are prepared to lead the Crooked House into any negotiations with the Magicians."

William shifted impatiently in his chair. "There are other things to discuss. Like my research of subject number thirteen?" Wren could almost see William's too-shiny eyes staring at some poor creature and his too-long fingers poking at its body.

Mary stiffened in her chair. "Research with Fiddler subjects is forbidden by Council Law. You know that, William, and no amount of discussion will change the matter."

"But number thirteen hardly qualifies as a Fiddler now, does he?"

Wren shivered. She wondered who number thirteen was. No one should have to be William's research subject.

"Enough, William," Cole said, and his gaze flared with animosity toward William before his countenance settled into his usual calm collectedness. "You may leave us now," he said to Wren. "Get some sleep. Be ready two hours past midnight."

After that, the Council members focused on each other, discussing the supplies they would need for the journey. Wren paused at the door for a moment, looking out on the clear blue sky. Somewhere up there was the gateway, waiting for her to do whatever she was supposed to do. However she was supposed to do it. She smothered a desperate laugh. It seemed to her like the Ashes had made a terrible mistake.

She told Simon as much when she found him in the library later and recounted what had happened in the Council Chamber. She had ignored the twinge of guilt for disregarding Mary's instruction for secrecy. Surely Mary hadn't meant that she should keep the trip a secret from *Simon*.

"This is incredible," Simon said, shoving aside the tome he had been reading to scribble frantically in his notebook. "You are going to have to take notes on everything you see. You'll be more aware of your environment this time, and you'll be able to—"

"Simon." Wren cut him off. "Don't you get it? I won't be able to do anything if I can't work the stardust. Or the starfire, or whatever it is."

Simon paused, chewing his pencil. "You're right. We need to do some preliminary research." He squinted at the pocket watch that he always kept in his vest pocket. "We have the rest of the afternoon and evening to study." He jumped up, muttering about which section would most likely house books on the Crooked Man and Weather Changers. Wren followed after him, but she felt tired. Something had gone wrong inside of her. Something that kept her from using the stardust. She doubted anything in the library could fix that.

When Wren dreamed that night, she knew immediately that she was in Nod. The landscape in front of her had no color, just shadows of black and gray. The air felt different, colder somehow, and unwelcoming. She stood on a flat plain that looked as though it had been cleared by a forest fire. Beyond, she could see what must have once been a sizable city. Singed piles of clay bricks littered the streets, which ran in narrow grids between the remains of buildings covered in charred ash. The dream carried her forward, as though some force was pulling her, leading her to what she needed to see.

The last row of buildings faced a structure made entirely of jagged spikes, which were melded together into a massive defensive wall. Wren walked along the length of it, the prickling bladelike points stark against the pale gray light. She came upon a single small door, barely big enough for her to slide through. On the other side, she froze, her knees tingling as she teetered on the edge of a giant canyon.

Below her, the burned-out ground dropped away into a huge cavern, like someone had cut a deep bowl into the earth. The edges on either side were layered in shadows, down to the darkness where Wren lost all powers of discernment. But it wasn't the natural out-cropping that set her off balance as she peered over. It was the mechanism that rose from the depths.

The device was huge—the length of two football fields at least—and its foundation was submerged in a large glowing pool. Above this, solid steel cones connected by spiraling cables sprouted upward. Wren didn't have a name for half of the things she saw on the device and could only guess at what they were intended to do. There were gears. Pipes to let off steam, perhaps, or excess gas. Coils to provide power. And bulb-shaped protrusions that seemed to have doors where a person could climb inside. Wren bent to examine the dirt, sending a little clod tumbling down toward the device. The soil seemed earthlike. She could almost hear Simon's lecturing voice telling her to grab a sample so they could study its composition, but she knew she couldn't bring any substance back from her dreams. And the glowing pool far below— was it an element? Neon, maybe, or phosphorous? As she peered down at it, Wren saw the liquid become agitated, as though the small handful of earth she had sent tumbling down was now causing turbulent waves in the pool below. A crackling noise accompanied the waves, sending sharp echoes up toward Wren. She got to her feet, her sense of wonder evaporating in the face of the horror that now confronted her.

A giant spidery creature emerged from the liquid, followed by another, and then still more until a whole slew of them began to climb. Their metallic legs were shiny against the shadowed earth behind, and they moved gracefully, at odds with their mechanized appearance. Wren stood rooted to the spot while the battalion of beasts scaled the wall opposite, the tentacle-like reach of their steel-plated legs easily covering the distance.

Wren scrambled back, hunting for the door through the thorny wall. Now she knew the purpose of the awful spikes. But before she pushed her way to safety, she took one last look behind her. She saw that somehow the beasts were communicating with one another, synchronizing their movements toward the other side of the chasm. And Wren's heart sank. There were people there. They had appeared from somewhere, approaching the pit as she had, but she doubted they knew what awaited them in its depths.

She opened her mouth, and at first no sound came out. She pushed harder, forcing out a strangled cry. "Run!" she called to the people. "Hurry!"

She saw the foremost among them glance her way, a tiny face across the distance. The person must have sensed her warning, because they all turned and sprinted in the opposite direction. A screeching rent the air behind them, as the first spiders reached the spot and sprang forward. Wren screamed in horror as she saw the giant beasts quickly catch up to the helpless people. Below them, some of the spiders had altered course, skittering off to the right to circle around the canyon toward Wren.

"No!" she gasped, shoving her way through the tiny door among the thorns. She stumbled through it, but this time there was no burned-out city in front of her. Instead, she was in a wide-open marsh, where gray-black flowers covered the spongy ground. On shaky legs, she staggered toward a solid rock, sitting down and willing herself to wake up. If only she would wake up. The scene had shifted, but the sounds had not. No matter how she ran in the dream, no matter how the foliage around her changed, from forest to field to marshland to mountaintop, the screams of the spiders hunted her, until finally, an exhausted Wren woke up in her bed at the Crooked House with her heart pounding and her forehead feverish. She sat up slowly, waiting for her breathing to return to normal.

The window in the corner of her room revealed

a midnight sky sprinkled with comforting stars, but
she didn't want to go back to sleep. What did it mean
that she was dreaming of Nod again? And what were
those horrible creatures? If what she had seen really
was happening on Nod, something was terribly wrong.
She looked at the little clock on her bedside table. She
still had two hours before she was to meet the Council. Wren buttoned up her apprentice robe and pulled
on her boots. She wasn't the only one in the Crooked
House who had dreamed of Nod. And it was time for
them to talk.

# THREE

*Little Jack Horner*
*Slept in the corner,*
*Hid from everyone's eye.*

Wren turned the corner of a long-abandoned corridor in the lower levels of the Crooked House and immediately ducked back, reaching behind her to motion Simon flat against the wall. He had been hard to wake, but he'd seen sense when Wren explained about the dream.

"Liza's here," she whispered. "She's leaving his room." Liza had been tending Jack since their return, and she was a strict nurse.

"My patient wants no visitors," she had said after Wren's last attempt to see Jack. "That hasn't changed any of the times you've come, darling, and I don't expect it to now. Poor boy has enough healing to do without being badgered by every Fiddler in the Crooked House." From that, Wren had guessed that she wasn't the only one trying to visit.

Liza seemed to pity Jack. Wren guessed that the Fiddlers would feel a whole lot of other things besides pity once they found out just how much Jack had been trying to help Boggen. For now, that wasn't common knowledge. The Council knew, of course, but Wren doubted many others were aware of the details of Jack's betrayal. She peeked back around the corner in time to see Liza disappear in the opposite direction. Wren still wasn't quite sure how she felt about what Jack had done. He had lied, stolen, and betrayed them, but he had also been tricked and manipulated by Boggen. Wren wished they could rewind the whole thing and go back to the days when their biggest worry was how to escape the Mistress of Apprentices' notice during work duties.

"Now's our chance," she whispered to Simon. "While he's alone."

"Are you sure this is a good idea?" Simon asked as he followed her down the hall. He had been remarkably reluctant to visit Jack, which was atypical for Simon, who was usually curious about anything. "Won't it be awkward?"

Wren choked out a laugh. "*You're* worried about a conversation being awkward?" Simon was the king of the uncomfortable pause, seconded only by his ability to monologue on subjects of interest only to himself. But, for all of that, his words made her think. Jack might be tricky to handle. She would need to be firm.

Wren knocked once on the green door but didn't bother waiting for a response. If Jack had Liza keeping visitors out, he probably wouldn't welcome the two of them in. Wren didn't care. She knew that Jack was physically recovered by now. He was probably wallowing, and she meant to snap him out of it long enough to get his help figuring out what was happening on Nod.

Every thought of bossing Jack around flew out of her mind when she saw the figure on the bed. He was propped up by a mountain of pillows, and his thin, gaunt face gave no sign of the merry Jack she'd once known. He looked about half his previous size, and his skin was a sickly gray color.

No wonder Liza pitied him. "Jack," Wren gasped.

"You look terrible," Simon said as though he were making a log note.

Jack rolled over on one side, dislodging the pillows and giving them his back. "I said *no visitors.*" He pulled the blanket up over his bony shoulder.

"Jack, are you okay?" Wren crept around to the other side of the bed. "Baxter said you were getting better. That you were healed."

"Baxter's wrong." Jack flipped away from her.

"But—" Wren began, but Jack immediately cut her off, pushing up on one elbow and lashing out at her.

"Why did you come here, Wren? To gloat?" He spit out the words like they were poison. "Liza says Fiddlers have been lurking outside every day. Have you been with them?" He pointed a skeletal finger at Simon. "You, too. Don't you have some other unique specimen to observe? Instead of poor, stupid traitor Jack?"

"Simon," Wren said. "Can you give us a minute? Wait outside and let me know if Liza comes back."

Simon stopped staring at Jack and stared at Wren.

"Please?" Wren asked, hoping to forestall Simon's litany of questions. For once, Simon didn't demand logical reasoning for her request. He gave her a sharp nod and disappeared.

"Jack," Wren said after Simon was gone. "This isn't like you."

"What do you know about what I'm like?" Jack's mouth twisted down into a frown. "You followed me to the gateway, and now you think you know all about me?"

"I know Boggen tricked you." Wren sat gently on the edge of Jack's bed. "Just like he tried to trick me."

Jack didn't say anything, but he sank back against the pillows.

"I know about the mental hospital," Wren said, looking not at Jack but at the worn edge of the blanket. "I know what Boggen promised you. I know that you were lonely and desperate, and he came to that awful place and promised you a home—a place to belong. I understand why you did it, Jack."

"Who else knows?" Jack demanded.

"No one," Wren said simply. She hadn't told the others what the Ashes had shown her about Jack's past. She figured it was Jack's story to share and had decided to leave it out of the narrative she gave the Council. "I told them that Boggen had you under a spell to make you do what he wanted." She shrugged and looked up at Jack's too-skinny face. "I mean, isn't that the truth? Boggen *did* have you under a spell."

Jack heaved forward, his breath coming in dry,

hacking coughs. And then Wren realized that he was laughing. At her. "Aw, so little Wren is going to *pity* me now? Lucky me."

Wren didn't say anything. She knew that what Jack had done was wrong. He had deceived them all, lied to every last Fiddler, including her, in order to get what he wanted, not to mention the fact that he had risked the well-being of everyone on the planet in order to win Boggen's approval. But Wren also knew it could just as easily have been her. She, like Jack, had dreamed of Nod, and when the most powerful Magician in ages had reached out to her in her dreams, she had found it nearly impossible to resist. How much more difficult must it have been for Jack, who had been desperate for someone to notice him? To believe in him? She pushed aside her defensiveness. She knew that somewhere in that husk of a person was the boy she used to know, her friend.

"Boggen used you, Jack, and had he lived, he would have simply thrown you away afterward." She swallowed and didn't turn her gaze from Jack's haunted blue eyes, which seemed too large for his face. If kindness wouldn't motivate Jack, then it was time for some tough love. "Don't throw yourself away by rotting down here in this sickroom. You're a Fiddler apprentice. Act like one."

Jack sighed, and it sounded like he had been holding in all the air in the room. "What's the point?"

"What do you mean?" Wren asked, alarmed. Jack had loved everything about being a Fiddler.

"I mean," Jack said, and his voice cracked on the words, "how can you be an apprentice when you can't use the stardust anymore?"

"What?"

"It's gone," Jack said. "I can't work the magic anymore. I'm burned out, or at least that's what Liza says."

Wren felt like someone had punched her in the stomach. You could *lose* the ability to work stardust? She would never forget the first moment she had learned there was magic in the world and that she could play it. It was as if everything had gone from a 2D black-and-white comic to a vibrant three-dimensional world. How could one survive going back?

"Oh, Jack," she said in a low voice. "Is Liza sure?"

"Go away" was all Jack said, slumping under the covers. "And don't come visit me again."

Wren didn't know what to do. She couldn't very well tough-love Jack into helping her now that she knew what really ailed him. She got to her feet and moved silently toward the door. "I won't visit until you invite me," she said, promising herself that she really could do that. "But"— she paused, one hand on the door handle—"when you're ready to talk about Nod, I need your help. Something awful is happening there. I saw it in a dream." She shut her eyes and pulled the door open. It was her last shot. If Jack really had given in to despair, there was nothing she could do. She was halfway through the door when he spoke.

"Wait," Jack said. "Tell me about the dream."

Wren breathed a sigh of relief, turned back around, and allowed herself to remember the dream. She didn't like to, especially because of the way it had morphed into new landscapes on Nod, one after another, but always with the horrifying pursuit of the spiders.

Simon reentered the room through the half-open door and perched on the corner stool, his notebook flipped open. Even though he had already heard about the dream earlier, he took meticulous notes, overriding Wren's objections with the claim that "anything could be significant." Wren closed her eyes, letting the dream wash over her, describing the scene in detail as she imagined her way back through the burned-out city and to the edge.

"The edge? The edge of what?" Jack's voice interrupted Wren's recollection, but she kept her eyes closed and tried to remember the details.

"The edge of the land," Wren said in an even voice. "It might be a mine. Or maybe a quarry. Whatever it is, it's definitely man-made and bigger than any excavation I've seen before." She described the device to them with as much detail as she could remember and then forced herself on to the spiders. If she could get all the words out, she'd be done, and perhaps she wouldn't need to relive the dream again. She shivered as she thought of the way the beasts had scaled the wall opposite her, the tentacle-like reach of their steel-plated legs. She heard again the screeching calls they made to communicate with one another. And the screams.

"There were people on the other side of the chasm." Wren's voice cracked at this part. "I just stood there. I watched them hunt the people, and there was nothing I could do."

"Did the people see you? What about the spiders?" Simon asked.

"Yes." Wren nodded and opened her eyes. "At least I think the people saw me. I know the spiders did."

She explained how the spiders had seemed to chase her through the dream world, the same way Boggen had once before. "It was like they knew I was a Dreamer." She dropped to the edge of the bed and looked at Jack. "We're both Dreamers, Jack. I know that's how Boggen communicated with you."

"Did it smell different?" Jack asked in a small voice. "Nod smells cold."

"Yes!" Wren seized on this. "Jack's right. It smelled like Nod."

"You can identify smells in your dreams?" Simon chewed on the end of his pencil.

"The point is," Wren said, ignoring Simon's speculative look, "what's happening in the dream is somehow happening on Nod." She felt her body relax, as though she had been carrying a weight for a long time and was only now noticing how tired she was.

"I bet the fence of spikes was built to keep the spiders out," Simon was saying. "And the spiders are clearly not organic beings. Where did they come from?" He had drawn a sketch based on Wren's description. It was eerily accurate. Panels of metal that had been bolted together formed a bubble-like body out of which sprouted eight furry legs. The underbelly of the torso was made of something clear as glass, with another similar section where the cluster of eyes were. "And what about the device? Where did *it* come from?" Simon ran his pencil over his far inferior sketch of the device. Wren didn't think it was possible to capture the scope and detail of that on a piece of paper.

"It's a well," Jack said, putting out a hand to reach for Simon's notebook. "There's seven of them on Nod." His words sounded raspy.

Wren nodded slowly. Her hunch had been right. Jack *did* have information that would help her. "What does the well hold? Neon? Phosphorous?"

"It's a well of magic. What else?" Jack barely got the words out before a coughing fit overtook him. "Boggen's trying to refine the stardust," he croaked. "The colony of Nod is on a very Earthlike planet, which is why the Magicians chose it, of course, but they didn't foresee the stardust problem."

"What problem?" Wren asked. "Couldn't they find any meteorites like we have here in the Crooked House?"

"They could find them all right," Jack said, pouring himself a cup of water from the pitcher on his bedside table. "But after a while it didn't do them any good.

Most of the stardust became corrupted somehow, and not too long ago, what little was left of the good kind began disappearing." He took a long drink. "Now the wells are nearly empty."

"Disappearing?" Simon's eyebrows knit together. "Like evaporating?"

Jack shrugged. "How should I know?" He studied Simon's sketch. "Do you think Boggen told me every detail of what was happening on Nod?" His mouth twisted in a bitter smile. "He only told me enough to get me to agree to help him." He yawned. "Now will you two leave me alone? I need to rest."

"You can't be tired," Simon said in his matter-of-fact voice. "It's a physical impossibility. You've been lying in bed for a month."

Jack shot him a withering look. "And what exactly do you think I should do? Get up and go to apprentice lessons so I can *watch* everyone else use the stardust?"

"Guys," Wren said, trying to get them back on track. "Nod, remember? The stardust there is disappearing?" She looked at Jack. "And corrupted? Did Boggen say what that meant?"

Jack shook his head, but Simon paged back through his notebook. "Didn't you say the stardust at the gateway was corrupted? I thought that was the whole reason the Council was going there. What if the same corruption—"

"Simon." Wren cut him off and darted a look a Jack. The last thing she wanted was for Jack to hear that they were going to the gateway.

"What aren't you telling me? Why are you really here?" Two spots of color appeared on Jack's cheeks. "Is this about the stupid gateway again? And the Council interfering? Cole *told* me that there was no way that creepy William was going to be able to conduct his research on me. He promised me." Jack was wide-eyed now, sitting up and pulling his blankets higher as though that would protect him from something awful.

"Wait," Wren said. "*You're* subject number thirteen?" She didn't need to see Jack's reluctant nod to know that she was right. She shivered. "No. Cole and Mary are on your side. They won't let William have you." She leaned toward him. "But surely there's more you can tell us about this corrupted stardust. Come on, think!"

"I have thought." Jack's voice was hard. "Don't you think I've thought about it every minute since that stupid gateway? You came here for my help—you, of all people—the least you could do is say thank you and then leave me alone."

Wren prickled. "What do you mean *you of all people*?" Did Jack think it was *her* fault that he couldn't work the stardust anymore? "*You're* the one who helped Boggen. *You're* the one who opened—"

"Just stop already, will you, Wren?" Jack sounded furious now. "I know exactly what I've done, and I know exactly what it's cost me." Jack slouched down and pulled the covers all the way up to his nose.

Wren shut her mouth with a snap. She hadn't meant to let her emotions get the better of her. She felt the little box of trapped feelings quivering inside her, leaping about at the thought of Jack being angry with her when *he* was the one who had helped Boggen, but she forced it to shrink back to its usual quiet state. She took one step toward the lump on the bed. "I'm sorry, Jack. I really am." She spoke to the top of the comforter and the tip of Jack's nose.

The covers were silent. Jack didn't even move. "Good-bye, Jack," Wren finally said, and she turned to follow Simon out of the room.

# FOUR

*I sing, I sing*
*From morn till night.*
*From cares I'm free*
*And hid from sight.*

"Wren," Cole said, greeting her with a smile. "You're right on time."

Wren stifled a yawn. She and Simon had talked over what Jack had said and what her dream might mean until the very minute she had to say good-bye and go meet the Council. Now she was regretting her lack of sleep. Wren had followed the Council's instructions carefully, slinking through the passageways of the Crooked House in predawn stillness, and arrived at the hidden cavern without much incident.

Across from her stood the ship that was obviously

intended to take them to the gateway. Beyond the ship was a yawning hole that opened up to a starry sky and a view of the valley Wren had never seen before. They were somewhere on the far side of the Crooked House, where aurora colors were just beginning to flicker across the landscape.

The ship itself was compact but impressive, with a wooden body shaped like an oblong tub. Ropes and wires stretched up to a balloon that ran the length of the vessel. Triangular sails sprouted from the sides— Wren guessed that these were to catch the energy of the aurora—and in the back was one massive propeller.

"You must fall asleep with the stardust apportioned here," Cole was saying to Astrid. He held out a finely worked silver compass that had two scales dangling from chains on either side. The apparatus looked vaguely familiar to Wren, and she wondered where in the Crooked House she had seen it before.

"This device allows a non-Dreamer to reach out to a Dreamer while he sleeps," Cole said. "Make your first attempt no later than twelve hours from now. And then try every subsequent hour."

"I will do as you say." Astrid spoke in a low, firm voice. She was the Council member Wren knew the least, but Wren had no doubt she was as brave and focused as the rest of them. She would need those qualities. Astrid was the only Council member who was staying behind to keep things running at the Crooked House.

"We will be able to travel the aurora tonight and then will return on a subsequent night. So look for us here each morning at dawn," Cole said, skimming over some papers Astrid had handed to him. "If anything goes amiss . . ." He paused, one hand hovering over the paper. "You know what to do."

Wren swallowed hard at those words. *If anything goes amiss!* The last time she had flown the aurora she had been so intent on stopping Jack she hadn't thought of the danger. But now it hit her full force. She was about to fly through outer space. To an unknown galaxy. In a spaceship that looked like it belonged on the high seas of the Caribbean. The wonder of what it meant to be a Fiddler hit her anew. She was going to be up there, among the stars she had studied for so long, warping through space like her favorite sci-fi characters.

"Feeling all right?" Mary said, coming up behind Wren and laying a hand on her shoulder.

"Never better," Wren said with a grin. "When do we leave?"

"We should board now," Mary said, giving her a warm look. "Your service to the Crooked House will not go unnoticed." Near the ship, William, the third Council member who was traveling to the gateway, was conducting a last-minute diagnostic. He tugged on cables and muttered to himself about sail circumference and properties of stardust energy, giving Wren a gruff nod as she followed Mary to the rope ladder looped near the bow. Mary carefully unwound it and began to climb, stopping only to flip open the hatch that led to the main body of the ship. Then she turned to Wren. "Welcome aboard."

The airship seemed little bigger once they were inside. A polished ramp led up to the main deck, which was built of what looked like weathered wood planks, strengthening Wren's impression of an old-fashioned pirate ship. On the upper level, a control panel was situated alongside a multigeared wheel connected by thin ropes to the sails. Dials and pressure readers encircled this, and a familiar-looking star map was pinned under a protective plastic cover. The sails themselves seemed to be made of canvas, but the blue-black glimmer of their stardust coating revealed that they weren't ordinary sails at all. Below stairs there was a small galley, a cramped captain's cabin with a seating area arranged around a table filled with books and maps, and a collection of small cabins with bunks for sleeping and even smaller closets laden with supplies.

Mary showed Wren to one of the cabins. "Make yourself comfortable, dear," she said, consulting the small hourglass that always hung at her waist. "Departure time in a quarter of an hour. I'll be in the captain's cabin if you need anything." Once Mary had left, Wren explored her cabin. There was a snug bed that fit the length of the room, and opposite that was a rather large window shaped like an octagon. Wren opened the plated shutter, revealing a breathtaking view of the night sky. The stars were brilliant, beckoning her closer with their hazy flickering, and she could see the glow of the aurora growing brighter against the horizon. No sooner had she settled in than she heard a clanking sound and the deep rumble of Cole's voice, blending with the higher nasal tones of William's. Someone shouted muffled orders. Then the door to her cabin opened and closed before Wren could even respond with surprise.

"Hello? Is someone there?" Wren couldn't see any-one, but with the door's opening came strange sounds, a fluttering whisper, and then a loud bump and a muf-fled groan that sounded remarkably like Simon.

"Simon?" Wren whispered. "Is that you?"

"Hang on a minute," Simon's voice said, and then the shadows shifted, revealing a lantern hanging in midair, and the sound of a match striking against something.

"What is going on?" Wren demanded as the cabin bloomed with lantern light. She could hardly believe what she was seeing. In front of her, Simon appeared, as though a cartoonist had sketched his outline in charcoals.

"Pretty cool, huh?" Simon said with a grin. "I found an old cloaking rhyme in the library archives, but this is my first successful execution of it." His voice turned lecture-y. "What you have to do is pinch your fingers like this—" He held out his hand but Wren swatted it aside. Though Simon looked almost see-through, he felt real enough.

"A cloaking rhyme? Is this for real?"

"I couldn't miss out on seeing the gateway a second time. I thought stowing away made the most sense, since I didn't want you to get in trouble for telling me the Council's big secret." Simon's voice sounded uncertain. "Do you not want me here?"

"No! Of course I want you here!" Wren cried. She realized the truth of the words as she said them. Having her best friend with her made the whole trip turn from an intimidating task into a fun adventure. "It's great that you sneaked on board. I just can't believe there's a rhyme that can make you invisible."

"Well, not completely. Ordinary firelight reveals the illusion," Simon said, dropping a blanket that shimmered under a coating of stardust onto the floor, uncovering a cage with two falcons roosting inside. "I thought you could use some company. Cleansing the gateway is a big deal, after all."

"Coeur!" Wren leaped across the cabin in one bound and stuck a friendly finger into her falcon's cage. She had finally decided on her falcon's name—it meant *heart*, which Wren had picked because of the courage her bird had shown. Coeur ruffled her feathers in response, and Wren moved closer, but she didn't have time to say anything more, because just then she heard voices passing by her door.

"Hide!" Wren hissed as Simon grabbed the birdcage, throwing the stardust-coated blanket over it.

Wren blew out the lantern and tumbled onto her bunk, holding her breath in the darkness.

Her door opened and closed a second time, but this incident was much less eventful. "Weather Changer, check!" William's nasal voice called, and then the door shut with a slam. Even so, Wren stayed on her bed, silent and still, until the airship began to rumble and jolt as unseen apparatuses sprang to life. Then came the whir of an engine. The wall next to her bunk hummed with the workings of the airship, and Wren could feel the thrust of a propeller. The boat began to slowly rock back and forth, then gave one final jerk before gently spiraling up.

"We're in the air!" Wren said excitedly, easing over to the porthole. The brilliant hues of the aurora surrounded her, whisking the vessel up into the starry night sky. The last time she had traveled to the gateway hadn't been so comfortable. The airship exhibited none of the strange gravitational effects she had experienced on Jack's platform. "Isn't it beautiful?" She looked down at Simon, who had lit the lantern and was hunched near the birds, already writing in his notebook.

"Want to take a look?" she offered.

"Hmmm," Simon said after he joined her by the

window. "It appears that there is a current flowing through the aurora. I wonder how the Fiddlers are piloting this craft." He rummaged through his pack until he found a pencil sharpener. "Aurora current paired with stardust sails . . . very curious." He expertly sharpened the pencil until the tip was a point and began working sums in his notebook. Wren couldn't hear what he was saying, but there were murmurs of *acceleration* and *speed* and *force*.

"Simon." Wren grabbed his pencil out of his hand. "Just take a minute and look out the window. We are flying through outer space." The same wonder she had felt the last time bloomed within her. "Unbelievable," she breathed.

"On the contrary," Simon said. "It is believable since we are actually experiencing it." He grabbed for his pencil, but Wren pulled it out of his reach.

"All right, Wren," he said. "It's amazing. Glorious. Magical. Do I need to get a thesaurus? I'm overwhelmed. We are flying through outer space." He grinned at her. "Now give me back my pencil so I can figure out how."

Wren had no recollection of how long the journey had taken with Jack, and on this second trip, time moved surreally. The minutes passed, but each one was wrapped up in the wonder of riding the aurora, of leaving the atmosphere and entering the blackness of space. Whatever protection the airship had against shifts in gravity didn't seem to extend to the temperature, and soon Wren huddled on her bunk with the falcons, piling the blankets and her apprentice cloak around them against the icy chill. Wren reached to stretch the cramp out of her hand and immediately recoiled. The metal wall of her cabin was so cold it burned.

"What was the gateway like?" Simon asked in a shivering voice. The invisibility rhyme was beginning to wear off, and even without the lantern lit, Wren could see the outline of Simon's features, though they were a little grainy.

"I didn't get a close look," Wren said. She chose as few words as possible. Talking made her feel even colder. "But the room it was in looked like a cavern. Maybe it was an asteroid, I don't know. And the gateway itself was a web of stardust."

"The gateway must sustain an Earthlike atmosphere," Simon said. The cold didn't seem to affect him as much. He had pulled the collar of his cloak up past his ears so only the tip of his red nose poked out, but he kept up the same lecturing tone. "Or else humans couldn't survive there. Even Magicians like Boggen need air to breathe."

Wren managed a noncommittal grunt. Simon seemed to think the whole endeavor was a curious scientific experiment, and Wren wished she could find some of his detachment. Instead, her sense of adventure was diminishing under the burden of the Ashes' command to cleanse the gateway, and the weight of what had happened there with Jack. She wanted to make up for all the trouble she had caused. Without her help—unwitting though it was—Jack would have never made it to the gateway in the first place. He wouldn't have lost his magic, and Wren wouldn't be on the cusp of losing hers. Something inside shifted at that, and Wren felt guilt tighten around her chest. Was it her defensive spell that had backfired and caused Jack to lose his magic? Would the same thing happen to her? She pressed the guilt down and curled herself like a comma around the roosting falcons.

Simon was still working equations in his notebook when Wren's eyelids began to grow heavy with sleep. "Don't forget to reapply the stardust," Wren mumbled. "I can see you clearly now."

Simon looked up, startled, then set his notebook aside and began rummaging through the pack he had brought. "Good idea, Wren," he said, setting to work immediately. Wren watched him for a while, the way he mixed a few drops from some bottle and a sprinkle of something that smelled like spices from another, before spinning it all together with stardust and singing the rhyme:

*I sing, I sing*
*From morn till night.*
*From cares I'm free*
*And hid from sight.*

Wren yawned, feeling the exhaustion of the past hours catching up with her. "That's amazing," she said sleepily. Simon was smearing the smoldering stardust across his skin, and whatever the stardust touched vanished as though it had never been. She watched him as he disappeared from sight, and then a blanket floated up from the floor and through the air, as Simon placed it over his other belongings. Soon, the only thing that gave any evidence Simon was in the room was the methodical scratching of his pencil. But even that blended in with the hum of the airship, lulling Wren into a most welcome sleep.

# FIVE

*Little Jenny Wren did dream*
*Once upon a time.*
*In came Robin true of heart,*
*And taught her how to rhyme.*

**W**ren took a deep breath and looked around her.
Jack had put words to what she had always
recognized. The air in her dreams of Nod smelled
different—smoky, almost, and very, very cold. She
braced herself, waiting for the horror of the spider
dream, but she wasn't in the burned-out village. She
was standing on a hill covered with a spongy plant. Off
in the distance, beyond a thick forest, there appeared to
be a city. Spindly buildings reached toward the gloomy
sky, with balconies and bridges connecting them. She
waited, wondering if the dream was going to show her

something more, but she had barely taken a few tentative steps toward the forest's edge when a crashing
sound came from behind her.

"My calculations were a little off this time, I see,"
said the person who was clambering toward her. Wren
took a step back, wishing for the cover of the forest.
Light shone from the open doorway that the stranger
had left ajar. Wren could see the outline of a low building that blended in with the rocky landscape.

The figure was drawing closer, and Wren could
see that it was a girl of about Wren's own height. She
wore a leather vest with a number of pockets and straps
that looked handy for carrying tools. It was belted at
the waist over fitted gray pants tucked into boots. Her
long black hair was restrained by a pair of large tinted
goggles that she pushed back to reveal her face, which
Wren instantly recognized.

"Robin!" Wren exclaimed, running to meet her.
She hadn't seen Robin in her dreams since before the
gateway, when Robin had contacted Wren to warn her
about Boggen's imminent return to Earth.

"Not here!" Robin yanked Wren's hand and pulled
her back through the doorway into the room beyond.
It was a small space, shaped like an octagon, ringed

by walls alternating with four glass-paned windows. Now that she was inside, Wren could see that she was in a strange combination of laboratory and storeroom. One bay was piled with an array of different-sized goggles, all the way down to a minuscule wire monocle no bigger than Wren's thumb. Another had maps and charts tacked up with tools that looked like telescopes arranged below them.

Robin was fidgeting with a candle, except in place of a lit wick it had a blue gas flame. She flipped through some parchments and made a notation using a quill dipped in ink. "That's better," she murmured. "The coordinate where Nebula 14765 crosses the Pearl Galaxy." She smiled up at Wren. "Next time I will be more precise. Of course it helps that you've seen my astrolab. That should make it easier for me to bring you here."

"Have *you* been doing that? Bringing me to Nod in my dreams?" Wren rubbed her arms. "I'd just as soon not be brought to the pit of giant spiders."

Robin pointed Wren to a roughly carved stool and leaned herself up against an old worktable. "What spiders?"

Wren should have felt reassured to see Robin. She

was, after all, a friend. But watching Robin's expression go from curious to wary as Wren recounted her dream did nothing to ease her prickle of fear at the memory of the spiders.

"It could be one of Boggen's wells," Robin said, running her palms across her forearms as if she was fighting off a chill. "The glowing liquid you described sounds like starmilk, a byproduct of the refining process, flawed as it is." She tapped her lip with a forefinger. "I wonder if there's more information in his lab. Now that he's ill, his defenses might be down, and it would be a good time—"

"Wait, *ill*? Boggen's not dead?"

"I don't wish any living thing dead, but I wouldn't mourn Boggen's passing." Robin gave her a bitter smile. "For now, he's only very sick. His henchmen found him collapsed outside the gateway. It seems he tried to force it open, and his spell backfired."

Wren stared at the instruments on the table next to her. *Boggen is still alive.* And it seemed that Robin didn't know about Jack. Or her part at the gateway. "He wants untainted stardust, doesn't he? That's why he wanted to open the gateway?"

Robin nodded. "I believe so, but who knows what he will do now?"

Something Robin had said tickled her memory. Jack had used that same term. "You said something about *refined stardust*. Has Boggen found a way to cleanse it? Is that what's in his wells?"

"We know very little about his wells," Robin said slowly. She got to her feet and reached for one of the charts on the wall. "Boggen keeps them a secret from everyone, even his most trusted advisors. We have a general idea of where they might be located, but it's all simply guesses at this point." Robin spread the chart out on the table. It was a hand-drawn map with names of places like the Murkish Wood and the Valley of Lights. Between a very darkly shaded area labeled *Upas Poisonwood: Keep out at all costs!* and something called Phosphoric Lake was a circular symbol marked *Well I?* There were three more scattered across the page. "However he tries to refine the stardust, it's still tainted." She tapped the roman numerals marking the potential locations of the wells. "We must stop the corruption from spreading else we risk another plague." She waved away Wren's questions. "Let's just say that the early Magicians' efforts to manipulate the stardust went very, very badly. It's a lucky thing Boggen didn't force the gateway open or he would have no doubt brought the same corruption to Earth."

"But that's the problem," Wren said in a small voice. "It seems the gateway itself has become tainted. The Ashes told me that soon it *will* spread to Earth if we don't cleanse it."

Robin's face grew worried at Wren's words. "The Ashes?" she said in a cautious voice. "You mean, the Ashes that belong to the Crooked Man?"

Wren nodded. "Yes. They seem to know a lot about the gateway. Why are you looking at me like that?"

Robin swallowed hard. "The Crooked Man is no friend of anyone on Nod. Legend says he's cursed this planet and one day he will destroy it with his starfire." She shivered and then tried to laugh it off. "Of course legends can mean many things, but all of them say his Ashes are not to be trusted."

Thoughts swirled in Wren's mind. What was Robin suggesting? That the Ashes meant to *harm* Nod? Wren had thought they meant to save it! And what did it mean that the Crooked Man would destroy Nod? She knew so little of him, only what vague references she had heard in the Crooked House. Now she wished she had asked more questions. Robin moved to an instrument that was like a compass with metal scales on either side, the sight of which snapped Wren's thoughts into focus.

"Hey! We have one of those in the Crooked House." She thought of what Cole had said to Astrid before their departure and things clicked into place. "Is *that* what you use to meet me in the dream?"

"Yes," Robin said, adjusting a gear on the side of the strange candle. The blue flame flared. "No one here really practices Dreamopathy anymore, but I'm trying to figure it out. Experimenting. But you're a tricky one. I can't quite find you in the dream sometimes. I almost think I need to be asleep myself."

"You're not dreaming?" Wren asked, staring at Robin and realizing that while the dream smelled like Nod, it didn't exactly look like the other dreams. In this one she could see shades of color: the blue of the gas flame, the warm orange of the light, the copper glint as it shimmered off the metallic walls.

"No," Robin said, looking at Wren curiously. "I'm on Nod. You're the one who's asleep." The pan next to her sizzled. "We don't have much time, though, before the dream will take you back. What I came to tell you is that there's someone helping Boggen on Earth. Someone who intends to open the gateway."

"I know," Wren said in a quiet voice. "But he failed." She thought of Jack, ill and magicless, and her heart squeezed with guilt and pity. She thought of how little

Robin knew of what had really happened. How could she explain any of it to her Magician friend? She imagined the conversation. *No, Robin, it only* looks *like Jack was helping Boggen. He was really deceived the whole time. And me? Well, yeah, I sort of helped him find the gateway and ruin it and everything, but I promise! I'm on your side!* Wren shook her head. "You don't need to worry about him anymore."

"I wouldn't be so sure about that," Robin said. "Boggen may be keeping to his sickbed, but the rest of his minions aren't. Something is going on at the gateway. My informants tell me that Boggen's henchmen have a new device that will force the gateway open any day now."

"No!" Wren shook her head. "The gateway's magic is tainted. The Ashes said that the corruption will only spread. If the gateway opens—"

Robin grabbed Wren's shoulder, glancing anxiously at the blue flame, which was slowly disappearing. "We have to find a way to keep it closed." Robin shook Wren as if she could shake her all the way awake. "You've got to stop it on the Earth side, Wren! Before it's too late for both Nod and Earth." The room was growing dim, shadows swirling about, and Wren knew the dream would soon end. "I'll see if I can pilfer some more stardust and try to meet you here again, but you have to try. Find a way—"

Robin cut off with a strangled cry. Her eyes grew wide as she stared past Wren. Wren was fading from the dream. She couldn't move, couldn't speak, could only watch as thick cuffs appeared on Robin's wrists, and a rope bound her arms to her sides.

"You!" Robin spit to whoever was lurking in the shadows. "You've been spying on us? Why?" A dawning realization crossed Robin's face. "Oh, no! What have you—"

A voice came from somewhere Wren couldn't see. "I do what I must," it boomed, sending the shadows shaking. Wren tried to reach out, tried to help Robin, but the whole scene was shrinking as though Wren was seeing it from a great distance. It was too late. Whatever magic held her in the dream was nearly gone. The colors blurred together, blotting out Robin from view, and then everything went dark.

When Wren woke in her bunk on the airship, she could feel the imprint of Robin's hand on her shoulder. She rubbed the spot as if she could somehow clasp the girl's hand. Robin was in danger. Someone had come, had shown up at that last moment when Wren was waking and had taken Robin, and Wren was the only one who knew. The tight fist of fear clamped around her chest as the rest of the dream came crashing back into her mind. Robin wasn't the only one in trouble. Boggen was still alive. And he had found a way to force the gateway open. For all she knew he had already done so, and a whole army of Magicians was waiting for them there. She tossed aside the blankets and hurried to the door.

"Simon," she hissed at the space under the window, but there was no sound. Either Simon was invisible and asleep or he had left her cabin. Wren threw her robe over her shoulders. She couldn't be bothered with Simon right now. She had to get to Cole and Mary. She yanked the door open and saw that she was already too late.

# SIX

*I saw a ship a-sailing*
*A-sailing on the sea.*
*And, oh! It was a-laden*
*With secrets kept for thee!*

A h, the Weather Changer joins us." Fiddler William's nasal voice now sounded treacherous. With a whispered rhyme, he wove a shimmering loop of stardust and, before Wren could do anything but utter a cry of protest, bound it tight around her wrists. Mary and Cole had similar bonds around their mouths and torsos, fixing them upright against the chairs that surrounded the galley table.

Mary opened her eyes wide and shook her head at Wren, but Wren had no idea what that was supposed to mean.

"Boggen's alive!" Wren shouted desperately, as William shoved her roughly onto the bench seat under the big octagon-shaped window. "And he's figured out how to force the gateway open!"

William laughed mercilessly. "A little behind on your information, Weather Changer," he sneered. "Mary and Cole already suspected Boggen was alive. Soon we will all get to meet him." He patted the glimmering golden key that lay on the table in front of him. "And Boggen will have no need to force the gateway open. Not since I have this."

"No!" Wren gasped, realizing what he meant. "You can't open the gateway to Nod." She squirmed against the stardust bonds, but they burned hot against her wrists. "The stardust on Nod is tainted. The gateway is the only thing holding it back from Earth, and even it is corrupted. William, the Ashes already warned us. You can't—"

William's slap took her breath away. Her cheek burned with the force of it.

"Don't tell me what I can't do." William towered over her, and Wren hated herself for cringing away from him. He muttered a rhyme, and Wren felt the stardust ropes warm against her lips. She knew better than to struggle, but she tried a tentative whisper. She might as well have been mute. More bonds squeezed against her torso and waist, fixing her as securely to the bench as any metal chains.

Seeming pleased, William took a step back. "The Ashes are fools, and their Crooked Man is a liar who means to destroy Nod. You would do well to remember that." He gave Cole and Mary a scornful look. "And the Fiddler Council's worthless deliberating only impedes progress. Their fear holds them back." He pulled out a pair of leather gloves from a pocket in his jacket. "With access to Nod and all the Magicians have learned, think of what we could accomplish! The taint on the stardust is nothing to fear. With proper research and refinement, I can use it to the Alchemists' advantage." He pulled the gloves on, adjusting each finger meticulously. "Once I have perfected living stardust, none of this will matter. You will see."

Cole gave a muffled shout, wriggling in his chair, and then his face creased with pain as his stardust bonds burned him into submission again.

Wren darted worried glances at both of them. She could see angry red marks on their skin, the evidence that they had not gone easily into captivity. Wren's heart sped up. Not all of them were captives. Simon was out there somewhere, an unknown stowaway, and invisible to boot. She glanced around the room, wondering if he was with them even now. *Simon.* She willed him to be smart. *Keep yourself hidden.*

William was leaning over the control panel, his gloved fingers sliding easily over the levers. How could he be so stupid? Wren remembered what she had learned about the Civil War, how the Alchemists fought against the Magicians, who wanted to subjugate ordinary people and who had even tried to use dark magic to steal the stardust from living things. In the Crooked House, that was one of the most forbidden areas of research, but apparently William thought he knew better. Wren had to stop him. She flexed her wrists. The stardust flared with light, burning into her flesh—not with the heat of a fire, but with the precision of an electrical burn. She stilled. There had to be another way, and she had to figure it out fast, because they were nearing the gateway.

The huge octagonal window loomed over William, silhouetting his form with a brilliant display of stardust swirling in a rainbow net that waved gently like underwater coral. A huge asteroid-like object blossomed in the distance, growing ever larger as they drew nearer, until the entire view was dominated by the rocky outcropping. The net itself had caught on one of the formations that dotted the asteroid, and their vessel steered closer, aiming for one of a thousand clefts in the rock. The window was dwarfed by the scope of what must be the gateway's exterior.

Wren cast a questioning look over at Mary as if to ask for confirmation, but Mary only gazed ahead with tired, worried eyes. It had to be the gateway. Wren shifted to get a better view but was immediately slammed against the frigid metal wall as something clanked in the belly of the airship. The vessel stopped its forward motion and tilted to one side, sending the papers on the table sliding to the floor. If Wren hadn't been bound fast, she too would have tumbled over, and it gave her a tiny flare of satisfaction to see William jolt to one side, unsteady on his feet.

"Prepare for landing," he hissed, covering his mouth, a gray look on his face. Wren's stomach also felt the change in motion, and she pressed her cheek up against the icy wall, counting the long seconds. All of a sudden, it was over. The ship had stopped.

Wren's mouth felt dry and her knees wobbly. She

peered out the window. The last time she had been at the gateway, she and Jack had fallen off Jack's vessel, and she had blacked out before arriving. The Ashes had brought her to the platform that held the gateway. She felt a twinge of unease at what William had said. She hardly believed he was trustworthy, but what did she really know of the Ashes? Robin had said something similar, that the Crooked Man meant to destroy Nod. What if the Ashes had their own reasons for saving her and Jack, for sending her to the gateway?

Wren couldn't see the front of the airship, but they had pulled up alongside a shiny silver platform covered with grating. It formed a ramp that led up to an arched entrance that framed a familiar-looking space. Wren couldn't see the entire cavern, but she did see that the gateway still held, its thick web of stardust stretching over the portal to Nod—the place where Boggen had whispered his evil lies and Jack had nearly died. William dragged Cole and Mary out first, using stardust to hurry them along.

Wren glanced around desperately. Did Simon see what was going on? Would he come up with some kind of rescue plan? *Now's our chance!* She pretended the force of her thoughts could somehow reach her friend. *Now! While William is distracted!* But whether Simon was aware or not, it didn't matter. William returned and jerked Wren to her feet, pulling hard on her stardust leash.

"Time for our Weather Changer to show us what she can do." He yanked her after him, and Wren dragged her feet, trying to do anything to slow him down, but she only succeeded in increasing the burn from her bonds. It wasn't just that William planned to open the gateway; he planned to make *her* do it. William shoved her toward the open hatch, not waiting for her to clamber down the ladder, and she tumbled to the rocky floor with a thud, her stardust bonds searing her flesh with fire. She could see the gateway, pulsing with a sickly green light, the aftereffect of what had happened here with Jack and Boggen. She could see the scorch marks on the floor, the spot where she had funneled stardust into Jack's chest, and she wanted to cry. Was it all for nothing? The tight box of emotions inside her leaped and hopped with fear and tension and worry. But she shoved it all away when William began to pull her with brute force toward the gateway. When they were standing in front of it, so close that Wren could sense the thrumming of the magic in the gossamer web, William leaned close, the stench of his breath causing Wren to gag.

"I will loosen your bonds," he said, "just enough so you can work the rhyme." There was a flare of stardust, and she felt the pressure leave her mouth and wrists.

"I won't do it," Wren said as soon as she could speak. "I'd rather die first."

"That's what the others said, but I think you'll be easier to persuade." William's laugh was hard. "You may be brave enough to lay down your life for what you've been told is the good of others, but will you pay such a price with the lives of your friends?" A knife appeared from his jacket pocket, and in two strides William was next to Cole, holding it up to his throat. Wren felt hot tears spring to her eyes.

Cole looked at her steadily, no falcon on his shoulder this time, and he shook his head slightly. Wren knew what he meant. He too would offer his life to protect Earth from a plague of tainted stardust. Wren wavered. Could she really stand by and watch Cole die? But Mary was there, too, her face pale and determined, and though she was bound like a prisoner, she still somehow managed to look like a queen. She gave Wren a confident look, her eyes shining with encouragement.

"I won't do it, William," Wren said, licking her lips. "I'll never help you!"

William sighed heavily. "I thought you would be foolish." He resheathed the knife and moved to return to the airship. "I'll have to get the other."

Before she saw him, Wren knew. There was only one other friend she had here, one other person William could use against her. Simon must have put up a valiant fight. He wasn't even conscious, and his pale face was marked with stardust wounds. The invisibility tincture had worn off, so when William tossed his limp form out of the airship, he was clearly visible. And then came the cage carrying their falcons, tumbling onto the cavern floor next to Simon, where Coeur let out an enraged squawk. Wren glanced around, desperate. Were the Ashes nearby? Would they show up with their Crooked Man and the promised starfire and save them all? But nothing happened.

Wren looked up at William, hot tears streaming down her cheeks. "You are a horrible person," she said, the words thick on her tongue. "You would kill all these innocent people. Destroy all these lives?"

"No," William said, folding his leather-clad fingers and looking at her calmly. "*You* would kill them. Or perhaps you've had a change of heart?" He held out the golden key to her. "First you will cleanse the gateway. Then you will open it." He grabbed Wren roughly by the elbow and shoved her toward the gateway. "Do it," he said.

"Do what?" Wren said hollowly. "The Ashes never told me how to cleanse the gateway. They said the Crooked Man would tell—"

"Shut up!" William said, scraping his hands through his hair irritably. "We don't need the Crooked Man. I found an ancient Magician's rhyme that should work. You will use that."

Wren stared through blurry tears at the crumpled paper he handed her. What choice did she have? As if to remind her, he pulled out his knife and pointed it menacingly toward Simon. She scrubbed at her eyes to clear her vision and then she took the stardust he handed her and stumbled toward the gateway, moving as if in a trance. William told her the rhyme to say, and she forced the words out. He told her how to weave the stardust, and she did. Or she tried to. The stardust sat limp and unmoving in her hands. She let out a strangled laugh through her tears. "I can't," she said. "The stardust won't respond." Relief flooded through her. She wouldn't have to do this awful thing after all. She couldn't.

"Impossible!" William said at first, but then as he realized that she really was trying and failing to work the stardust, he turned a scrutinizing gaze on her. "You, too, are losing the stardust," he said in an observational voice.

Wren redoubled her efforts. Now that he'd discovered her secret he'd probably kill them all. She slapped at the stardust, her sobs morphing into angry words like swords and then into ice that became a hard lump deep within her. William might force her to do this, he might think he had won, but he was wrong. She would figure out a way to make this wrong right. Just like she would figure out a way to make it up to Jack and Simon and all the others who were pawns in this terrible war.

And then it was over. The stardust had escaped her hands, and Wren fell to the floor with it, a crumpled heap of exhaustion, waiting for William to do whatever horrible thing he planned next. But there was no horrible thing. Instead, William was studying her clinically, almost compassionately, one forefinger pressed against his top lip. "You may be burned out already."

He shook his head as though coming out of a trance. "No matter. Your loss of magic will make for interesting research later." He studied the gateway for a moment, and Wren felt a glimmer of hope. If he wasn't going to kill them, would William take them back to Earth? Even being his next research subject would be okay if only he would give up his dangerous plan. But he seemed to come to some sort of decision, and he shrugged his shoulders as though sloughing off a heavy weight.

"We will deal with the taint later." He hefted the golden key. "For now, we open the gateway," he said— and shoved it into the lock.

The gateway shimmered and then exploded into a blinding flash of green light. Wren shut her eyes tight and put her hands up to her ears to block out the shattering sound that accompanied the light. She felt her body blown back with the force of it, the cavern around her swimming with clouded colors.

"Get back in the ship!" William shouted. He grabbed her by the elbows, and the cavern blurred around her as she was jostled up into the airship, then shoved through a doorway and onto the floor. Wren felt icy metal against her cheek, heard the rumble of the airship's motor, but everything felt wrong, somehow. The atmosphere hummed with the energy of stardust, but there was a discordant note as well. The air felt electric and volatile. Wren opened her eyes. Simon's crumpled form was next to her, and beyond him was the dented cage where the falcons lay silent. She was back in her cabin, but the stardust bonds were gone.

Wren dragged herself to the door but wasn't surprised to find it locked. She crawled back to the window, looking out at the gateway cavern, which was rapidly disappearing behind them. She grabbed at the wall, reaching for a handhold to steady herself. But then the whole ship jolted with a violent lurch, so forceful that Wren was catapulted to the floor. She worked to pull herself, inch by inch, back up to the window, but she saw only empty space beyond the trailing stardust web. The gateway was gone, replaced by a diminishing cluster of pulsing green stardust. She felt like someone had punched her hard in the stomach. William hadn't just opened the tainted gateway. He'd destroyed it. And now they were stuck on the other side.

"Wren?" Simon's bleary voice came from his spot on the floor.

Wren shoved aside her fear and guilt and turned to

her friend. "Are you okay? What did he do to you?" she asked, taking in the welts on his face and his blooming black eye. Simon ignored her question, pressing himself up to a seated position.

"The gateway's open, isn't it?" Simon said it as though it was an irrefutable fact.

Wren nodded shamefully, and began woodenly telling the halting story of what had happened at the gateway. "I couldn't cleanse it. The taint is spreading."

"It's not your fault. William is the one who's responsible," Simon said, and Wren was thankful for his words, even if they rang false to her own ears. Whatever happened now, whatever happened because of the gateway being gone—it would be because she had failed to cleanse it.

Simon rummaged through his pockets, pulled out a tiny bottle, and peered at it through his good eye. "I think I have enough invisibility tincture to cover us."

"It doesn't matter," Wren said. "We're locked in."

The airship had shifted directions, and the window showed a different view, a reddish-orange globe looming in front of them.

"That's another planet." Wren stumbled over the words, hardly believing what she was seeing. She hurried toward the window, where the fiery hues were taking on the shape of atmospheric clouds. The journey on this side of the gateway hadn't taken nearly as long. Where in the universe were they? She knew in her head that Nod was somewhere in another galaxy, but to see in reality that the gateway had taken them to uncharted space . . . "It's amazing," she breathed.

"So that's it," Simon said as he moved to join her. "Nod, land of the Magicians."

# SEVEN

*This little Fiddler went to new worlds.*
*This little Fiddler stayed home.*
*This little Fiddler had stardust.*
*This little Fiddler had none.*

As they drew near the planet's surface, Wren pressed close to the icy window to get a better view. Rolling brown hills spotted with reddish clay outcroppings gave way to a brilliant green carpet of vegetation. She couldn't tell if it was trees or bushes or plain old grass, but it stretched for miles, broken only by circles of pearly white, which she had to assume were lakes of some kind.

"Nod must be Earthlike," Simon said, chewing on his pencil eraser. "I mean, of course it's Earthlike if people can live there, but for even plant life to be similar . . . I wonder if the animal life . . ." He trailed off, his eyes growing wide.

Simon had been a bundle of nonstop talking and hypothesizing since they had first entered Nod's atmosphere. Wren felt the same nervous energy and stuffed it far down inside, tuning out Simon's endless theories.

The green vegetation soon disappeared into a flat ring that encircled what was clearly a city. The dusty plain ended in a wall of thick bricklike blocks stacked on top of one another. Towers dotted the wall's surface at regular intervals, but Wren saw no roads entering or exiting the city.

Above the wall, Wren spotted the arched catwalks she had seen from afar in her dream crisscrossing a horizon full of spindly towers. It was as though at that moment everything became real. She was about to land on another planet. Even the threat of the tainted stardust, even the guilt of not being able to cleanse the gateway, couldn't compete with the wonder of it.

Nearer and nearer they came, until Wren thought that the airship would surely scrape the top of the wall. There was a horrible jolt, as if their vessel had struck a solid mass, and she could smell the acrid tang of oily smoke. A horn began to sound, which she and Simon uneasily concluded had to be an alarm, and the next moment the airship began to move, but not as before. An invisible current seemed to catch them up, one that drove the ship along even as its engines hummed to a halt below them. Once they passed the wall, the light faded, as though they'd come under a thick veil of clouds. The airship soared over bridges and past brick and glass outcroppings as something—or someone— took them deeper into the heart of the city.

As the ship tilted to turn, Wren got a clearer view of the land below. Some of the arched bridges ended in spiraling ramps that angled down toward the ground. Narrow bricked roads intersected around buildings with sloped walls, giving everything the off-kilter feeling of a house of cards. Remarkable glass domes topped many of the structures, some trailing gusts of steam into the blue sky. Far below, vehicles moved through the streets. Wren squinted, wondering if she could be seeing them correctly: carriages drawn by actual horses inching along the narrow roads.

The clouded sky was smudged with a brilliant orange and smoky gray, the steam from the buildings enhancing its resemblance to a dingy watercolor painting. The city seemed to stretch on and on. Rain began to fall,

coating the window with tiny droplets, and then everything disappeared as the ship entered a dark tunnel.

"I think we're here," Simon said.

"Wherever here is," Wren said. The airship was
moving very slowly, descending past hammered-metal
walls that shimmered in the blue light of lanterns hung
at regular intervals. It docked with a gentle bump, and
Wren heard William's voice shouting something from
beyond the door. Outside, a group of what must be
Magicians approached the ship. Their long black jackets fastened up the front with an array of buckles, and
leather caps with goggles attached fit snug against their
scalps. They pressed in around the airship, carrying
narrow spears tipped with glowing stardust.

"They don't look like a welcoming committee,"
Simon said.

Then William appeared below, pulling Cole and
Mary behind him until armed Magicians surrounded
them all. Wren wished she could hear what they were
saying. William was shoving Cole and Mary forward,
one hand spread as though he were offering the Magician soldiers a delightful gift.

One of the soldiers jabbed his weapon toward Cole
and Mary. He might have been the leader, because he

wore a red scarf around his neck where all the others had gray ones. He motioned to his underlings, and they surrounded Cole and Mary, herding them toward a far door.

The last Wren saw of her friends was Cole's dignified form disappearing through an archway. As the soldiers turned, Wren saw that their glowing spears were attached to backpacks that they wore strapped over their long fitted uniforms.

"Are those stardust-powered *weapons?*" she asked Simon, but his attention was directed somewhere else.

"It looks like William is arguing with them about something." William was frowning, his arms folded across his chest stubbornly, while the red-scarfed captain pointed at the doorway. But whatever argument had occurred, William seemed to have lost, and the entire party headed toward the archway.

Wren watched them go. She was listening so intently to what was going on outside that she wasn't prepared for what happened next. There was a heart-stopping bang on their cabin door, which burst open the next moment, sending Wren scrambling to hide. She was halfway across the room when she realized who was standing in the doorway.

*"Jack?"*

Jack stood there, fully dressed in his apprentice cloak, with a pack slung across one shoulder and his familiar crooked smile on his gaunt face.

"Nice to see you, too," he said, as though they had merely bumped into each other in the Crooked House.

"Excellent stowaway skills," Simon said politely, as though Jack's surprise appearance were a matter of course, and went back to his notebook like Jack had been with them all along.

Wren was not so unruffled. She glared at both of them. "What are you doing here, Jack?" she said when she could find her voice.

Jack snorted. "Same thing you are. Saving the world." He raised one eyebrow as he moved to join them at the window. "Though I must agree that I was a much better stowaway than Simon was. I mean—" He stopped short as he saw the cage with the sleeping falcons in it. There was an awkward pause.

Wren cleared her throat. She had killed Jack's falcon in order to stop him from helping Boggen. The cocky smile disappeared from Jack's face.

"Why are you really here?" Wren asked.

When Jack turned around, his face was somber. "I'm

here to make things right." He waved a hand to forestall a reply. "Look. I know you probably won't believe me. I don't blame you, but I couldn't just sit there in the Crooked House when I knew you guys were going to the gateway, could I?" He looked at Wren as though to plead his case. "And good thing for you I *did* come along. Because it means I'm here now to rescue you."

Wren leaped to her feet. Jack's arrival had distracted her from what was important. "We shouldn't be standing here chatting. We've got to decide what to do next. The Magicians have Mary and Cole"—she hardly thought William was worth saving—"and I doubt William has forgotten about us."

"I've got it all figured out," Jack said, patting the white rope that hung looped about his shoulder.

"Um, guys?" Simon said from his observation post by the window.

"Simon, come on!" Wren interrupted him. "You've got to stop taking notes. Now is our chance to get out of here!"

"I'm not so sure about that."

Wren raced to the window. Not all of the soldiers had left. The captain had returned, and even with the window closed, it was very clear what he was doing.

He was ordering his troops on board the airship.

"I hope you really do have this figured out, Jack," Wren hissed, grabbing the falcon cage and stumbling over Simon's discarded pack. "Come on! We don't have any time!"

"This way," Jack said, pointing to the far side of the ship.

As they moved down the passageway, Wren could hear footfalls above, and the gravelly voice of the soldier in charge. Wren wondered how long it would be before they came below deck. There were shouts and the sound of running feet.

Jack paused, one ear cocked toward the steps that led upward. He snaked them through the galley kitchen and into one of the sleeping cabins, where a porthole stood open. They were on the side of the ship opposite the landing platform, and the scaffolding dangled into darkness broken by gleams of metal framework. It seemed the hangar was built to house much bigger airships. Who knew how high up they were? Jack tied one of the ropes to the pipe below the window.

"This is your brilliant plan?" Wren hissed. "Dive out the window into who knows what?"

"Whatever's out there sure beats what's coming for

us in here. Besides, it's a docking station, not a bottom-
less pit. We just have to make it to some of that metal
scaffolding over there," Jack said, tossing the rest of the
rope out the porthole and tugging hard on it to test his
knot. "The rope should hold all of our weight, but try
not to wiggle. Or else it will swing."

"And if we fall?" Simon asked, but without any
of the fear that was inching up Wren's spine. Simon
sounded like it was merely a matter of clinical interest.

"Don't" was all Jack said, and then he gave Wren
a crooked-smiled salute before propelling himself out
over the edge. Simon and Wren looked at each other
after Jack disappeared.

"We can't take the falcon cage that way," Simon said.

"You're right." Wren bent to open the door, carefully cupping her hands around a dazed Coeur and
setting her on the window ledge. "They'll stand a better chance if they're free." Coeur ruffled her feathers
and then launched, followed by Simon's bird, and then
Simon himself, until only Wren was left in the room.
She stood at the window watching the others, who
were working their way down the rope toward the
precarious metal latticework that made up the docking station, and her knees grew weak. Heights hadn't

bothered her too much before the gateway, but now things were different. Her mind flashed back to the time when she had tackled Jack and fallen into the darkness. She could almost feel the invisible pressure that had nearly squeezed the breath out of her. Her chest felt tight, and little spots danced before her eyes. What was wrong with her?

"Wren," Jack's loud whisper came from below. "Where are you?"

Wren peeked back over and saw that the rope was empty. It disappeared into the shadows below the airship, but her friends weren't on it or the metallic framework beyond. Wren hesitated a moment longer, fighting hard for control over the panicked feelings, and then she won, shoving them deep inside. She could hear the soldiers calling to one another right outside the captain's rooms. She flung a leg over the edge and eased herself down, one hand over the other, slowly making her way lower, and not a moment too soon. Somewhere above her, she heard a door bang open and the guttural sound of the soldiers talking.

"Hurry!" Jack hissed from below. "They still might see us."

Wren willed herself to move. Her palms burned

with the friction from the rope. Her body swung. The rope twisted.

"Hold the rope," Simon's voice said from just below her. "Come on, Wren. You can do this."

Another few handholds, and then she was down. Just in time, too. The end of the rope dangled above a small platform that was connected to the larger landing dock by a narrow strip of metal.

"How did you know this was here?" Wren asked Jack in a shaky voice as she found her footing.

"I didn't," Jack said with a smirk.

"Captain!" a soldier's voice called from above. "You need to see this."

"They've found the rope," Simon said, shouldering his pack.

"Come on," Wren said, pointing toward an opening on the other side of the platform. Beyond it, she could see a familiar smudge of orange-streaked sky. "Follow me!"

# EIGHT

*There was a house on Scavenger Hill,*
*And, if not gone, it sits there still.*
*It grew so tall, it reached the trees,*
*So build a nest there if you please.*

A damp cloud of mist enveloped Wren as she and the others raced away from the docking station. The opening led to a metal mesh balcony high in the air, and as Wren hurried along it, she saw that it bridged the spires of two spindly buildings. Both were constructed at odd angles, with glass bay windows protruding like tumors. There were no cries of pursuit from behind. At least not yet.

"We need to get down to the street level," she called over her shoulder. Far below, she could see a maze of bricked roads and narrow alleyways that crisscrossed between cluttered city blocks. Lamps flared on the corners, sending pools of light into the overcast sky. The streets were bustling with activity. With luck, they could lose themselves among the crowds.

"The falcons will follow us from the shadows," Simon said, puffing up behind her. "They don't want to be seen in this place."

Wren nodded in response, too out of breath for words. She didn't blame the birds. She waved at Coeur, watching her form coast stealthily along the rooftops, and hoped that they'd be able to find each other again. One of the tight curving staircases appeared in front of them, and Wren ducked down it, beckoning for the others to follow. From somewhere above, she heard a voice calling and heavy footsteps. Perhaps the soldiers had discovered their trail, but it wouldn't do them any good. Once on the ground, Wren hustled toward the intersection, where a throng of people was going about its ordinary business. Soon, she, Jack, and Simon were just another group jostling through the crowd.

Up close, the Magicians seemed ordinary enough, even if their clothing was a bit odd. Wren saw men wearing tall hats that matched dark jackets with tails and women with corseted waists and ruffled skirts.

Some of the scene was familiar, as though Wren had stepped into a setting from more than a hundred years ago on Earth, but it all felt not quite right. The top hats had goggles strapped to the front, for instance, and the women's petticoats were tucked up at the corners, revealing fitted leather pants. The children ran to and fro wearing vests covered with buckles and pockets. And there were other things that were completely foreign. The sleek three-wheeled cart that sped by, for instance, and the unrecognizable contraption that stood on a street corner, whirring and ringing to the delighted cries of children.

Simon paused to study the machine. "I wonder what its purpose is," he said, adjusting his pack and pulling out his notebook.

"Nod doesn't seem so bad," Jack said, coming up beside Wren and grinning at the children. He took a deep breath. "And something smells really good."

Wren's stomach growled in response, a reminder that she hadn't eaten in what felt like forever. In the center square, near a stone fountain, merchants were selling their goods, calling out prices for white cheeses, fruits, and some kind of roasted meat on skewers—the source of the mouth-watering smell.

"Please, can we stop and get some?" Jack plucked at Wren's sleeve, his tortured face focused on the food stalls.

"And pay for it with what?" Wren said in a sour voice. She was as hungry as he was.

"Maybe we could barter?" Simon suggested.

Just then, a crowd of boys and girls descended on the marketplace with a chorus of whoops. They slid down gutter pipes as though they were spiders, slipping down into the market's center. The vendors did not look pleased to see them, but they made no move to stop the new arrivals from pressing in and taking their food.

"Some pies, I think," the boy who seemed to be their leader said, swiping a whole platter full of baked goods into an open sack. His companions did the same, taking fruit and cheese without even asking. "Thank you very much, kind sirs," the leader said with a dramatic bow. "Your generosity is, as ever, most unwillingly given but greatly appreciated."

The other customers pressed to the sides of the market, making room for the strange group, until Wren realized too late that she and Jack and Simon were standing on their own in the middle of the square.

"Whatcha staring at?" the leader said in a gruff voice, but then his eyes softened when he looked carefully at them. "New recruits?" he said with a grin, tossing each of them an apple. "I can pick 'em out a mile away." His friends were finished collecting their loot, and had begun to scale the brick walls again. "Well?" the boy asked them. "What are you waiting for? Get your food, and then come with me. I'll get you settled."

Wren looked at Jack and Simon, who shrugged. Jack was already stuffing his face with one of the meat kabobs, and it took all of Wren's willpower not to follow suit. From somewhere behind them, the sounds of the bustling market were overtaken by something else. The blast of a strange horn echoed through the square, followed by a ripple of worried mutters among the crowd.

The boy in front of them darted a glance back the way Wren and the others had come. "You wanna wait for Boggen's soldiers to get here? Suit yourself." And then he dashed toward a metal ladder, which snaked up the side of a building like a fire escape. That decided it for Wren. She turned to the others. "I think our chances are better with the kids than with Boggen's soldiers."

Jack grunted agreement around his mouthful of food, Simon nodded thoughtfully, and they all hurried to follow after the strange boy, who was already halfway up the building, climbing as quickly as a cat. Wren went first. It took all her attention to focus on the slick footholds in front of her. *Don't look down,* she told herself. *Anywhere but down.*

Painstakingly, Wren made her way upward, and after a few very long minutes, she had joined the others on the rooftop. Most of the pack of kids were already slinking across it. When the leader looked back and saw them following, he gave them a funny sort of salute. "Good. Glad to see you made the right decision." He winked. "This way to the Nest." And then he was racing down the slanted side of the roof. A little staircase connected to the peak and Wren, Jack, and Simon hurried up it. There was no space for conversation or questions. All of Wren's energy was focused on keeping up with the others. Trotting over the steep rooftops. Dodging laundry lines and steaming pipes. Scooting around inconveniently placed chimneys and avoiding the odd apartment with windows glowing blue green. She lost count of how many rooftops they crossed before dropping back down into an alley.

Yellowish lanterns lit up the corners, casting reflections that glistened wetly in the gathering puddles. Finally, in what appeared to be a forgotten corner of the forgotten street, the wild race stopped. The children pushed and shoved their way into a jumbled mess of a building, which stretched up for five or six stories at least, its strange curved architecture towering over the small figures, while their leader turned to face Wren and the others.

"So," the boy said, adjusting his jacket and tightening the belts and straps on his vest. "New recruits. What neighborhood did you come from?"

Wren and Simon looked at each other. Jack had already slumped to the ground, the rooftop flight seemingly taxing his physical reserves. Wren didn't know how she was going to bluff her way through this one. She wanted to trust the boy. He looked friendly enough. Wren fidgeted under his gaze. With anyone else, she wouldn't have squirmed. With Simon, for instance. Or Jack. But this boy made her feel odd inside, almost like she was off balance. She felt the heat rise in her cheeks. She was being stupid. Or overtired. All of this because a boy with the most striking eyes she had ever seen was looking at her, was scrutinizing her, actually, and saying nothing.

Wren started to get annoyed. Was he going to just sit there and stare? She took the foreign feelings and shoved them deep down in the tight-lidded box inside her. Whatever the feelings were, they were a distraction. She folded her arms and stared right back at him.

"We're not from Nod," she began.

"Outsiders?" The boy's face crinkled in alarm. "You three are the worst Outsider spies I've ever seen. Nearly got yourself caught back there."

Simon cleared his throat. "Yeah. Um. Thanks for your help . . ." Wren stared at him. *Simon* was going to try and smooth talk their way past this?

"Vulcan," the boy said. "My name is Vulcan."

Jack choked back a laugh. "That's your name? Seriously?"

Wren couldn't stifle her own grin as Jack did an exaggerated *Star Trek* Vulcan salute.

"You have a problem with it?" the boy said, a dangerous-looking half smile on his face. "What are your names?"

When they told him, he frowned. "Those are old-fashioned, even for Outsiders."

Simon nodded. "You guys were really impressive, the

way you travel over the city." His voice turned curious. "Tell me, is that your usual mode of transportation?"

Wren rolled her eyes. Simon was seriously going to conduct research at a time like this?

Vulcan grinned at them. "That's the Scavengers at their best. The city may not want us, but we own the place in our way." He gestured toward the crooked building in front of them. "The Nest, for instance. All the grown Magicians wanted to condemn it after the plague, but we claim anything condemned." His face grew hard. "Boggen owes us."

Simon was scribbling furiously, not bothering to hide his notebook, and Wren could guess what he was writing. *The plague?* As in the tainted magic? She was trying to think of a way to ask Vulcan more about it without giving anything away, but he had already moved on, frowning at their clothes. "The Outsiders must be losing their edge. Those clothes stick out worse than anything I've ever seen." He grinned again. "Come on. I'll help you out. We outcasts have to stick together."

Vulcan led them through the door and into a wood-paneled entryway cluttered with odds and ends. It appeared to be the back entrance, with mops and brooms tottering in one corner and a trash bin in the other. The walls were lined with cubbies, but Wren could make no rhyme or reason of them. There were books stacked three rows deep, precariously balanced atop one another so as to utilize every possible space. Spools of thread filled the nook closest to her, and then there was one with jars and small rumpled envelopes. There were rolls of parchment, globes, goggles, and spectacles. The ones near the stairs seemed to contain articles of clothing, and Vulcan quickly pawed through these.

"I heard that an Outsider was just taken prisoner." Vulcan's voice came from within one of the cubbies. "You know anything about that?" He emerged with a basket of boots that he dumped on the ground. "Find a pair that fits."

"Who took him prisoner?" Wren asked, hoping that if she could ask enough questions, they might continue playing the part of the Outsiders, whoever they were.

Vulcan shook his head. "Who else?" Simon and Jack were looking at him blankly. Wren wished they could at least try to play along.

"Boggen's henchmen," Vulcan said, as though this would bring clarity. "His security force? How is it you guys were in the marketplace, anyway? I thought you people liked to come and go through the catacombs."

Wren cleared her throat. "We got a little turned around, that's all."

"Well, if anyone else in the marketplace puts two and two together, Boggen will be after you next. He's really cracking down on the Outsiders, looking for one of their leaders—called the Knave of Hearts, I think?" Vulcan was tossing articles of clothing to each of them while he talked. "But I don't intend for Boggen to recognize you. New recruits are always arriving at the Nest"—he gestured to the building around them as he said this—"so you might be able to blend in. If anyone asks, tell them you're too sad to talk about it."

"What?" Simon was tugging on a pair of weathered boots. "Why would we be sad?"

"You Outsiders haven't heard of the Nest?" He looked a little insulted, and then his mouth softened. "This is where Nod's orphans come," Vulcan said. "Any new recruit who lands here has something to be sad about."

By the time they were finished, Wren was outfitted with skirt and shirt held together in the middle by a thick corseted waistband. Over all of this, she wore a vest, but Wren's hung loosely, like a many-pocketed overcoat. She tugged on a pair of boots, folding the tops down at the knees as Vulcan showed them, and watched the others. The boys were wearing ill-fitting jackets with longish tails, and normal-looking pants tucked into their boots.

Vulcan stepped back and surveyed them with a grin. "Not so bad. Not bad at all." He began heedlessly shoving supplies back into the cubbies, adding to the cluttered jumble of goods. "You guys hungry?" Vulcan asked as he wedged a wad of clothes behind a stash of umbrellas and took up the satchel he had filled in the marketplace.

"Yes!" Jack finally spoke. "Yes, please."

"Okay," Vulcan said. "So every new recruit needs to know that we run a tight crew here at the Nest. There are three hundred Scavengers, and even though the city merchants are required to give us food, we have to find everything else we need to live on our own. For however long you stay with us, you're part of our crew." He stopped, giving them a serious look. "Silver's the captain, and though she might look friendly, she's not. When she says 'Jump,' you say 'Onto which rooftop?' Got it?"

Wren exchanged an amused look with Simon. Jack grinned and ran his hand back through his hair, messing it up. Even though Wren didn't know the expression, Vulcan's meaning came through loud and clear. Silver was the boss. At least for now.

With that introduction complete, Vulcan led them through a long, dimly lit, darkly papered hallway that smelled like boiled potatoes. They climbed up a scarcely used stairwell to a room crowded with more cubbies. Their contents overflowed so much that they nearly blocked out the weak lamplight filtering through the narrow floor-to-ceiling windows in each of the walls. Hammocks were strung at varying heights between them, and the result made Wren feel a touch claustrophobic. A few boys dozed in their hammocks. One was hunched over a worktable in the corner, and when he saw them enter, he hurriedly covered what he was working on and scowled at Vulcan.

"They're clear," Vulcan reassured him. "They're with me." He turned to Wren and the others and said under his breath, "Some of us Scavengers can be a little . . . protective . . . of what's ours." He ducked under an unoccupied hammock and down a hallway that ended in a cramped room filled with boys and girls of

all ages. Wren recognized some of them from the marketplace. The foods they had acquired were piled up
on wide platters in front of them. Other kids perched
on stools or crowded into window seats, gnawing on
the meat skewers. As if in response, Wren's stomach
growled embarrassingly loudly.

"Dig in!" Vulcan said, shoving his way through to
the table. "Rocky!" He gestured to a boy whose cheeks
were stuffed with food. "Pass that down here." While
the boy complied, the girl on his other side studied
them over the full table.

"Silver," Vulcan said respectfully. "We've got some
new recruits."

Wren could see where Silver got her name. Smooth,
nearly white hair hung past her shoulders. She took
a slow sip from a dented tin cup and finally nodded
approval.

"Welcome," she said, spreading a hand toward their
empty plates. "There's plenty of food. Eat."

Wren was glad that Silver's first command was something she wanted to comply with. She didn't waste any
time. There was bread and some kind of meat pie. The
food on the stick resembled chicken, and the fruit tasted
just as sweet as fruit from home. The pie was good, if
a little spicy, and Wren was so hungry she didn't really

care about that. As the other kids finished eating, they moved on to other activities. Some younger boys were hunched over the floor playing a game that looked like marbles, except with balls that glowed blue in the dim lighting. Near them, older kids had fiddles out and were playing a merry tune, and a handful of girls around them had started dancing.

Wren felt people watching her, and she wondered if her costume was fooling anyone. The real Scavengers were similarly dressed. Leather and ruffles, patched and mended fabrics, buckles and straps all over the garments, and pockets everywhere—the waist, the shoulders, and any other place anyone could conceivably want to have a pocket. Wren wondered what it was that everyone put in them. She had seen Vulcan tuck something from one of the cubbies inside one boot, and a spyglass dangled from his belt. Wren wondered what kind of place Nod was that they needed so many tools. Or weapons. Half a dozen times she started to ask Vulcan questions and as many times, she stopped herself. Surely even the outcast Outsiders, whoever they were, knew the basics of how Nod worked.

With her hunger satiated, the reality of their predicament began to settle in. They might have escaped Boggen's soldiers, but they still were alone in a city of

Magicians, all of whom could hate the Alchemists for all she knew. And while they had found a temporary reprieve at the Nest, they couldn't stay here forever. At least she hoped not. They needed to figure out how to rescue the others and get back to Earth. Next to Wren, Vulcan was pouring a black liquid that looked like tea from a steaming pot. He handed her a cup, and Wren decided to take a chance on some careful questions.

"This Outsider prisoner you heard about," she said, blowing on the hot liquid. "Do you know where he's being kept?"

Vulcan gave her a curious look. "Where all the prisoners are kept," he said, and Wren felt her heart leap. *All the prisoners* could mean Mary and Cole as well.

She took a sip of the scalding liquid. "I see," she said, thinking fast. "I'm afraid we've gotten so turned around I don't know where we are exactly." She gave an embarrassed cough. "But we really do need to get to the prisoner. Do you think you could show us the way?"

"To the House of Never?" Vulcan set his cup down, a gleam in his eye. "It would be my pleasure."

# NINƐ

*Hickory dickory dock,*
*The three climbed up the clock.*
*The clock struck one,*
*Away they run,*
*Hickory dickory dock.*

It was late when they finally arrived at the House of Never. The city sprawled around them in ripples of buildings and alleys, which Vulcan navigated with familiar ease until they began to slowly ascend, the streets swirling upward toward a hill in the center. The buildings here were quiet, no evening lamps lit inside, and at their center a huge brick-and-glass monstrosity loomed over it all. The core of it reminded Wren of a monument, with smooth sides that stretched up to a tapered point, but wooden turrets and outcroppings bulged from the sides, interspersed with large glass-paned additions. The largest of these additions, a big circular window, was constructed of familiar-looking black-and-white glass.

Wren recognized it immediately from her dreams. She remembered how Boggen had looked silhouetted by the black-and-white glass, how angry his face had been when he discovered that she had traveled through the dream. "That's it, isn't it?" she asked, even though she already knew the answer.

"The House of Never," Vulcan said. "Boggen's headquarters." He ducked through a crumbling portion of the brick wall that surrounded the House of Never. He swung himself up to a bridge as if they were in a playground rather than a prison. Vulcan paused at the foot of a spiral staircase. "This will take you to the upper levels, where they keep the prisoners." He shifted from one foot to the other. "Do you need an extra crew member for your mission?"

"Shh," Simon said. He seemed to be listening for something off in the distance.

Wren exchanged an alarmed glance with Jack. The last thing they needed was someone from Nod tagging along to discover that they were, in fact, Alchemists.

However nice Vulcan seemed, he was still a stranger.

"No," Wren said quickly. "I think we can take it from here."

"She's right," Jack said. "We've got our . . . um . . . Outsider plans. Top secret, you know. Can't tell anyone. Nope." Jack was rambling now, and Wren stomped on his toe to get him to stop. "But thanks for the offer," Jack finished with a pained grimace. His words sounded fake-cheerful, and Wren could tell by the look on Vulcan's face that they might have made things worse.

"O-kay," Vulcan said slowly, turning away from Jack and giving Wren a crooked salute. "Good luck. And you know you can always find me at the Nest."

Wren watched Vulcan disappear into the shadows with a fleeting sense of regret and some other emotion she couldn't quite put her finger on.

"Oh, come *on*," Jack said. "Stop staring at him and let's go." Wren blushed, and then quickly scaled the ladder with Jack and Simon following quietly behind. They hurried along a catwalk that skirted a wooden turret. If they could cross over to that bridge there, and then swing up to the parapet outside it, they'd be almost on the upper level. Ducking under the cover of one of the many roofs, she waited for the boys to join her.

"We should put on the invisibility tincture," Simon said, and pulled out a little bottle from one of his many pockets. Jack and Wren stood shoulder to shoulder with him, forming a little circle that would hide the glistening stardust from sight as Simon worked the rhyme and showed them how to apply it. Soon, they were as unnoticeable as the shadows, darting upward as quietly as possible. After Wren climbed up the final ladder, she leaned against the wall at the top to catch her breath.

"Jack?" she asked, when she heard the sound of someone bumping into a wall, followed by a muffled groan. She recognized the sound of Simon flipping a page in his notebook, which meant that he was somewhere nearby as well.

"Hey," Jack said. "Did you see that twisty little staircase?" He paused, out of breath. "There's a door there. I think maybe we can get in that way."

"Excellent!" Wren said, listening carefully to Jack's instructions. It was difficult to follow someone you couldn't see.

Jack's discovery turned out to be a stroke of luck. The rooftop below them was shabby and untended. It looked like it had once been a main part of the building, but in the intervening years someone had built two bulging turrets to either side, leaving a sliver of a path between them that led up to a forgotten door. But that was where their good fortune ended. The door was shut tight, and there wasn't even a lock to try to pick. Jack claimed he could have easily done so if there was one.

Wren peered through the smudged window but couldn't make out anything. "I guess we can try the rooftop," she suggested. Back at the Nest it had seemed like a good idea to go to the House of Never and then figure out a way in, but now it seemed like they might have made a wasted trip.

"Why don't we just break the window?" Simon asked.

"And announce to Boggen's soldiers that we've arrived?" Wren said. "I don't think so."

"What else is being invisible for?" Simon asked, and Wren could almost hear the smile in his voice. Before she could say anything else, there was a crashing sound of tinkling glass.

"Simon!" she gasped. "We didn't even—"

"It wasn't Simon." Jack's voice held an unmistakable

grin. "He's right. We're freaking invisible!"

"Shh!" That was Simon. "Someone's coming."

Wren crouched up against one of the turrets, instinctively hiding even though the henchman peering out the window couldn't see them.

"No one's here," he said in a voice with a heavy accent. "The exterior is empty."

"Are you positive?" A woman's voice this time. The first man jerked aside, and another face peered out. The woman had a bright red scarf tied smoothly over her scalp. Wren had seen one of those red scarves before, back at the airship. Whoever wore it seemed to be the leader among the soldiers. The woman moved toward a pipe fixed to the wall near the window and spoke into it. "Glass exterior broken on floor twenty-seven, witnessed by Delta and Omega. No evidence of nefarious activity." She flicked a switch next to the tube, and another voice filled the air, with the tinny sound of a radio.

"Report accepted," the voice at the other end of the pipe said. "Delta and Omega: confirm status of prisoners and report back, please."

"Right away, sir," the woman with the red scarf said. The two guards swiveled and moved away from the window. Wren inched forward, glass crunching under her boot. It sounded excruciatingly loud in the quiet night air, but they didn't have much choice. Those soldiers were going to check on the prisoners, and if they moved fast, they might be able to follow them.

The others must have had the same idea, because just in front of the window she bumped into someone.

"Ow," Jack moaned, as his scalp met her chin.

Wren groaned.

"Wait," Simon whispered from somewhere behind them. "I heard something."

"Of course you heard something," Wren said. "This is a bad idea. All of us bumbling about like this." Apparently, invisibility had its drawbacks. They needed a plan.

"No," Simon said, his tone uncharacteristically forceful. "I heard it earlier, too. I think the falcons found us."

Wren scanned the silent, dark sky. She didn't know what Simon was hearing, but they were losing time.

"Okay, listen to me. Jack and I are going to catch up to those guards and follow them to the prisoners. Simon, you do what you need to with the falcons and keep an eye on the exit. Everybody, be smart, and we'll be back here in—" She faltered halfway through the window. It wasn't like they had a way of keeping track of time. "Well, whenever we're done, I guess. Be careful, Simon." But Simon was already gone, his footsteps climbing higher up one of the ladders, toward where the falcons might be.

Once she was through the window, Wren saw that the pipes against the wall indeed seemed to be some kind of messaging system, with a callboard and a flashing little flame that showed somebody on floor thirteen was using it. But she hurried on. They might already have lost the guards.

"Wren?" Jack's hand smacked into her ear. "Oh, sorry."

"We've got to figure out a better way of doing this," Wren said. "Here, give me your hand."

"What?" Jack sounded confused.

"Hold my hand," Wren said flatly. This was not how she had imagined her first hand-holding experience with a boy would go, but there was nothing she could do about that. Finding Cole and Mary was too important.

Jack grabbed her wrist, but Wren shifted and slipped her hand into his. "This way we can stay together without being loud enough for the guards to hear." She tugged Jack toward the doorway. "Or getting smacked in the head."

"I said I was sorry!" Jack said as they stumbled out into a well-lit hallway.

"Shut up," Wren said. She had been wrong. The guards hadn't gone far. In fact, they were patrolling the hall right in front of them.

Wren watched the guards make a circuit. They walked the hall, turned a corner, and then returned within two minutes, paying special attention to each door along the way. A few more minutes passed, and then they returned, completing the same route like clockwork.

"Mary and Cole have to be somewhere back there," she whispered to Jack.

"They sure aren't leaving that area alone," Jack said. He must have been scratching his skin, because little flakes of stardust were sparking in the air, and if Wren looked at just the right angle, she could see a flicker of his outline.

"Stop."

"Stop what?" Jack sounded annoyed.

"Stop whatever it is you're doing." Wren reached over and grabbed what was becoming a clearly visible sleeve. "The invisibility mixture is coming off you." She waited until the guards completed another circuit and then told Jack: "Now."

They made their way to the crossroads, which was lit by lamps that glowed bright blue from behind arched glass ceiling panels—so bright, in fact, that Jack's halfway-there arm floated along noticeably beside her. Wren was grateful the lamps weren't candles or torches, or else they would both have been entirely visible.

"Let's split up," Jack whispered when the guards had rounded the corner again. "You go that way. I'll try the other."

"Be careful," Wren said reluctantly. "They might not be able to see you, but they'll still feel you if you bump into them."

Wren made her way alone to a wide wood-paneled door and tried the handle. Locked. Of course Jack was nowhere to be found, now that she could have used his lock-picking skills. She lifted the flap near the top of the door and peered through the tiny window in the center, but to no avail. Either the room was empty or the guards liked to keep their prisoners in complete darkness.

The next door was much the same. They weren't going to make any progress looking into dark rooms. Just then Wren heard the sound of metal on metal—keys jingling toward her. She pressed back against the wall. It wasn't time for the guards to come this way! But no guards appeared.

The jingling drew nearer and nearer.

"You find them?" Jack asked, the black shadow of his sleeve waving in front of her face and producing a ring of keys out of midair.

"Where did you get those?" Wren gasped.

"I don't only pick locks," Jack said mischievously. "I pick pockets as well. Believe me, it's a lot easier when your target can't see you."

"Jack!" Wren said in mock disapproval, but she was really only disappointed she hadn't thought of it first.

"All those rooms are dark," she said, pointing behind her. "Let's try these." Now that she was closer she could see a flicker of light coming from the crack under one of the doors. She grabbed the keys from the air and hurried toward it. The low sound of music drifted out. When she stood up on tiptoe to peek in, she saw not the dour prison she had expected, but a finely furnished room and a long table set with china and goblets. Seated at the head of it was none other than Cole. And next to him, Mary.

"What's in there?" Jack asked, and Wren could feel

him squeezing in close to get a look.

"Well, isn't that nice? There they are feasting, while we're barely making do."

Wren didn't bother to point out that Jack hadn't exactly been starving back at the Nest.

"Hold on," she said, feeling him tug at the keys. Mary looked older somehow, and the lines around her mouth were stark in the lamplight. Cole was sitting stiffly in his seat, his food untouched before him. They were alone. William and the soldiers who had captured them on the ship were nowhere to be seen.

"Well?" Jack prompted. "What are you waiting for?"

"Nothing," Wren said.

The third key Wren tried fit into the old-fashioned lock, and she gave it a hard twist, hearing the tumblers engage. The sound was loud in her own ears, and the two figures at the table swiveled their heads toward the door like hawks hunting prey.

Wren stepped inside, tucking the keys in her fist to hide them.

"Who's there?" Mary said, half rising to her feet. "William? Enough of your games." Mary's voice sounded strong, but lines around her eyes deepened.

"Let's be done with this," Cole said, putting an arm protectively around Mary's shoulder. "We have not changed our minds, William. I'd sooner die than help you with your twisted research."

Wren saw Mary reach for her stardust, could see a tiny flare of light when she began to work it in a rhyme, but then the dust sparked a dangerous-looking orange color and burst into flame.

"Ow!" Mary hissed, sucking on her finger.

"The shield is impenetrable," Cole said. "Attempting to work the stardust will only further injure you."

Wren moved closer. From the look of Cole's skin, he hadn't exactly stopped trying to use magic. His hands were covered with burn marks that matched the one Mary was nursing.

Cole and Mary were still barred from using stardust, and they were defiant toward William. That was all the confirmation Wren needed. Fancy dinner or not, Cole and Mary were indeed prisoners.

"Cole," Wren said in a low voice. "It's Wren. And Jack's with me." Behind her, the door swung shut.

"We've got to be kind of quick, though," Jack said. "The guards are bound to notice that their keys are gone soon."

"Wren!" Mary's face broke into a smile. "We thought you were lost!" And then surprise: "Jack? What are you doing here?"

"We're here to rescue you," Jack said impatiently. "But we've got to hurry."

Cole and Mary exchanged glances. "I'm afraid that's impossible," Cole said in a grave voice.

"If only we could leave," Mary said in a weary voice. "But many lives depend on our remaining here. If we come with you, William and Boggen will kill them."

Wren and Jack sat on the floor near the table, and even though Mary and Cole couldn't see them, they had circled their chairs to face them. In case any guards peeked in, it would look like Cole and Mary were merely having a quiet conversation. Cole told them how William had immediately offered to help Boggen in return for unlimited access to Nod's research logs. With his newly granted authority, William had imprisoned Cole and Mary and demanded that they begin helping him run Boggen's experiments. "As we suspected, what's left of the stardust on Nod is now tainted. Boggen is exploring whether it can be used without extreme side effects."

Mary frowned. "A Magician first tainted the stardust

long ago. It seems she thought to create living stardust from the creatures here. It did not go well. I knew her as Svana, though she went by many names over the ages. Here, she is called Mother Goose."

"Mother Goose!" Wren thought of all the nursery rhymes she had read in preschool. "You mean she's real?"

"I assure you she was. Poor Svana," Mary said. "Her curiosity and intellect were unparalleled, but without limits they led her to dark places." She shook her head sadly. "Her intentions may have been good—I don't know—but William's certainly aren't. Boggen's wells of stardust have been emptying, and now he's appointed William to experiment with the tainted stardust." The more Cole and Mary talked, the more it became clear that things were bad on Nod. The little remaining untainted stardust was rapidly disappearing from the wells, and with the gateway open, Cole and Mary feared what the taint would do as it grew.

Wren heard the shuffling sound of Jack shifting next to her, and Mary turned toward him.

"Did Boggen ever talk about any of this, Jack?"

"Why are you asking me?" Jack said in a hard voice. "Do you think he told me the truth about anything?"

Wren was surprised at how bitter he sounded. Mary didn't follow it up with a question, just let his words fall in the still room.

"Who knows what Boggen intended?" Cole said after some time. "But this new method of research—experimenting on kidnapped human subjects—is evil."

Mary's face grew drawn. "Magicians from the poorest parts of the city have been disappearing. Imprisoned until they are needed as human tests for William's research."

"Disappearing?" Wren echoed. She felt strange prickles up and down her spine.

Mary shook her head. "I don't know where the prisoners are taken," she said. "But the man in the cell next door is hunting for news of them. He's one of a group of Magicians who want to overthrow Boggen. They call themselves Outsiders."

Wren nodded slowly. "They have some kind of spies here in Nod." She explained what little Vulcan had said about the Outsiders. Jack cleared his throat next to her. "What do you intend to do, Cole?"

"Me?" Cole shifted back in his seat. "Not much from here, I'm afraid. What you two have done to reach us is admirable and very brave, but we can't go with you.

William has us trapped here as surely as any prisoner."
He gave a halfhearted smile. "You saw how trying to
work the stardust burned us? It would incinerate us if
we were to try to escape."

"So he's just going to keep you locked up here
forever?" Wren got to her feet. "That's stupid. We'll
figure out a way to get you out of here. Rescue the
others. Defeat the shield. Hide you in the city somewhere. Come back with more Alchemists. I don't
know." Wren's voice grew frantic as she realized the
grown-ups actually intended to stay locked up in their
little prison. In that moment she understood that she
had been counting on the fact that once they found
Cole and Mary, everything would be okay. Once they
found Cole and Mary, she wouldn't have to figure
everything out on her own. Once they found Cole and
Mary, somebody would be able to help her before it
was too late and she lost her ability to work the stardust. Now she knew better. There wasn't anyone else.
She had to figure this out herself.

"As wonderful as rescue would be," Cole said in a
soft voice, "there are more important things at stake.
Boggen's, and now William's, research no doubt cen-
ters around extracting living stardust. Their prisoners

face an awful fate, and the repercussions of that kind of twisted magic could destroy the entire planet." He shook his head. "There isn't time to wait for help from Earth. The Crooked House has its own set of problems to deal with now that they know the gateway was destroyed." He nodded, forestalling Wren's questions. "I've been communicating with Astrid through dreams, and we'll find no help from there anytime soon, I'm afraid. No. It isn't the Alchemists who can help us now. It's the Magicians."

# TEN

*Goosey, goosey, gander*
*Whither dost thou wander?*
*Upstairs and downstairs,*
*And up and over yonder.*

Wren didn't know how much time had passed while they talked to Mary and Cole. After a while Mary drew Wren over to the far side of the room, where a beautiful wooden bureau stood under a round mirror. "It seems that many Magicians in the city don't know about Boggen's horrible research," she said, taking her burned finger and scraping at the edges of a brick in the wall, "but the Outsiders do. They've known for several years that Boggen was testing tainted stardust on his prisoners and have worked to thwart his plans. You must do what you can to help them." She leaned toward the wall, patiently wiggling the brick out of its place. Wren waited, staring straight in front of her. Despite the invisibility mixture, the mirror revealed Wren's reflection, down to the look of surprise on her face. She hadn't known that the magic didn't extend to mirrors. That could have ended badly.

"Wren," Mary said as she eased the brick farther out, sending bits of dirt crumbling to the floor. "I'd rather you were back home safe in the Crooked House, but perhaps fate would have it this way for a reason. Nod is full of injustice. Innocent people are suffering. The Wren I know cares about that."

"I do care about it," Wren said, and the words came out all wobbly. "I just don't know if I can do anything." Her throat felt tight, as though it would tear if she forced the words out. She wanted to tell Mary. Mary might understand. She wanted to scream: I can't do it! I can't work the stardust anymore! But if she let that out of the box inside her, who knew what else would come out as well? Instead she worked her mouth wordlessly, watching tears wash paths through the invisibility tincture on her face.

"I believe in you, Wren," Mary said. "I always have." Her voice grew soft, and there was a humble note in it that Wren had never heard before. "I'm not able to show it very well. I have probably been too gruff with you. There," she said as the brick came all the way out. A few moments later a voice whispered through the hole.

"Mary," it said. "Courage and Peace."

"Courage and Peace to you as well, Auspex," Mary said, as though it was a formal greeting. "I have someone to introduce you to."

But they never got to the introductions. The prison door slammed open, and Wren gave a loud cry of surprise. Mary shoved Wren away from the mirror and then covered her mouth as if it had been she who'd cried out.

"Why, William! You do frighten a woman so. What with your grand entrances and all." Mary fanned her face with one hand as though overcome with shock and stealthily shoved the brick back in its spot with the others.

William stood in the entryway, his lean form now covered with a strange mix of metal and leather that made him look little like the researcher he was. "Captains!" he whined at the two soldiers hovering in the door behind him. "What is the meaning of this? A code came through that the prisoners had escaped."

"Crew Member Flint's keys were stolen." The fierce captain's face crumpled worriedly. "And with the report of the broken window, we sounded the alarm. We know your orders were that no one engage with the prisoners."

"My orders"—William slapped the guard across the face—"my orders are that you not summon me for crew members' mistakes. Or do you not run a tight ship?" He scoured the room with his gaze. Wren stared at the floor, hoping any tear tracks that might reveal her face would be dismissed as nothing more than a trick of the light. "Are the other prisoners in their cells?"

The two guards shared uneasy glances.

"Go see," William said in a deadly quiet voice. "Leave. Leave now."

The two guards scurried out, and William sauntered into the room, plopping down into a seat at the head of the table.

Mary turned back to the mirror, primping her hair as if that was what she had been doing all along. Wren gaped at her. She had never in all her time with the Fiddlers seen Mary primp. Mary puckered her lips as though she had just applied lipstick, but all the while she was working hard to finish putting the brick back into place.

"Go. You and Jack. Get out of here," she whispered to Wren while William tried to persuade Cole to join him at the table. "Find Auspex in the cell next door. Help the Outsiders. We'll try to make contact somehow." With practiced ease, Mary leaned forward, wiping a finger on one lip as if to fix a blemish, and used her skirt to dust the dirt off the loose brick. Then she turned around and glided over to join Cole, who stood planted in front of the fireplace in such a way as to hide the telltale fabric of Jack's sleeve.

"—haven't eaten any of Boggen's feast?" William was saying with a frown. "Now, now, I thought good Alchemists had better manners than that."

Wren crept quietly toward the open door.

"And I never expected good manners from a traitor," Mary was saying in a frosty voice. "You've hijacked your fellow Alchemists. Allied with Boggen. Imprisoned us. Threatened us"—she wrinkled her nose in distaste—"and you expect us to help you after treating us in such a fashion." She folded her arms primly across her chest. "I've quite lost my appetite. But please, enjoy the welcome of our table. You obviously feel free."

William reached for a piece of fruit and began peeling it with a slim knife he took from his belt. "Perhaps you could play the part of a princess in the Crooked House, but not here, Mary." He gave Mary an indulgent smile, and two bright spots of color appeared on her cheeks. Wren would have bet anything it wasn't embarrassment but anger that fueled her.

"On Nod, a princess's charms run thin." He let his boots drop to the floor with a thud. "Cole. You must see my wisdom. Help me with my research, or you will join my other test subjects. Those are your choices."

Wren froze, her back pressed up against the wall. She was so close to William she could have reached out and grabbed his leather-clad arm.

"We've made our choice," Cole said in an even voice. "And it hasn't changed. I would rather die with the prisoners than help you."

"We'll see if you feel the same when you reach Boggen's stronghold. I think you will not find Boggen's other researchers to be such"—he paused, holding up his knife as if to examine its sharpness—"*welcoming* hosts." He gave both of the Fiddlers a wicked-looking grin and moved toward the door. He was looking at Cole when he said this, so he didn't see the tiny shadow in front of him, the quick flicker of movement that told Wren Jack was on the move. William stumbled, appearing to trip over his own feet. He caught his balance and scowled at the floor.

Wren held her breath. How could Jack be so stupid? To risk exposing them all for a laugh?

She reached out a hand, grabbing in Jack's direction and making contact. His hand found hers, and she squeezed hard, tugging him toward the open door.

"The stonework there is a bit tricky." Mary's too-polite voice was behind them now. "Do take care, William."

Wren slipped through the open door and pulled Jack around the corner, where they flattened themselves against the wall. William's guards were out here as well, several of them lingering in the hallway where Jack had picked their pockets. Others were rushing back toward the room with the broken window.

Wren could hear Mary's firm voice and William's whiny reply, and then he was there, too, his form blocking out the lights. He slammed the door to Cole and Mary's prison behind him, the sound of the lock turning soon drowned out by his voice as he called for his guards. "Prepare these two for transport to the stronghold," he said, ordering the others to join him in the control room.

Wren hardly dared to breathe while the patrols slipped by. A single movement could give them away. All it would take was one observant guard to see a shadow where no shadow should be and their whole plan would be ruined. Luck must have been with them, because the guards were nearly gone, and Jack, for once, didn't try to pull any stupid pranks. Soon, they were alone in the hallway.

"Did you see him trip?" Jack said with obvious delight. "I would've given anything to see him fall flat on his face."

"You about gave our freedom for it," Wren said. "The last thing we need is for anything to go wrong. You wait here. Don't move. I'm serious."

From the sound of Jack's soft laughter, Wren wasn't sure that he cared if she was serious or not, but at least he seemed to be staying put. She slipped over to Auspex's door, found the right key, turned the lock as silently as possible, and darted into the room, easing the door shut behind her.

Auspex's quarters weren't nearly so fine—a plain bed, a small writing desk, a tiny window. The man who must be Auspex was over at the wall, talking to Mary, Wren supposed.

"Hold on," he said. "Someone's in here now."

Wren could hear the low tones of Mary's voice, the rushed way she spoke. And Auspex himself was nodding, faster and faster. "Yes. Yes. I agree. Very well, Mary. Until we meet again."

And then Auspex swiveled toward the door. He was a middle-aged man, dressed in a gray shirt and pants, with a long leather coat over all. With his pointed beard and thick eyebrows, he looked to Wren like a pirate from a fairy tale.

"Wren?" he asked the wall opposite her.

"Over here," Wren said, and then realized that wouldn't do much good. "By the desk."

He turned in her direction and gave her a half bow. "Courage and Honor, Wren."

"Um, right. My friend's outside, and we probably don't have much time." Wren meant that Jack was probably about to do something that would get them all caught, but Auspex interpreted it differently.

"Of course," he said, grabbing a sheaf of papers from the desk drawer and stuffing it into one pocket. Then he moved to the wall opposite and carefully removed another loose brick, pulling something out of the depths and tucking it in his vest pocket.

Wren watched him gather his things, thinking that Boggen really needed to do something about his loose bricks, and then Auspex was ready.

"Very well." He turned to Wren with a smile. "Lead the way."

As he turned, she noticed something hanging around his neck, a talisman she had seen before, though she couldn't recall where. "That symbol," she said, describing the circular weave of bronze. "What does it mean?"

"This?" Auspex touched the symbol, which showed a bird in flight above a sword. "This represents the Outsider way of life: peace and courage, the two things we most prize."

"So if someone wears one of those, they're an Outsider, too?"

"Of course," Auspex said, listening at the door for a moment and then opening it a crack.

Wren followed him, racking her brain for where she had seen the symbol before. She thought it was from some time back in the Crooked House, but why there? Or had Vulcan been wearing one? She opened her mouth to ask Auspex if he knew Vulcan, but closed it again immediately. Questions for the Outsiders would have to wait. They had taken only two steps outside the prison door when Wren saw that they were in trouble. Jack hadn't been up to mischief. Wren could see him exactly where she had left him, his gaunt form leaning up against the wall, twiddling his thumbs. Which was exactly the problem. His invisibility mixture was wearing off.

"Wren!" he said, and a look of horror crossed his face. Wren looked down and saw the outline of her own arm.

"We've got to move fast." She grabbed Jack's elbow and propelled him down the hallway in front of her. Auspex followed behind, somehow moving silently despite their breakneck pace. They were almost back to the room they'd broken in through when Wren realized they had another problem. That room was apparently the control room. She could hear William's grating voice as they rounded the corner.

Jack came to an abrupt halt. "We've got to go back," he cried, but it was too late. The guard captain from earlier was patrolling the halls and had spotted them. The captain reached for the glowing stardust-tipped spear that was strapped to her back. Before she could raise something that looked like a whistle to her lips, Auspex was on her. He leaped past Jack and Wren, moving quickly and silently, and with one small movement locked the captain's shoulders in a grip that soon had her melting to the floor, unconscious.

"Or we could do that," Jack said, exchanging a stunned glance with Wren.

"She will wake after we are gone," Auspex said. "Though we must find a different exit, yes? Perhaps the roof?"

"I saw stairs earlier," Jack said, but before they could get out of sight, another patrolman was upon them.

"You two, go!" Auspex ordered, darting toward the guard. "If courage and honor favor us, we will meet again."

Wren was about to argue, but Jack grabbed her this time, half hauling her toward the stairs. "Are you crazy?" he said. "You think we can do anything to help that guy? He's practically a ninja." The stairs wound up and up, tightening in on themselves in a dizzying circle. "I thought Magicians would be different. Like they'd be throwing stardust around as weapons or something."

As Wren sprinted up the stairs two at a time, she realized that Jack was right on two accounts. First, it would have been foolish to stay and defend someone who was clearly capable of defending himself. They would probably only slow him down.

Second, and perhaps more troubling, was the fact that only one person in that hallway had tried to use stardust, and then only on a spear tip. Anyone looking on might have thought the rest of them couldn't work the stardust at all. Not burned-out Jack. Not the mysterious Outsider. And certainly not her. She wondered if Simon and the falcons were still out on the roof somewhere. Was he okay, or had he run into trouble, too? Wren worked her legs harder, passing Jack as she pushed the door open to the rooftop and then came to a dead halt.

There were gas lamps blazing on the rooftop, and they showed everything in stark relief. The spindly spires of the city, Jack's grainy silhouette next to her, and the pair of guards who stood blocking their way.

# ELEVEN

*What did she dream?*
*She does not know.*
*The fragments fly like chaff.*
*Yet strange her mind was tickled so,*
*To do anything but laugh.*

Wren instinctively reached for Jack's hand. What were they going to do? There was nowhere for them to run. If they went back down the stairs, they'd be in the midst of Auspex's fight. Wren was surprised when one of the guards lowered his lance.

"What are you two doing up here?" he asked, frowning at Jack. "Apprentices are supposed to stay on the lower levels."

"Right," said Jack, giving his trademark smirk and looking for all the world like he wasn't worried in the least. "But give a guy a break. I wanted to show her the rooftop at dawn. Even apprentices have to bend the rules every once in a while."

The younger of the two guards laughed at them. "Sure, I guess so," he said, but the older officer didn't look so persuaded.

"Rule breaking leads to disorder. This should be reported."

"Aw, come on," the friendlier one said. "They're just kids. Don't you remember what it was like to be a kid?"

"I remember what it's like to be caught and disciplined, Titus," the older guard said in a harsh voice. "Escort them back to their quarters. Avoid Level Nine. Butcher's patrolling there, and he's not happy." He looked at Wren and Jack. "Next time, you won't be so lucky."

"Oh, we'll make sure there isn't a next time," Wren said, and meant every word.

Titus saluted his commanding officer and then led them over to an entrance that they would never have discovered on their own, concealed under a shiny copper rooftop. He waved his wrist over a sensor of some sort that unlocked the door, letting them into a steep stairwell that wound around and down. Titus didn't say much as they descended, so Wren examined the glowing lance that bobbed in front of her. It seemed to be strapped to a pack of some kind. She hesitated. Was it full of the tainted stardust?

"Hurry up," Titus said. "You can be back in your rooms and get some sleep before morning duties begin if you don't dawdle." He grinned up at Jack. "You remind me of myself. I always had night escapades. Keep things lively. Otherwise apprentice ops never get any fun."

Jack laughed as though he knew what Titus was talking about, and Wren hoped that his bluffing would keep them going long enough to figure out a way out of the House of Never. She stumbled and caught herself on the handrail. The exhaustion of the past days was catching up with her. She hadn't exactly been sleeping well before leaving the Crooked House, and the adrenaline of their close call was evaporating, leaving her with the mind-numbing debilitation of too many sleepless nights. And for what? They hadn't helped Cole and Mary escape. Who knew if Auspex had broken free, and even if he had, he wasn't likely to wait around for them. He'd be off to wherever the Outsiders lived, and Wren wouldn't even have a chance to figure out how to help him. And now she and Jack were stuck here, having to rely on their wits to get them out and back to Simon. Was he still somewhere out there waiting for them? What if he had been taken prisoner? She panicked at the thought. What *had* happened to Simon?

Titus stopped to wave his wrist in front of another panel. "That way your reentry isn't recorded on your chip," he said, winking at Jack. "For old times' sake." Wren could see that his wrist was marked with some sort of glimmering tattoo. She gathered that it was somehow connected to stardust, since it shimmered with magic.

"Thanks," Wren said.

"Stay out of trouble, you two," Titus said as he opened the door and ushered them through before letting it shut behind them. Wren could hear his footsteps echoing in the stairwell and waited, back pressed up to the door next to Jack, letting her eyes adjust to the dimness. As soon as Titus left, they could return to the stairway and get out of this place for good.

"I think we might have a problem," Jack whispered.

"You think?" Wren snapped back as the shapes in the room took form. They were standing at the edge of a huge room that must be a dormitory of sorts. Hammocks were strung across at all heights, each occupied by a sleeping figure. It reminded Wren of the Nest, except this time they had no Vulcan to guide them through.

"Titus is probably gone now," she whispered. "Let's go back out before we wake someone up." The apprentice nearest them shifted, sending Wren's heart racing, but then the movement turned into the deep, even breathing of sleep.

"And that would be the problem," Jack whispered. "There's no handle on this door. Just one of those panel thingies that Titus swiped."

"No!" Wren hissed, feeling the thick, cool surface of the door for herself. But Jack was right. They were trapped. "Come on," she whispered.

Very carefully, very silently, Wren led the way around the room. It was long and narrow, so it took them some time to traverse the length of it. While the hammocks were like the Nest's, the floor was swept clean and empty.

"Oof," Wren said, as her knees met something hard, and she discovered wooden shelves, piled high with blankets and cushions. Past that was another door, equally smooth and handleless, and then more shelves. The whole room was like that. Hammocks of sleeping students, shelves with soft blankets or clothes, and more completely unopenable doors.

"Do they just lock them in all night?" Wren said in exasperation when they'd made it back around to the front. "What if there's a fire?"

"Well, they can get out with their sensor thingies," Jack said. "Though if every movement is recorded, I bet they stay right where they're supposed to be. Which works out well for us. We just need to wait for morning, and then we can slip out with one of the apprentices. Or apprentice ops. Or whatever they're called. Simple."

He plopped something soft into her arms, which turned out to be a set of the blankets and cushions they had passed.

"Sure," she said with a silent laugh. "Simple." Nothing about Nod was simple.

"No big deal," Jack said, and she could hear the cocky grin in his voice. "If we got past those guards, don't you think we can fool a couple of apprentices?" He yawned. "Besides, there's no use worrying about it now. Not when we can finally get some sleep."

★ ★ ★

Wren woke up to find herself alone in an empty room. Where were the others? Where was Jack?

Wren got to her feet and padded over to the single window, which took up an entire wall. A wind must have come up and blown Nod's typical rainy cloud cover aside, leaving a clear night with a bright round moon twin to Earth's shining in the velvety sky. Clouds scuttled across it, sending strange shadows playing over the cityscape below. But as Wren watched, an eerie feeling grew inside her. It wasn't only the clouds but the buildings themselves that appeared to be moving. Spires twisted and curled upward. Structures creaked and groaned, sprouting turrets and extra floors like trees growing buds. Bridges poked out where bridges hadn't been before. The wind seemed to call them, as every passing gust brought more stonework alive and whispered low, crooning music through the air.

Wren flung open the casement and leaned outside to get a closer look. The city streets were empty. No Magicians were about. No people as far as the eye could see. Only the strange organic buildings, creaking mysteriously upward and outward under the moon's watchful eye. The music began to change, the low notes climbing higher and closer together. The buildings cracked open and burst with shattered glass and splintering wood, erupting in explosions of crushed brickwork.

"Beware the stardust," a voice boomed, coming from all directions at once. "Beware the magic."

Wren reached for the windowsill as the ground below her began to move, as though a huge earthquake was picking up the building and shaking it all around. She grabbed for the pouch of stardust around her neck, forgetting for the moment that she might not be able to do anything with it, but it wouldn't have mattered anyway. The little pouch was gone, and with it, the last of Wren's calm.

"Help!" she screamed, but her mouth felt like it was full of cotton. "Help!" She tried to cry louder, but all that came out was a strangled yelp. The sound of the wind was changing, the low moaning rising higher, pulsing with the rushing rhythm of waves on the ocean.

Wren stumbled back from the window and the rising tide. A high wall of water was crashing toward them, and she could feel the jolt of the moment it struck the boundary wall around Nod. The wave crested and foamed, rushing over the sides like a massive waterfall, flooding the tormented streets. The falling buildings were caught up in the rush as the tempest tossed and turned, heading directly toward Wren.

Her feet felt stuck fast, as though someone hadn't only taken Wren's voice, but her movement as well. A silent scream bottled up inside her, until she felt like she, too, might self-destruct, like all the buildings of Nod. She shut her eyes, waiting for the end, wondering where the others were and if they had somehow escaped. But nothing happened. The water never hit her. And when Wren opened her eyes, she was out on a barren hilltop, the smell of her dreams of Nod sharp in her nostrils. She cried out in pain as the back of her neck cramped tight.

"I know you are here, Weather Changer."

Wren froze. This wasn't the voice that had warned her about the magic. This was a different voice, a voice she recognized. This was Boggen's voice. A little weaker, perhaps, but his. And he knew her.

"You are mine, Apprentice. And I will find you."

Wren tried the trick she had learned before, shutting her eyes tight and willing herself somewhere else. The landscape around her shifted. An abandoned city street. A wide-open plain. The side of a clouded pink lake. Boggen's voice didn't come again, and Wren took that as a good sign. She kept shifting locations until she finally found herself really awake.

She was lying in the cramped corner where she and Jack had piled their blankets the night before, but this time she wasn't alone. The pearly gray light of dawn was shining weakly through a many-paned round window at the top of one of the walls. She could now make out clearly what they had only been able to guess at the night before. Neat rows of hammocks were strung four deep and five across, like regimented bunks.

As she lay there she could feel the memory of her horrible dream creep back, the lingering clench of fear on her neck. Boggen had found her in her dreams. And what had happened before that? Why did she feel as though if she turned around quickly enough, she would catch sight of that ominous wall of water? And why did the music still thrum inside her, as if her blood pounded with the rhythm? *Beware the stardust. Beware the magic,* the voice had said. What did it mean?

On Earth, she had dreamed strange things, and it turned out they were visions of Nod. So what did it mean if she had a strange dream about Nod on Nod?

The rope ladder that hung from one of the hammocks twisted in the air, shifting under the weight of awakening apprentices.

"Jack," Wren whispered, punching the lump under

the blankets next to her. "Get up."

Jack gave a muffled moan and sat up.

"Shh," she said. "The others are waking." They didn't have much time. They were going to have to come up with a plan, or at least some excuse for why they had suddenly appeared in the middle of the night. Maybe they could say Titus sent them. Maybe—

"We can hide under there," Jack said, looking wide awake now and delighted at the challenge in front of them. He pointed to one of the shelves Wren had stumbled into the night before. In the light of day she could see it was a low bench that ran along the length of one wall. Sets of boots were tucked neatly under it, but the benches were deep enough that they might be able to squeeze beneath them.

"Let's go," Wren said, not wanting to waste any time. They scooted over. "I'll take this one," Wren said, clearing aside the boots and then sliding back as far against the wall as possible as Jack did the same with the bench next to it. From underneath, Wren reached out and tried to rearrange the boots, wiggling them back into place so that they would provide some measure of concealment. And she finished just in the nick of time. As she wedged the final boot in place, a buzzer, which must have been an alarm clock, sounded. She couldn't see much, but she could hear the sounds of people waking. Bare feet hit the floor in front of her as an apprentice clambered down the nearest rope ladder. She could see the end of it swinging as more kids awoke. There was the sound of hurried chatter, the opening and shutting of cupboards and closets. The sound of buckles and jangling metal. What were the apprentices doing in the House of Never? Were they guards in training?

Then one of them started to head her way, his bare feet coming closer and closer until Wren realized in one horrible moment the flaw in their plan. *The boots!* The apprentices would need to put on their boots. A hand snatched up one pair of boots, and then someone dropped down on the bench above her. She could see the buckles and laces and the hands working to put the boots on. The glimmering blue of the tattoo on the apprentice's wrist shimmered at her in the shadows. Others joined him. Boys' voices mostly.

"I wonder what the summoning is for," one of them said.

"A special op?" another answered. "Think you can handle that?"

"I don't think," one joked back. "I *know* I'm ready."

Another loud buzzer drowned out the rest of their chatter, and then there was a mad final rush for boots as the rest of the boys grabbed theirs. Wren shut her eyes tight, as if not being able to see them would keep them from noticing her, but she needn't have worried. Soon, the boots were gone, and the whole herd of apprentices was forming a line near the door panel on the opposite side of the room.

"Wren, now!" Jack hissed at her, and Wren realized he was right. If they didn't move fast, they'd be stuck in the room alone. She slithered out from under the bench, keeping close to the wall. Peering out from behind a cupboard, she could see that the boys were all individually scanning out of the room. A dozen were left, exiting one by one, and taking with them any chance of escape.

"Let's go!" Jack was next to her now, and they slipped across the room, making their way from cupboard to cupboard in case anyone turned around. There were only five boys left.

"Wait," Wren said, pausing at one of the open cupboards and grabbing two garments from inside. "Put this on." She shoved one at Jack, who hurriedly flung it over his shoulders as they crept toward the final closet, the one closest to the exit. There were only two boys left now. The jackets she had grabbed were identical to the ones the boys wore—made of leather, fitted with straps and buckles down the front, and stopping near their knees. Wren wondered if it was some kind of apprentice cloak for the House of Never. And then it was time. They had to make a break for it. She slinked forward, creeping up behind the last boy as he scanned his wrist tattoo. Right before the door shut behind him, she wedged her booted foot in the gap.

*Got it.* Now they just needed to wait a few seconds for the boys to get wherever they were going, and they'd be home free. She listened for the sound of the boys' footsteps on the stairs to fade, but they weren't fading. Instead, it sounded as if there were more of them. Wren peeked out the crack. Another troop of apprentices were coming from the floor above. This one was a group of girls, and Wren was relieved to see they all wore the same buckled cloak that the boys did. She just might blend in. Each girl's hair was pulled back in a tight knot at the nape of her neck. Wren wondered how many apprentices there actually were and how long she and Jack would have to wait. Seconds later the panel on the door started beeping at her, increasing in loudness.

"It must be a sensor of some kind," Jack said from over her shoulder. "To keep the door from being propped open." Wren ducked back, panicking, as one of the girls drew near to investigate the door.

Jack pushed past her. "Oops!" he said, winking at the girl. "Moving a little slow this morning."

The girl gave him a stony look, but his bluff must have worked, because she kept moving, joining the seemingly never-ending line of boys and girls headed down the stairs. Jack waved to Wren and they fell in with the others, Wren hastily smoothing down her hair and trying to work it into a knot like the other girls'.

The stairwell had plenty of doors, but none that seemed to lead outside. Down they went, plodding after the other apprentices, looking for a chance to escape that never seemed to come.

# TWELVE

*Jack be nimble.*
*Jack be quick.*
*Jack beware of trap and trick.*

The steps kept curving down and around, down and around, circling in on themselves. Soon, the stairwell changed from sterile metal to earthen walls with wooden steps. The air grew damper. Then they were funneling through an arched doorway, older boys who must be leaders of some kind holding the door for the others to pass through. Beyond, Wren found steps leading deeper beneath the surface.

The girls near her were whispering. "The catacombs!" one said in wonder. "Have you ever been down here before?"

"Never." The other girl shivered. "And I wish I wasn't now."

Wren looked around curiously. They were passing through a string of forgotten, empty rooms. They
moved past piles of discarded wood and other places
where it looked like fire had left sooty markings on the
floor and walls. There were a few faded papers tacked
up against walls and bits of rubbish in the corners.
Whatever had once happened in the catacombs, they
had been abandoned long ago.

They tromped through a warren of empty rooms,
past store cupboards and wide gathering places.
Through what had obviously once been bathing rooms
of some sort. In and down. Around and through.

As they moved deeper, Wren could hear snippets of
conversation.

"He's called a quarantine," the boy in front was saying. "We haven't had a quarantine since . . ." His words
trailed off as he rounded the corner.

"What's a quarantine?" Jack whispered to Wren.

"I'm not sure what it means here," Wren said quietly. "Back home it's when they isolate people for some
reason. Usually because of disease."

As they moved farther into the catacombs, the spaces
around them seemed to become more purposeful, with
wide-open rooms designed to house large numbers of

people and faded signs indicating assigned seats. Then the rooms gave way to smaller passageways that resembled tunnels.

Wren wondered where they led. Could she and Jack escape through them, or would they just end up wandering forever beneath the city?

The damp earthy smell tickled at Wren's nose. No old papers dotted the walls here. Instead, someone had carved things into the stone. Silhouettes of men and women. Smaller figures that were obviously meant to be children. There were names below most of these. And dates.

"Do you think . . ." Wren began when they passed the fifth such monument.

"Um, yeah," Jack whispered. "Tombs. This whole place officially gives me the creeps."

Wren shivered. She thought Jack was probably right. The entire passageway felt like a huge underground crypt. The statues. The numbers. The regular nooks carved into the wall as if— "You mean, you think there are *bodies* back there?"

"Skeletons, probably," Jack said matter-of-factly.

Wren felt a tickling at her ear and stifled a squeal, jumping around to see Jack grinning at her.

"Feeling a little nervous, Wren?" he said, waggling the falcon's feather he had poked her with. "Don't worry, the scary skeletons can't hurt you. They've been dead for, what? Many years, I'd say."

"I'm fine," Wren said, smiling at the girls in front of her who had noticed her squeal and were now scowling at her. "Really." Wren spread her hands innocently. "Just a practical joke, that's all." She laughed weakly in Jack's direction. "He's full of them."

"Now's not a good time for joking," the frowning girl said. She spoke with a slight accent. Her forehead crinkled into a frown. "What unit are you from, anyway? I don't think I've seen you before."

"Hey, look," Jack said, pointing up ahead and providing a welcome distraction.

They had arrived in a circular room with passageways sprouting off in different directions like the spokes on a wheel. The boys in charge were directing everyone to gather in the middle of the space, and Wren was glad to yank Jack in the opposite direction from the curious girls.

Seizing the moment, she pulled Jack into one of the dark tunnels. She didn't want to risk anyone else noticing that they didn't belong.

"Shh!" Wren said when Jack began to protest. "This might be our chance to escape."

Jack looked pointedly down the black tunnel ahead of them. "Escape where?"

Wren ignored him. It was a good thing they had ducked aside, because the unit leaders seemed to be organizing everyone in groups and taking attendance. She pressed back against the wall and felt carved letters beneath her hands. The main room was lit with flickering gas lamps, and their glow spread far enough to barely make out the words:

*To commemorate the end of the Great Plague of Magic from the Noddian year 231, in which 14,792 Fiddlers met their demise. Let it be remembered that tainted stardust was the cause of such deeds, and most solemn caution must forever be implemented to ensure that no Plague of this kind shall ever threaten our colony again. We honor the victims and their families with this monument, and we warn the generations to come not to follow in the wicked and foolish ways of Mother Goose, who brought this Plague upon our great colony. We do hereby declare a Memorial Day on the twenty-seventh of each month to grieve our losses and celebrate the successful containment and end of the Most Grievous Plague. Signed forthwith: The Most Solemn and Most Reverend First Council of Nod, this twenty-seventh day of the eighth month, in the 232nd year of our colony.*

Jack snickered. "Mother Goose?"

Wren shushed him. "Remember what Mary said?" The fact that the nursery rhymes she had grown up with had dire significance hardly surprised her anymore. She read through the engraved words again. Almost 15,000 people had died. How awful!

"Attention, please!" a familiar, unwelcome voice called out in the big room.

Wren peered around the corner. William was there, wearing the same leather coat he had worn in Mary and Cole's cell the night before. He stroked his pointy white beard while he waited a moment, but Wren didn't know for what. All the units were already in perfect attention.

"You apprentices have been assigned to my research team," William said in a too-pleased voice. "And what I say will be obeyed without question, is that understood?"

"Yes, sir!" the units answered in unison.

"Good. Your first assignment is to excavate these crypts." William pulled out a pair of thin gloves and situated them snugly on his long fingers. "We will be studying the tainted stardust, particularly how much of the taint is required to cause a plague of this nature. Obviously, some Noddians were exposed to the taint and did not die. Others"—he spread his gloved hands—"well, others, not so much. Your job is to determine why. Now. Let us look at a sample together."

Wren watched in horror as William turned to one of the crypts and pressed on a stone lever. Then, he carefully slid out a long tray.

"Ah," William said, his eyes alight. "The remains of our first subject. Come closer, apprentices, and watch carefully."

Wren wondered if the other apprentices were feeling as queasy as she was. She had done her fair share of dissection in her biology and anatomy studies, but this was a human cadaver!

"William always was a turd," Jack said, wearing a pinched expression.

Wren stifled a relieved snort when suddenly a burst of static rent the stillness of the catacombs.

Some of the apprentices jumped back, startled, but William merely looked annoyed.

He pressed a button on a device resembling a walkie-talkie. "What is it?" he snapped.

"William," the voice rasped, and Wren felt her neck throb with pain. Jack gasped, too, and clutched at the back of his head.

*Boggen!* Wren would know that voice anywhere, but it was especially recognizable after last night's dream. Only this was no dream. She stifled a moan as the spot on the back of her neck where he had once marked her burned like it was on fire.

"You, too?" Jack whispered, his face lined with pain.

Wren nodded. Whatever Boggen had done to mark her as his apprentice in her dreams, he must have done to Jack as well.

"William, my apprentice is in the catacombs with you." Boggen's voice sent stabs of fear through Wren's body. "The one that I have marked."

William's gaze was sharp now, scanning the rows of boys and girls in front of him. "Is this true?" he asked. "Which of you is it?"

Vehement denials came from the orderly regiments.

"Bring me my apprentice." Boggen's voice echoed

throughout the chamber.

"We've got to run!" Wren said, stumbling to her feet. "Or they'll catch us for sure." She knew even as she spoke that trying to escape was probably futile. The units were already fanning out in orderly patrols, and there were far more of them than there were tunnels to search. It wouldn't take them long to find Jack and Wren.

Wren pointed down the dark tunnel in front of them. "This looks like as good an escape route as any."

Jack shoved at her shoulder. "Then you take it." It took Wren a second to understand what he meant.

"No, Jack," she said. "You can't sacrifice yourself."

"Why not?" Jack's half smile looked a little forced. "He's marked us both, but apparently the mark can't tell him the difference between us. All he said was that his apprentice was here. If he has me, maybe he'll stop looking for you."

Wren grabbed his hands, pleading with him. "We don't know how the marks work. Besides, if Boggen gets his hands on you, just think what he'll make you do. You'll be like Mary and Cole, forced into who knows what kind of research!"

"So what?" Jack shrugged. "I can't work the magic anymore. He can't use me to do anything useful. For all Boggen knows, I'm still on his side." His voice grew sly. "I could be like a spy on the inside, you know?" He gave a weak laugh and then reached out and squeezed her hand. "But you. You he'd use for sure. Make it count, Wren." He winked at her, and then he stepped out into the circular room, calling out in a loud voice, "I'm here. I am Boggen's apprentice."

Wren reached a useless hand out after him, but she knew she couldn't throw away the chance Jack had just given her. She would come back for him. She *would* rescue him. Her last sight of Jack was one of the unit leaders grabbing him by the elbow and dragging him up to William.

"Ah," William said. "What a pleasant surprise to find you on Nod, Jack."

Wren shut her ears to the horrible sound of William's laughter and fled into the darkness of the tunnel.

# THIRTEEN

*One for sorrow,*
*Two for joy,*
*Three for girl,*
*Four for boy,*
*Five for silver,*
*Six for gold,*
*Seven for secrets, yet untold.*

Wren stumbled down the dark corridor, the sound of Jack's final declaration echoing through her mind. What would happen to him?

She calculated her options, darting around another corner. Cole and Mary would be of little help, still trapped as they were as William's prisoners. With luck, Jack would end up with them, which would make rescuing them slightly easier. Wren started to jog, sending little puffs of dirt up where her feet fell. She *was* going to rescue them. First, she'd have to find Simon. She hoped he'd had a better time of it last night. Maybe he had gone back to the Nest.

She was taking whatever path led upward, hoping that the sloping tunnels would eventually lead her to ground level. Soon the tunnels grew lighter, as dirt-smudged grates near the ceiling let in daylight. She must be getting closer! Wren passed what seemed to be a bird in flight carved roughly onto one of the earthen walls. She recognized it immediately. Auspex had worn the same symbol around his neck. She remembered how Mary had said that their only hope for help lay with the Outsiders now. Vulcan had thought Wren and her friends were Outsiders. Perhaps he knew where she could find the real ones. Wren moved a little farther down the tunnel, stopping to check the grates to see if any were loose. On her fourth try she found one. Wiggling it sent dirt cascading down over her hair, and she jerked her head down to keep it out of her eyes. A few more jostles. Moving it just a little. And then it was out.

Wren eased herself carefully through the hole, looking quickly to see if anyone was around, but she seemed to be in an abandoned part of the city. She replaced the grate, dusted herself off as best she could, and made her way down the street. Boarded-up buildings stared hollowly at her as she moved from shadow to shadow. She felt the uncanny sensation of eyes watching her from somewhere within, and she quickened her pace. There were no gas lamps here. No vendors selling goods. Just echoing, empty streets. On the corners, she saw broken hourglasses and apparatuses that looked like they belonged in the Crooked House, abandoned and rusted with disuse. It seemed that without enough stardust, whole parts of the city had fallen into ruin and disrepair.

Wren wandered for what felt like most of the morning, first turning right, then left, always keeping the House of Never behind her. Her clothes soon grew damp with the ever-present mist of the city, and her tiredness returned. Shivering, she realized that to get back to the Nest, she'd need to think like a Scavenger, and a Scavenger would never wander through the streets on foot.

She spied a thick drainpipe with tiny footholds on either side and began to climb. *No problem. You've got this.* She willed her trembling body to be strong, shoving her anxiety back down into the cramped box of emotions she kept tight reign over. Hand over hand, foot over foot, she scaled the pipe and eventually pulled her shaky self up onto the rooftop. From there, she could see that she was on the far side of the House of Never, opposite from where they'd arrived the night before. In fact, she wasn't far from the thick wall that ringed the city.

All her street wandering had only taken her farther away from the Nest. Sighing, she decided to continue traveling like a Scavenger, keeping the House of Never fixed on her left and hurrying over the rooftops, stopping only to painstakingly navigate the jumps between buildings.

Finally, a familiar landmark came into view: a glass rotunda she remembered seeing the night before. Below her, she saw signs of movement on the streets— carriages rumbling by and people going about their business. Wren's relief was almost palpable. Only at the sight of other people did she realize how foreboding the feeling of being watched had been. Her relief was short-lived, however.

"Hey, you," an angry-sounding voice said, and Wren froze behind a chimney pipe. It didn't work.

"I said: hey, you," the voice insisted. "What are you doing in Scavenger territory?"

Wren opened one eye and then the other, peeking around to see a boy in rough clothes and an older girl with silvery-white hair standing on the roof, legs apart and arms folded across their chests confrontationally. Wren recognized the girl's hair immediately.

"You're Silver, right?" Wren said, weak with relief. "I've been looking for the Nest! Can you take me there? I need to talk to Vulcan."

It turned out that Wren was closer to the Nest than she'd thought. As the pair of Scavengers led her over rooftops and across buildings, Wren learned that the boy's name was Rocky. He looked familiar, too, from when they'd all crowded around the dining table back at the Nest. He was Silver's brother, and they had joined the Scavengers two years ago when their parents disappeared. When Wren asked what had happened to them, Rocky's voice grew hard.

"Nothin' but theories," he said. "The leaders say they prob'ly went outside the Wall when they shouldn't have." He picked his way past a line of drying laundry. "Bad things happen outside the wall and all, but I know my ma and pa better. They never would've done somethin' like that."

Silver's voice grew furtive. "More and more people have started disappearing. You're not supposed to ask questions, but we Scavengers aren't too good at following rules." She gave a low laugh. "I know our parents are still alive." Silver neatly leaped a gap between buildings. "And I think Boggen and his henchmen know they're still alive as well."

"Wishful thinking," Rocky said, his hand resting on a fire escape. "They're probably dead, like everyone else who was working in the stardust labs during the plague." He shrugged at Wren. "Long-term side effects of the taint. That's what all the secrecy is about, y'know. If people found out that the plague was still killing folks, there'd be a full-scale riot."

"I think Silver's right," Wren said carefully. "I've heard rumors that Boggen is imprisoning people."

Silver stopped, whirled around, and eyed Wren suspiciously. "Where did you come from, anyway?"

Wren dodged the question. "I'm looking for the Outsiders. You should, too. They know more about Boggen's plans."

Silver grunted, seemingly pacified, and Wren decided not to volunteer any more information. Instead, she followed them silently down the fire escape into the familiar alley that led to the Nest. She added Rocky and Silver's parents to the list of people who needed rescuing. If they were still alive, that is. But all of this dropped out of her mind when she reached the ground and saw who was in the courtyard outside the Nest.

"Simon!" Wren ran toward him, leaving a puzzled-looking Rocky and Silver staring after her.

Simon stood up from where he had been feeding Coeur and his own falcon, Leo, and grinned at her. "Wren! You're back!"

Wren felt like hugging Simon tight around the neck, she was that glad to see a friendly face, but Simon had stuck out his hand awkwardly, so she pumped it up and down instead. "You made it out of the House of Never!"

Simon nodded and looked behind her. "Where's Jack?"

"He's okay. For now." Wren eyed Rocky and Silver nervously. "It's actually a long story."

"We should go report to Vulcan," Silver said, elbowing her brother. "Tell him what this one said about Boggen's plans."

"I have to finish feeding the falcons," Simon said.

"We'll be right behind you," Wren told the others.

As soon as they were out of sight, Wren leaned close to Simon. "Where did you go? What happened to you last night?"

"The falcons were roosting on a building next to the House of Never." Simon was carefully laying out strips of dried meat for the birds. "They were nearly starving, poor birds, so I brought them back here to feed them." Once he had arranged the meat to his satisfaction, he looked up at her with interest.

"What about you and Jack?"

Wren sighed heavily, watching Coeur and Leo swoop down to grab the meat in their talons. "Jack is with Boggen," she finally said, and Simon's head shot up.

"What?"

Wren explained what had happened. "He sacrificed himself so that I could escape."

"Sacrificed himself *or* wanted to reunite with Boggen," Simon said, and Wren felt a thread of suspicion reverberate inside her.

"I think Jack's changed. He's different now." She willed her words to be true.

"I hope you're right," Simon said quietly. They talked over the rest of what had happened, what Wren had learned from Mary and Cole and what Simon had

observed of the city. He told her that the neighborhoods appeared to be laid out according to castes.

"They seem to be a pretty divided lot," he said,
methodically laying out more strips of meat. "I think
Boggen likes it that way, because if the different groups
are suspicious of one another, they can't unite against
him."

Wren watched Coeur swipe a slice of meat and then
soar up to the roof to feed. They needed help, and Wren
would rather take help from kids like Vulcan, Rocky,
and Silver—kids who had good reason to work against
Boggen—than anyone else they had seen on Nod.

"I told the birds to stay close," Simon was explain-
ing. "Vulcan said it was dangerous for them to leave
the city or fly too high. Actually, it's quite interesting."
His voice grew animated. "Apparently, the Magicians
have created a unique design that keeps the entire city
shielded from above. I think that's how the Noddians
detected our airship. Remember that big jolt we felt
when—"

Wren cut him off. "Forget the architecture of Nod.
Tell me about Vulcan. You've spent more time with
him. Can we trust him and the other Scavengers?"

Simon sat back on his haunches, looking thoughtful.

"I think so." He scratched his head. "We might have to. He knows something's up. There are no falcons on Nod, for one thing, and we have two."

Wren nodded, watching Leo follow Coeur up to the roof.

The falcons wheeled overhead, diving down to gather more meat. Wren could tell they felt confined, only allowed to fly up and down the street outside the Nest. Just like all of them. Mary, Cole, Jack, and even Rocky and Silver's parents. All of them were trapped in this strange city with only Wren and Simon to save them. She looked back at the Nest, squaring her shoulders. Maybe she and Simon wouldn't have to do this alone after all.

"C'mon," she said to Simon once the falcons had finished their meal. "It's time to talk to Vulcan."

# FOURTEEN

*There was a Crooked Man*
*Full of crooked ways.*
*His bowlfuls of starfire*
*Will bring the end of days.*

Vulcan sat across from Wren and Simon, pouring some of the hot tea he had served them the day before. Rocky and Silver had returned and led them to a cramped room in a corner of the Nest where gray daylight filtered through grimy windows.

"Alchemists," Vulcan said, his piercing green eyes sending Wren's thoughts scattering. "Actual Alchemists. Here on Nod." He blew out his breath. "I almost wouldn't believe it, except that you've been acting so suspicious. Outsider spies not knowing how to find their own people!"

"We are telling you the truth," Simon said. They had laid everything out for Vulcan—what they knew of the stardust taint, Boggen's desperation, and William's horrible research—but he still seemed most concerned about something Wren had accidentally let slip: the Ashes.

"The Ashes told us—" Wren had said, and Vulcan immediately made a strange *X* with his hands, as if to ward off evil.

"The Crooked Man's Ashes?" Vulcan's mouth was tight.

"What is it with Magicians and the Crooked Man?" Wren said, remembering that Robin had responded similarly.

"Well, nothing, if you don't mind death and destruction." Vulcan set his mug down carefully. "Don't you have the Legend on Earth?"

Wren shrugged. "What legend?"

"The Legend of Starfire." Vulcan's face was very solemn as he began a rhyme:

*There was a Crooked Man*
*Full of crooked ways.*
*His bowlfuls of starfire*

*Will bring the end of days.*
*Destruction and ruin, oh, Listener, take heed!*
*For woe to those who with the Crooked Man must*
*plead.*

When he finished, the room was very still. "There are tons of rhymes like that, warning of the Crooked Man's destruction. I know you said those Ashes helped you, Wren, and I suppose I believe you, but now believe me—they mean only to destroy Nod."

Wren nodded slowly and took a sip of her tea. She couldn't very well tell him what she was thinking, that trying to cleanse the gateway seemed like the opposite of destruction. Whatever else they meant to do, she thought the Ashes did intend to save Earth's stardust, but little good that did them here. The Ashes couldn't help her now. Vulcan could. And he seemed ready to rally the other Scavengers and attack the House of Never all on his own. All of the Scavengers were orphans. All of them had lost parents. She didn't blame him for hoping that his parents might not really be dead after all.

"You'll help us, then?" Wren asked when he was done cursing Boggen for the fifth time. They had finally convinced Vulcan that rushing off impulsively might just supply Boggen with a whole bunch of new, young research subjects.

"Of course," Vulcan said. He told them that he thought he knew somewhere they could find help, a shop that had connections to the Outsiders. He brought sandwiches, and they sat for some time eating while making companionable conversation. Vulcan seemed keenly interested in everything they could tell him about Earth. That, and perhaps something else, too.

"He likes you," Simon said matter-of-factly after Vulcan cleared the table and left to return the dishes to the kitchen.

"What do you mean?" Wren said, her cheeks flaring with heat. She knew very well what Simon meant. She just wasn't sure what to do with it.

When Vulcan bustled back into the room, Wren could hardly meet his eyes. His extraordinarily green eyes.

"All right. Let's go," Vulcan said with a grin, leading them out into the maze of city streets. They were crowded with people. Men wore brightly colored tailored jackets and vests and escorted women in dresses of fine silks that trailed over the ground. Children in crisp matching uniforms ran down one street, and Wren and Simon were accosted by dirty urchins hawking papers on another.

As Wren became more accustomed to the sights of the city, she began to notice things. The way certain streets were nicely kept, with well-scrubbed people walking under tidy storefronts. Whereas others seemed forgotten, with garbage in the gutters and dirt-smudged people selling goods on every corner. Perhaps this was what Simon meant about there being such a strict caste system on Nod.

"Citywide search for the Knave of Hearts," a ragged-looking boy crowed at Wren, shoving a paper in her hands. She stopped to stare at it.

"'Knave of Hearts.'" Simon read the front headline. "'Wanted dead or alive for crimes against Boggen. Any information about his whereabouts will be richly rewarded.'" The article went on to say that the Knave had been involved in union meetings and speaking out against the leadership of Nod, all of which amounted to treason.

"Five pence for the paper, miss." The toothless boy's hungry eyes were on her.

"They're done with it," Vulcan said, shoving it back

at the boy and walking briskly away. "You want to draw attention to yourselves?" he scolded.

"Hey!" the boy said. "No reading for free. 'Tisn't fair." But Wren was hurrying after Vulcan.

"The Knave of Hearts," she began. "You said—"

"If we find the Outsiders, we'll find the Knave," Vulcan said confidently.

Simon kept his head down as he pushed after Vulcan through the crowds. It seemed that they weren't the only ones on the move. They met people with suitcases and trunks on their backs and saw carriages laden with household goods. They passed a store where a worried-looking shopkeeper was locking up the front gate. Another had a sign posted: "Temporarily Out of Business. Please Call Again Later."

"Where is everybody going?" Wren asked no one in particular.

"Haven't you heard, dearie?" A wizened old man pulling a cart full of crates and baskets behind him said. "The Crooked Man's star is in retrograde." He placed a finger alongside his nose. "Nightmares and hauntings and all. The plague is coming for sure. Add that to Boggen's men on the hunt, and you'd be stupid to not do something about it. Hurry on home to your ma."

"But where is everyone going?" Wren asked again.

The man stopped wheeling his cart and peered closely at her face. Wren took a step back, but the man reached out with a grubby hand.

"Hey!" Wren said, pulling back when he touched her forehead.

"Nope. No fever. No plague yet."

"Do you mean the plague of magic?" Simon turned from examining the cart and directed all his powers of observation at the man. "Is it returning?"

The man cowered, as though by making himself small, he could keep bad things from happening to him. "I guess we'll find out soon enough," he said. "I shouldn't be standing here talking. Told my wife I'd get our stock locked up before nightfall." He gave Simon a wary look. "You two, watch yourselves now." And then the man was gone remarkably quickly, pulling his cart behind him. Wren watched him go. What did the man mean? She wished he had stayed longer. They had so many questions.

"Another plague of magic?" she finally landed on. "Do you think that really might happen?"

"I don't know." Simon shook his head soberly, until he was bumped from behind by a man with hooded eyes and a nasty-looking device strapped to his side. "Maybe once we find the Outsiders we can find some answers."

Wren agreed with him. She looked for the Outsiders' symbol—the outline of a bird in flight over a sword, which made Wren think fondly of her falcon. Knowing what symbol to look for didn't help very much, however, as there were images of all sorts on buildings here. There were bird shapes and owls and swans. Other birds that were surely swooping hawks and some that were little chicks. Clearly, birds were very important to the Magicians on Nod, which was odd considering their conspicuous absence. She stopped when she finally caught up with Vulcan, who was standing in front of a bakery, staring up at the symbol discreetly etched on the awning over its doorway.

"This is it," he said, turning around and smiling at Wren.

"Thank you," she said, ignoring Simon's knowing grin.

She pushed the door to the quiet shop open, making her way into the fragrant interior. Her stomach rumbled as she took in the display cases full of freshly baked loaves of bread.

"Hello?" she said, but there was no response.

"I think they're closed and forgot to lock up," Simon said, pointing to the snuffed gas lamps and the chairs propped up on top of tables.

"In the middle of the day?" Wren said. She'd never heard of a successful restaurant that wasn't open to serving customers. "Do you think they're worried about the Crooked Man's star as well?"

"Everyone should be worried about that star," Vulcan said.

Wren wandered slowly around the room as if the shopkeeper would suddenly pop up from behind the counter, offer them a pastry, and explain where to find the Outsiders.

Instead, she found something a little better. Near one wall, she heard the sound of voices. A whole chorus of them, cheering and chanting. Then the sound quieted down, and she heard the muffled tones of a woman speaking. Loudly.

"You guys." Wren pointed at a vent in the wall. "There *are* people here." She pressed her ear up against the elaborate grate. "Do you think they're above us or below?"

"Definitely below," Simon said without much consideration.

"How do you know?" Wren asked. To her, the

direction of the sound was unclear.

"Because of the stairs I found," Simon said with the tiniest suggestion of a grin playing around his mouth. "They go down. Not up."

"*Now* is when you're going to start joking around?" Wren said, but she secretly was pleased. This felt a bit like old times, when she and Simon were sneaking around the Crooked House looking for answers. She hoped that this time the answers might be more welcome ones.

The stairs looked ancient. They reminded her of the catacombs, and she kept waiting to see statues and silhouettes carved into the stairwell's earthen walls. Instead, she soon found herself in a neatly stocked storeroom. Casks and barrels were stacked tidily against one wall, and shelves of crockery and baking supplies were piled on another. But it was the room beyond that held her interest.

She sidled forward to the doorway, and poked her head around just enough to see without being seen. A group of about fifty people was gathered there. The ones in the back stood, pressed in shoulder to shoulder, and those in front were crammed onto benches. Everyone was leaning forward, eagerly listening to the woman who stood up front.

"And it's not right to have different castes of people," she was saying, her voice strident. "Are certain people worth more than others? The divisions among us need to stop."

"But some division is good. Different neighborhoods for different work. Differences don't have to be a bad thing," a woman near the front argued. "The caste system has given us efficiency and progress."

The woman's face turned hard. "What exactly do you know about progress? I guarantee you everything Boggen has told you is a lie." She looked toward the back of the room, and for a heart-stopping moment, Wren thought they had been discovered, but she was only nodding at a man who stood next to a device. The next moment the device began whirring and projecting flickering images across the wall.

Grainy black-and-white photographs clicked past. All of them seemed to be taken from a distance, as though the photographer had been trying not to be seen. There were images of what appeared to be laboratories, with people of all ages being clinically evaluated. Whole factory floors of men and women, working with steaming vials at long tables. Wren recognized the scene from her long-ago dream, the one where she had discovered Boggen and his blackbirds. Had she seen him, then, in one of his research laboratories?

Another image caught her attention. This one showed a group of children standing in front of what could have been a large cut-out quarry. Wren nearly took a step forward and then stopped herself. She knew this place as well. More images followed, and Wren became certain. She had seen that group of children before in another of her dreams, long ago when she was on Earth. There had been children staring into the sky, children who had seen the candle that lit the path to the gateway. Children who had cheered, and—

She grabbed Simon's hand and pulled him a little farther back into the storeroom. "Robin was there."

"Where?" he whispered, his head popping up from behind his notebook. "She's here?"

"No. That place. In the images." She explained about the dream. "I never got a chance to ask her what it meant."

"They seem to be secret photos of Boggen's research projects," Simon said, consulting his notes. "Maybe those were children taken from the lowest caste on Nod? Or orphans from the plague?"

Wren crept forward into the doorway. Pictures were still streaming by. Some had older people in them, sitting in cages under the observation of Boggen's soldiers. And then the images stopped, landing on one where children no older than Wren and Simon were all crowded together in one room, waiting silent and hollow-eyed in line to receive an injection of some kind.

"What further evidence do you need?" The woman turned to face the audience. "Boggen has been free to indulge his terrible experiments for years, but it doesn't have to stay that way." She put her hands on her hips and stared at them. "Now is the time to act. Now. While Boggen is weak."

A rumble of discontent passed through the crowd.

"She's suggesting that Boggen is harming innocent citizens! That's treason!" a skinny man in the back row said in an angry voice. "There is no new information here. Boggen is doing nothing illegal. His administration has said over and over that research trials are only conducted on criminals or the insane." He coughed softly. "Those people aren't real Fiddlers."

"You make me sick," the woman next to him said in a broken voice. "Those *children* can't be criminals. Or insane. Boggen's been lying to us."

The skinny man gave her a pitying glance. "*If* you can believe those images." He pointed an accusing finger at the woman in front. "What proof do we have that those are authentic? She could edit them to show you whatever she wanted! *Her* kind doesn't care about progress. Those fanatics don't care about how Boggen's research could help all the citizens on Nod. They would have us go back to our Earth days, when we lived like ordinary humans."

The old woman in front of them guffawed. "And you think we're living better than that now? No public education. Barely any food in the poorest districts. Half of the city lost after the plague. That's no way to run things." The volume of the crowd rose as others began to air their grievances.

"Listen!" The woman in front raised her hands to quiet them down. "We must set our differences aside. We may not see eye to eye on everything. But our best hope for changing the system is by working together."

"And what if you're wrong?" It was the skinny man again. "Boggen's researchers say they're close to finding a way to purify the taint on stardust. Don't you see what that means? We could restore the city! Expand beyond the walls! Ensure that there would be no more plagues of any kind." He turned to face the crowd. "Don't you see Boggen's wisdom? He has to deal with the criminals and the insane anyway. We can't have them running loose on Nod, not when they might spread the plague to others. Why not contain them *and* work for the good of all Magicians at the same time?"

Murmurs rippled through the audience, and a few people nodded their heads.

"But it isn't for the good of *all* Magicians. There are no limits to how far Boggen will go in the name of *research*," the woman up front said in a stony voice. "Just ask those outside the city walls. They've seen it with their own eyes."

"Oh, and you have ventured outside the city walls, have you? Or are you just taking the word of the *Outsiders*?" The man spit the name out with a guffaw. "They would make up anything just to get us to stop using stardust. Reliable, factual evidence, that's the only thing that will convince me. You'd be a fool to believe this kind of Outsider rabble-rousing. Maybe it's not Boggen we should be investigating. Maybe it's fanatics like Winter and her Outsider friends." He pointed an accusing finger at the woman, and Wren could almost palpably feel the opinion of the room shift against her.

The woman looked determined. "Wait just a minute." She retrieved a carpetbag from the floor and began pawing through papers. "I have lists! Dozens of Magicians who have simply disappeared. Children left as orphans." She waved the papers above her head. "People who've gone missing all the way back to the days of Mother Goose."

"Missing persons? Or *plague-tainted criminals*?" the skinny man said, and stood up as though he was now making the speech. "Or perhaps they were foolish enough to wander outside the city walls." He shook his head and clucked his tongue disapprovingly. "It's tragic when a political group begins to make up lies to gain popularity."

Wren was riveted to the spot. She didn't know the whole story of what was going on, but she knew one thing: she detested that skinny man with the orange hat. His words were like a poison that manipulated the crowd before her very eyes. The tactic seemed familiar to her somehow, and it made her angry. The woman was protesting, but the hand holding the papers had fallen useless by her side.

The man was talking now about the good Boggen

had done, the way he had helped Nod recover from the plague and how his initiatives kept the city safe. "Or perhaps you'd rather we were still dealing with the plague? It might be returning, you know, and how will we manage it without Boggen in charge?" Buoyed by approving smiles from faces in the audience, the man continued. "For all we know, the Outsiders have patched together these photographs to manipulate us. Perhaps this is a test! Perhaps Butcher's spies are among us now to see who will be guilty of treason."

Wren could see worried frowns bloom on the faces nearest her, and the whispers grew louder. A few people even stood to leave, making their way to a side exit near the front. Wren could hardly believe what she was seeing. Were these people going to pretend not to have heard that there were *abducted children* in Nod? Were they going to ignore it altogether?

The woman did not look angry anymore. She looked desperate. "Please, stay!" she said. "Together we can change things! Don't be afraid!"

The skinny man strode to the front, making a show of putting on his overcoat and adjusting the bright orange top hat on his head. "Nice try, Winter. But until you have some eyewitnesses who have actually seen these research projects . . . until you show us definitive proof . . ." He turned toward the audience, giving them a rueful shrug.

More were beginning to leave. Winter's expression changed from determination to desperation, as though through sheer willpower she could stop the people from leaving. Wren didn't allow herself to think. She knew if she did, she would second-guess herself. So she was sure her face must look as surprised as Simon's and Vulcan's did when she strode out into the room and announced in a loud voice, "I've seen them. I've seen the children."

Every eye in the room was on Wren. Winter pulled her up to the stage, leaning close to whisper a threatening "You'd better be telling the truth" before thrusting her in front of the audience.

Wren swallowed hard. Public speaking usually didn't bother her, but public speaking on another planet in front of a bunch of unknown Magicians, including one furious-looking man in an orange top hat, was another thing altogether.

She took a few deep breaths. Her impulse to speak out to help the prisoners had rushed ahead of her brain. How exactly was she supposed to explain what she had seen without revealing too much?

Simon must have been thinking the same thing, because he was silently shaking his head from the back of the room. "Don't tell them about us," he mouthed at her. Like she needed the reminder.

"It was the day Boggen fell ill," Wren began, settling on a partial version of the truth. "My friend Robin took me to one of Boggen's projects"—Winter tensed at her side at the mention of Robin's name, but Wren plowed on—"and it was just as the photograph showed." She raised a hand to the man operating the device. "Could you go back a few?" The man, startled, pushed his eyeglasses up the bridge of his nose and bent over the machine, sending the pictures whirring in reverse.

"A little more," Wren said. "Now, stop." The picture stood frozen behind her, the faces of the children even younger than she had remembered.

"They were digging." She pointed to a spot on the cliffside. "I was standing about here. Then the gateway opened, and the children began to cheer." She looked back to the audience. The man in the orange hat was glaring at her. He opened his mouth to speak, but Wren knew nothing good would come of letting him do that.

"You think Boggen has been a good ruler?" she shot at him. "You think he's nice?" Wren realized what the man in the orange hat's words reminded her of now: the way Boggen had talked to Jack that day at the gateway, the way he had lied to Jack and promised him a home, when all the while he was just using him. "Did you know Boggen was planning to return to Earth?"

There were audible gasps and cries of outrage.

"That he made contact with an Alchemist apprentice? That even now he's recruiting Alchemists to conduct research on human subjects? I'd bet anything that the children I saw are only a small portion of his research pool."

The man in the orange hat's face went ashen. "How do you know—" he began, and then he caught himself. But it was too late. The crowd was in an uproar. The people around him were peppering him with questions, and others looked about ready to go to war.

Winter grabbed Wren harshly by the elbow. "Time to go," she said.

"But Simon's still in there!" She turned around, but the gathering had turned into more of a brawl. One man punched another, and someone else was throwing a chair.

"It's okay," Simon said, appearing at her other side with Vulcan behind him. "We're here."

"Anyone else?" Winter said with one eyebrow raised. When Wren shook her head, Winter gave her a grim smile. "Good. Then the three of you are coming with me."

Winter hustled them out a side door and down a gloomy alley cloaked in shadows. It was nighttime outside, and rain was falling hard.

"Hurry," she said, but Wren needed no coaxing. The shouts from the room they had left were pouring out into the streets, and Wren had no desire to meet angry orange-hat man in a dark alley. In front of them loomed a shiny carriage, slick with rain, with two horses hitched to the front of it. A man in a heavy black overcoat sat atop it, illuminated faintly by the lantern that swung next to him.

"Inside," Winter said, nearly shoving Wren up the small steps.

"Grovesnor Street," Winter shouted at the driver. "And fast." The little door slammed shut, and the horses began to move, leaving Wren, Simon, and Vulcan jostling about the carriage across from a very stern-looking Winter.

Wren was running through the options of what she could say, but Winter spoke first.

"Where's Robin? Do you have her?"

"Have her?" Wren repeated stupidly. "What are you talking about?"

"What about you?" Winter looked angry as she turned to Vulcan, and then Simon. "You haven't said much. Have you taken Robin?"

"Never heard of her." Vulcan shrugged.

Simon wiped drops of rainfall off his forehead. "No. But we've been keeping an eye out for her ever since we arrived."

Wren cringed. Simon was usually much more savvy than that. She tried to cover up his misstep.

"What about you? How do we know you don't have Robin?" she asked Winter.

But Winter wasn't distracted. "Since you arrived?" She glanced back and forth between Wren and Simon, and her eyes grew wide as she began to put things together. "You're the ones from Earth!" Her gaze lit on Wren. "And *you* are the Weather Changer!"

Wren and Simon exchanged glances. "What do you mean?"

Winter's stiff form relaxed back onto the carriage

seat, and she gave them a real smile for the first time that Wren remembered. "You're the Weather Changer!" she repeated, as though she could hardly believe it. "Robin's told me about you. And here I thought you might be more of Boggen's nitwits come to disrupt the rally."

As the cart rumbled its way down twisted alleys and over bumpy cobblestones, Winter revealed that she had met Robin when she began leading the rallies. "Robin was the first Outsider I met."

"Robin is an *Outsider*." Wren realized why Auspex's Outsider symbol had looked so familiar to her. Robin had been wearing the same token when Wren had seen her in the dream.

"Robin is a great many things. She was one of the first to discover Boggen's research projects and was passionate about freeing his prisoners. So are the Outsiders. We're all concerned about Robin's disappearance," Winter said with a frown. "It was dangerous work she was doing, trying to secretly gather information from the House of Never to prove what was going on. If Boggen found out . . ." She trailed off, her expression transforming into one of worried concern. "Well, you saw what he's done to his 'subjects.'" She reached for a rope that must have somehow been connected to the driver, because the carriage rolled to a stop outside an imposing townhouse. Its brick walls glistened in the gaslighted rain as Wren clambered out after Winter. The four of them entered the house.

Winter led them through dark, musty-smelling halls until they came to a large shadowed room, the corner of which was lit by a warm hearth fire. Several high-backed armchairs had been arranged there, and someone was sitting in one, drinking tea from the tray on the table next to him.

"Captain," Winter began, and the man before the fire set down his tea and turned to look at them. It didn't take long for Wren to recognize him.

"Auspex! You made it out!"

"Courage and Honor, Wren." Auspex's teeth shone white in the shadows of his face. "I am glad to see you are well."

After introductions and brief explanations were made, they settled in around the crackling fire. Auspex rang a bell, and a boy entered, returning a short while later with another tray full of food. Though Wren had difficulty recognizing the different vegetables on Nod, the meat in the stew tasted familiar, and she was sure there were potatoes in there. She hadn't realized how hungry she was until the boy set the tray down next to her, the rich aroma sending her mouth watering.

"Eat. Please," Auspex encouraged them. While they ate, he explained that he had escaped from Boggen's henchmen only to find that he could not locate Wren or Jack. "I knew I couldn't return to the House of Never," he said. "I'm so pleased that you found me, for I'm leaving tomorrow for the Outsiders' camp."

"You're going outside the city walls?" Vulcan wiped his mouth and stared. "What's out there, anyway?"

Simon was finished eating and watching Auspex carefully. Wren imagined he was taking mental notes while he listened.

Auspex smiled at them and shrugged. "Come see for yourselves." He leaned forward with a very serious expression on his face. "I must be honest. The Outsiders are not friendly toward the city dwellers, even less toward the Alchemists." He smoothed down his beard with one hand. "But if they hear that you also want to end Boggen's twisted research . . ." He trailed off, hopeful.

"Agreed," Wren said, but she didn't smile at Auspex. She trusted him as much as she had to trust anyone in this strange world, but that didn't mean she thought they were going to be friends. She had a sneaking suspicion that whatever he was saying, he wasn't being 100 percent truthful. The whole thing made her uncomfortable, including the part about going outside the walls. She hadn't been in Nod for very long, but it had been long enough to convince her that the world beyond the city wasn't safe. But then again, Robin was somehow connected with the Outsiders. Perhaps going with Auspex would help Wren find out what had happened to her. "When do we leave?"

"Tomorrow." Auspex explained that he had been gathering information about the nightmares inflicting the city. "We are concerned about what they signify."

"There was a plague," Winter began, but then stopped when she saw Wren's face. "But I see you know about that."

"But not anything about the nightmares," Simon said expectantly.

"Or why people are so worried about the plague returning. The whole city is in an uproar," Wren said, adding what the old man had said about the Crooked Man's star being in retrograde. She glanced at Vulcan, who was watching her, and shifted her gaze quickly back to Auspex. "Do you believe the Legend as well?"

Auspex sighed. "It has long been foretold that the Crooked Man will destroy Nod with starfire. All the signs indicate that this day is now approaching. We should have given up the foul stardust long ago." He turned to Wren and Simon. "We Outsiders don't believe in the use of stardust. We prefer to live naturally." He made a reverential gesture—somewhere between crossing himself and bowing. "We've seen the cost of using magic. The plague, for instance. One of the first symptoms was the nightmares, and now they have returned. After that came the insanity. Nod would have been better off if we had stopped using stardust long ago."

Winter cleared her throat. "Some of us are not as uncompromising as the Outsiders." She ignored Auspex's accusatory look. "While we do not shun the use of magic completely, we believe in better education. And, more important, in the abolition of the caste system and the ending of Boggen's forced research on unwilling subjects." She poured Auspex another cup of tea, almost as a peace offering. "On those things we can be united. We hope to work together to reform Nod."

They talked long into the night. Even after Auspex and Winter left to make preparations, Simon, Wren, and Vulcan continued the conversation. At first they talked about what they had seen and learned, what they thought might be beyond the walls, and what the nightmares meant. And then once Vulcan had nodded off to sleep, Wren and Simon talked about what might be happening on Earth and when they might see it again. And then their conversation dwindled to a halt, with sentences coming sparser and sparser, heavy quiet filling the space between them, until Wren's own head began to nod and she gave in to the undeniable desire to sleep.

Wren woke into one of the nightmares. The thick fog that had accompanied the tidal wave poured from the ceiling and crept down the walls to cover the ground around her. She wasn't in the room by the fire anymore. This time she found herself in the underground catacombs, where she watched from a very great distance as a group of Magicians tried to manipulate stardust. A voice came through the fog, almost as though a narrator in a movie was speaking over the scene.

"The use of stardust is a dangerous choice," the

voice said. "And one that the unwise will pursue at great cost."

The memorial on the wall that described the consequences of the plague of magic flared with a dark light. The engraved letters began to wiggle, jostling against one another. As Wren watched, the letters became bugs, small winged roaches that began to creep down the monument. The trickle became a swarm as the places where the letters used to be transformed into holes that poured forth more and more insects.

Wren tried to cry out, tried to warn the unsuspecting Magicians, but her voice was stoppered, and no sound came out. The insects clambered on top of one another, burying themselves several bodies thick as what looked like a carpet of moving bugs began to wash through the catacombs. Soon, the Magicians were overcome by it, the walls and tombs of the catacombs unrecognizable beneath a flood of the unstoppable black insects.

Wren tried her old tactics, the ones that caused the dream to shift back on Earth, but her efforts were fruitless. She was stuck fast, and there was no escape.

"Death and destruction will be the end of all who seek to use magic," the voice said, and the words were heavy with the threat. "Take heed."

As the voice spoke, the horde of bugs turned toward Wren, and it was like her earlier dream, except that instead of the wall of water, a wave of squirming roaches was cresting toward her. Wren tried to move, tried to scream, tried to cry out, but there was nothing she could do. "Take heed," the voice echoed again. Wren shut her eyes tight to brace against the first feathery touch of the bugs.

She awoke with a jolt and shot out of her armchair, her skin crawling with the memory of the bugs. "They were on me!" she yelped.

"Huh?" Simon sat bolt upright in his chair, woken by her squealing.

Vulcan mumbled and rubbed his eyes sleepily.

"The bugs! In the dream!" Wren scrubbed at her forearms as though she could cleanse herself. Her scalp itched, her back crawled, and the rub of her skirt against her calves felt like the wings of an insect.

Simon patted his coat pockets and then pulled out a green notebook, the one in which he usually cataloged new animal life. "Interesting," he said, jotting something down.

"Interesting?" Wren squealed. "What are you talking about?"

"We had the same dream. At the same time." Simon was scribbling without looking up.

"Me, too," Vulcan said with a yawn.

"Yes"—Simon chewed on his pencil eraser—"it's almost as though someone wants to communicate with us."

Wren stopped squirming. "You mean Boggen? But this was different. It wasn't Boggen's voice. And my neck . . ." She trailed off. "I can feel it when it's Boggen. This isn't him." She stole a glance at Vulcan to see if he looked horrified, but he merely appeared thoughtful.

"Lots of Magicians are Dreamers, and with the Crooked Man's star so close, I bet even more are open to it now." He explained how certain times of the month were better for meeting in dreams. "Usually, you need a cartoglobe, a special compass for communicating in dreams." He rubbed his chin. "But the same dream to multiple people at once? Even those who aren't Dreamers? That's new to me."

Wren moved closer and saw that Simon was sketching one of the horrible bugs she had just seen.

"What if those people were right?" she said slowly. "What if the plague is returning and the nightmares are a side effect?"

"Could be," Simon said, adding just the right amount of shading on the wing.

Wren peered closer. "That's really quite good."

"It's a German cockroach," he said matter-of-factly. "Must have come over here with the earliest Magicians. We have the same species on Earth."

"Ah," Wren said, but her mind was still working out what the dream itself might mean.

"Was someone talking in your dream?" she asked, as her skin stopped itching and she could actually process what she had heard.

Simon shook his head, laying his pencil flat to shade in the bug's body. "No. Just the bugs themselves. They were all over the horse carriages, and there wasn't anything anyone could do to stop them."

"Wait," said Wren. "You weren't in the catacombs?"

Simon stopped scribbling. "No." Neither was Vulcan. He had seen the bugs and heard the warning, but had been in the basement of the Nest.

Wren told them what she had dreamed. "Someone is manipulating the dreams, but each is personalized in some way. The voice in mine said that using stardust was dangerous."

Simon chewed on his eraser. "My dream was silent.

But I did have a sense of foreboding, as if using the magic would be a Very Bad Thing."

Wren thought about that for a while. The fire was still crackling in the hearth, and she stared at the hot orange flames. Why had she heard the voice but Simon hadn't? Who was using dreams to scare people? And was the warning against magic a prediction or a threat?

They sat like that for some time until Auspex came back into the room with two packs over his shoulder. "Time to go," he said.

# FIFTEEN

*Say, say, what shall I say?*
*The cat came out, he wants to play.*
*Do, do, what shall I do?*
*The cat will bite him quite in two.*

Winter burst into the room while Auspex was still making preparations to leave. "We all are in danger." She paused only a moment to catch her breath, but her sentences still came out in choppy bursts. "I just heard from my informants. Yesterday's rally was reported. Boggen's henchmen are on their way here even as we speak." She looked at Wren before grabbing a stack of papers off a crowded desk in the corner and shoving them into a bag. "They have specific orders to take into custody a girl with your description."

Auspex looked at her curiously. "Boggen knows what you look like?"

"He knows." Wren shared a panicky glance with Simon. "We have to get out of here."

"Of course," Auspex said, moving with fluid grace to gather his own pack. "Boggen's men will not track us where we are going."

"Good," Winter said, shutting her bag with a snap. "You take the children. I will remain here. Every neighborhood deserves to hear the truth about Boggen's research no matter the cost. We must act now," she said fervently. "Before Boggen can gather his strength and shut us down. If we can't hold rallies, we'll get the information out some other way."

"I'll stay, too," Vulcan said in a firm voice, and when Winter seemed about to protest, he cut her off. "I can help! The other Scavengers, too. We know every rooftop in the city and are welcomed by law in every marketplace. If you need to get information to people, we're your crew." He looked determined. "Most of us have had family members disappear in the last few years." He clenched his jaw. "Now we know why."

There was a pounding on the door, and the sound of harsh voices demanding entrance.

"They're here!" Winter shot a wide-eyed glance at Auspex. "The back door!"

But before they reached it, they could hear Boggen's

soldiers banging on it as well. Wren reached for Simon's hand. *They were trapped.*

"Is there a rooftop exit?" Vulcan asked, and no sooner had he said the words than Winter was leading the way up a crooked stairwell to a narrow area crowded with chimney pipes. From far below, they heard the sound of breaking glass as the soldiers began to force their way in.

"We part ways here," Auspex said, scanning the rooftops that sprawled in front of them. "The city wall is not far, and you two must go in the opposite direction. Courage and Honor."

"Courage and Honor," Winter said to Auspex, and gave Wren and Simon a salute before turning to go. Vulcan paused in front of Wren, hesitating, but then Winter hissed at him over her shoulder. "If you're coming with me, Scavenger, you come now."

And with a quick smile, Vulcan was gone. The tiny flash of disappointment Wren felt soon disappeared in the face of the daunting task of following Auspex over the rooftops. He was faster than any Scavenger, navigating gaps between buildings with ease and expecting Simon and Wren to follow suit. Soon, they had left the townhouse far behind, and, after pausing to listen carefully, Auspex pronounced that they were far enough away to return to the streets. "We need to cross the river before we reach the wall," he explained, shimmying down a gas pipe like a monkey.

It was early, and only a few people were out on the streets. Cleaning women on their way to assignments with brooms and mops over one shoulder. Magicians streaming toward the mills where scavenged goods were repurposed. Deliverymen on their rounds. But so far, no soldiers. Auspex set a steady pace. The ever-present rain made even the pearly morning light wet and damp. The smell of fresh-baked bread steamed out of storefronts, and the children who sold newspapers were already out with stacks of freshly printed paper tucked into their bags.

"Boggen hunts for a crew wanted for crimes against the state," the nearest urchin shouted, and the shrill pitch of his voice made Wren wince. "The Knave of Hearts and two Outsider escapees. Reward offered."

She and Simon pushed past, but Auspex stopped and took a news roll, handing the paperboy a fat coin. "Keep the change," he said, causing the boy's eyes to grow round with disbelief.

"Do you know who the Knave is?" Wren asked, as

they made their way down the street.

Auspex skimmed the paper as they walked. "I don't know the Knave personally," he said, turning a page. "But the name is respected among the Outsiders, not least because anyone whom Boggen wants that badly is a friend to us." He pointed to a sketch on the front page, and Wren's heart sank. The artist had clearly portrayed Auspex's profile, and the other supposed escaped Outsider looked exactly like Wren.

"That's a good likeness of you," Simon said politely over her shoulder, and Wren nearly jumped. Her nervousness had almost disappeared, but now she felt hunted, as if every face around her was sure to recognize her picture and start calling out for Boggen's soldiers.

"Perhaps the Outsiders will welcome you after all," Auspex said with a smile. He appeared calm, but he doubled his pace after this, leaving Wren to straggle along behind, nervous and out of breath.

The farther they went, the more crowded the streets grew, which made Wren feel a little bit better. She kept her head down and darted after Auspex and Simon. Suddenly, the movement of the morning traffic slowed to a stop, and Wren could hear the sound of a commotion up ahead.

"Wait here," Auspex ordered. With an easy move-ment, he clambered up the brick wall so that he could see above the crowd. "A blockade," he said. "More of Boggen's soldiers."

After doubling back and clambering through a nar-row alley filled with refuse bins, they finally drew near the river. The smell of garbage mixed with the odor of fish. Canalboats drifted past, and so did the small canoes that served as river taxis. Auspex hired one of these.

"Say nothing," Auspex whispered as they climbed onto the boat, with a meaningful look at the pilot. Wren perched precariously in the middle, Simon behind her, as the pilot poled them down the canal. Their silence gave Wren the opportunity to observe the city around her. They passed by buildings that must have once been brightly colored but were now weath-ered by the elements.

She knew that Nod had thousands of Magicians liv-ing in it, but now she saw that they were more than just Magicians—they were people, too. A mother stood on a balcony, hanging up laundry as two small chil-dren played at her feet. Older kids chased dogs on the waterfront, their happy laughter making her suddenly homesick. *Or Earthsick.* She wondered what her life would have been like if she had been born on Nod. The food was odd, of course, and the customs and clothing looked like a strange mishmash of history and sci-fi, but there were people here. People who lived and died at the mercy of Boggen.

The boat angled toward a lonely-looking dock. Auspex paid the pilot, and Simon clambered out onto the weathered boards, one hand extended.

Wren grabbed his hand, but as she followed after him she felt a sense of foreboding. The other parts of the city might be crowded or dingy. They might be weathered by the elements or not as well-kept as some neighborhoods, but the area where they now stood was nothing like even the shabbiest of the places she had seen. Wren instinctively squeezed Simon's hand as she looked at the bleakness around her.

"What happened here?"

The buildings, or what was left of them, were scorched with black stains. She could see through some entirely, where interior walls lay in shambles. And others stretched halfway up and then abruptly stopped. Refuse and clumps of forgotten papers had gathered in the gutters. The whole place had the feel of a forgotten ghetto.

Auspex replied in a whisper, even though the pilot was long out of earshot. "The plague happened." He took out a piece of fabric and began to unroll it. "Boggen will have to push his soldiers hard to follow us here." A faded map was painted on the fabric, and Auspex traced a route with his finger. "They had to quarantine the neighborhood and burn it to stop the plague's spread, and the superstitious folk in the city still suspect that it is tainted."

"That's horrible," Wren said. Any relief she felt at hearing that they had escaped Boggen's soldiers evaporated at the thought of exposure to the plague.

"Thousands died." The fabric hung limply in Auspex's hands. "Young and old alike. It was unstoppable."

"Was it viral or bacterial?" Simon asked, and for all his being in observation mode, his voice was reverent.

"Viral?" Auspex said, as though tasting a new word. "I don't know what you mean, but it spread like fire." He pointed to the blackened surfaces. "And fire was the only thing that stopped it." He paused ominously. "If it really ever stopped."

"What started it?" Wren asked.

"What do you think?" Auspex shook his head. "Stardust." He nearly spit the word. "You know what the colony was escaping. Years of civil war on Earth. Fighting against what they saw as too many restrictions on the use of magic." He sat down on a piece of broken stone. "Factions sprang up. Magicians argued about how best to use the stardust." He sighed. "Mother Goose was the leader of the most progressive. She said that a new planet with new life had new potential." He spread his arms out wide. "This used to be her part of the city—her launching place for expeditions into the wilderness."

Wren looked at the broken buildings and the refuse. "Was there an explosion?"

"Worse." Auspex studied his hands. "A mutation." He glanced up at them, and the fierce anger in his eyes frightened Wren. "Mother Goose's crew set no limits on their experiments. Everything was fair game. And since they had no qualms tampering with human life, do you think they cared about alien life? Her Beautiful Creatures, she called them." He lifted his gaze to the burned-out tops of the laboratories. "Half animal, half machine. They rebelled. And the animachines destroyed the outpost settlements. The city dwellers built their wall to protect themselves."

"Animachines?" Simon asked, so astonished that his pencil and notebook fell useless at his sides.

"Indeed. And worse even than rampaging monsters, the stardust grew tainted, mutated not to enhance life but to kill it." He rested his elbows on his knees, clasping his hands between them. "Many good Magicians perished destroying that strain of stardust." His mouth twisted into a bitter smile. "Small consolation that Mother Goose herself perished in the final efforts at containment." He sighed. "It came at the cost of thousands of lives, and the animachines were even harder to stop."

Wren didn't know what to say. What a horrible history!

Auspex glanced up at her, his bushy eyebrows raised. "In the end, we could not destroy them. Containment alone was the key." He got to his feet, stretching his arms behind his back. "The remaining factions united to construct the wall. They never venture outside it."

"You mean . . ." Wren began, feeling her heart begin to pound.

"Yes," Auspex said, and his words were grave. "The animachines are still out there. Multiplying, evolving over the years. They are the only true predator of humans on this planet." He barked a short laugh. "And we created them. We were handed a heaven and we turned it into a living hell."

Wren was only half listening. She was remembering what Vulcan had said about dying a horrible death outside the walls.

"Will we see some of these animachines?" Simon slipped his red notebook back into his pocket and coolly pulled out his green one. "Outside the wall?"

"Aye," Auspex said, remembering the fabric map in his hands. He pointed to a spot marked with an $X$ in the lower corner. "The wall was constructed as a permanent safety precaution. No need to go in or out. But one of Mother Goose's crew members thought differently. He secretly cut a passageway so he could pass back and forth unnoticed. He believed that the animachines could be reformed, that they would evolve to be compatible with human life, and for some years he traveled to and from the abandoned research outposts to continue his work."

"So what happened to him?" Wren asked as Auspex folded the fabric and set off down what must have once been a road.

"He learned otherwise."

Wren didn't ask any more questions, nor did Auspex speak again until they came to the wall itself. Up close, Wren could see that unlike the other buildings on Nod, which were constructed of clay bricks or wood, this was made of a dark stone that reminded her of lava rock back on Earth, and interwoven through it all was the sheen of stardust.

The door itself was little more than a filthy grate wedged in between the street and the wall. Auspex bent to unscrew it, and Wren reviewed her options. Was it too late to change her mind? To return to the Nest with Vulcan and come up with a different plan? She knew it was futile. The other Alchemists were counting on her. The Outsiders were her best chance of rescuing them, not to mention helping the prisoners and finding Robin. She watched as Auspex lifted the rusted piece of metal, strings of wet plant matter dangling from the grate. She tried not to think of what the mutant animachines would be like, tried not to wonder if she'd ever be back within the walls again. As she stooped to enter the dank hole, she felt for the pouch of stardust around her neck. She might not be able to wield it properly, but it was there. And that thought gave her a sliver of hope. After they had all passed through, Auspex replaced the grate and lit a gas lantern.

"Straight ahead," he said gruffly.

The tunnel was in much the same condition as the grate. The walls looked slimy and filthy. When her arm brushed against them, she felt slick wetness, and from then on was very careful to stay in the middle of the path. The dampness smelled like earth and mildew and forgotten things. Thankfully, the tunnel was short—only as thick as the wall itself—and then Auspex slid past her to work at the latches on another grate.

"No animachines roam near the walls, but when we enter the forest, you must take care." He rested an arm on the grate and turned to face Wren as if to emphasize the importance of his warning.

Wren felt like telling him he needn't bother. There was no way in the world she was going to run off on her own in the middle of a bunch of monsters. The only thing she was afraid of was losing her nerve and dashing right back to the tunnel. "I'll stay with you."

"We'll be at the Outsiders' camp by nightfall." Auspex leaned hard on the grate, which opened with the screech of reluctant metal, and then they were outside the Wall.

Wren took a few paces and then blinked against the brilliance of the light. It was almost as though someone had flicked a switch, and the gray, rainy atmosphere of the city had disappeared. Instead, her eyes fought to make sense of a landscape full of brilliant colors. She saw the red dirt she had noticed on that first flight into Nod dotted with brilliant yellows and greens. Large violet plants swayed at what must be a forest's edge, and it was to this Auspex led them.

"Why did the rain stop?" Simon asked, peering back to look at the city, which was still covered with mist.

"The rain is artificial," Auspex snorted. "Another invention of the Magicians." He nodded up toward the brilliant blue sky. "A way to keep the flying anima-chines out."

"Ah," Simon muttered, flipping back a few pages to add a notation. "So *that's* what the shield over Nod is for."

Wren hunched her shoulders and hustled after him into the cover of the wood. There were flying animachines?

She was glad Simon was with her, though of course

his nose was buried in his notebook. She never understood how it was that he managed to walk and write at the same time. The countryside around them had a strange topography. Nothing was recognizable, though plenty of things were Earthlike. She could see what appeared to be mountains off in the distance, and the tree line ahead of them indicated a forest. The earth itself was a burnt-orange color that rose in crests and was covered with a brilliant red shrubbery that was soft to the touch.

"What is it?" Wren asked Auspex, but he merely shrugged.

"Redbush, we call it. It's all over the flatlands."

"And that?" Wren asked, pointing to the lavender foliage growing on the trees.

"Purplevines."

She stopped asking after that. It seemed the Outsiders were no-nonsense about most things, including what names they chose for their biological discoveries.

The purplevines were breathtaking and gave the entire forest an ethereal feel, as though she were walking between swaths of wispy fabric in some outdoor temple. The trees grew dense here, shutting out the harsh sunlight and bathing the forest in twilight.

Low-lying yellow flowers bloomed at the roots of most trees. They were probably called "yellowflowers."

"How long have the Outsiders lived beyond the walls?" Wren called up to Auspex, who was setting a fast pace.

"Since the end of the plague," he said. "Malcolm was the first." Auspex stopped to uncork his canteen, taking a long drink and then offering it to Simon and next Wren. "He had a few apprentices. They found him when he died."

Wren lowered the canteen from her lips. "How did he die?"

"Upas trees," Auspex said. "The gas they emit is poisonous when inhaled."

"Could you describe them for me?" Simon asked, turning over a fresh page in his notebook. "And the qualities of their poison?"

Wren scanned the clearing. For once the Outsiders decided to pick a nondescriptive name?

"They're not in this part of the forest," Auspex said, noticing her alarm. "Else we'd already be dead. They have crimson flowers and emit a colorless gas that has a faint cinnamon odor. But by the time you smell that it doesn't matter anymore." He took the canteen back from Wren. "Anyway, it was a shame that we lost Malcolm. He was a brilliant Magician." He slung his pack over his shoulder and beckoned for them to walk next to him, as the path was wider here. Wren followed but did not stop to pluck the yellow flowers as she had thought of doing before. Deadly plants were not something to be trifled with.

"His apprentices were upset," Auspex continued. "The city dwellers responded callously to Malcolm's death and became more interested in preserving pure stardust than in discovering how to become caretakers of our new planet. Instead of joining with Boggen's forward push for progress, Malcolm's apprentices decided to leave." He smiled, the first genuine emotion she had seen on his face. "My grandmother was one of them."

"So there are lots of Outsiders, then?" Despite the fact that Simon seemed to navigate the terrain easily while continuing his note-taking enterprise, Wren had to struggle to keep up. The undergrowth had grown thicker, and she couldn't help but brush up against the yellow flowers. The purplevines that had once seemed so lovely now impeded their progress, and Auspex had to stop and cut their way through more than once.

"A fair number," Auspex said. "We don't take

censuses, you see, and life out here is dangerous. We lose many, but it's a good life, and stardust free."

Wren fell back then, letting him hack away at the vines unhindered. What would Auspex say if he knew she and Simon were carrying stardust around their necks?

"Here's a thick one," Auspex said, pulling out a cutting tool with several folding blades that he stopped to adjust. "The purplevines grow back within twelve hours," he said with a grunt as he clipped the vine in two. "Impossible to trim. It gets harder to pass this way with every year."

"I thought the Outsiders didn't like the city," Wren said. "Why do they go there?"

"Do you not study ecosystems on Earth?" Auspex looked puzzled. "He, at least, seems a born naturalist." He gestured toward Simon, who looked up from his notes, blinking.

Auspex continued. "What the city dwellers do affects us all. We Outsiders have been cleaning up Mother Goose's mistakes these hundred years past, and the animachines still run free. What new wretchedness is afoot in Nod with every passing decade?" He frowned. "Stardust taints everything, and until the city dwellers come to believe that for themselves, no one on this planet will ever have peace. There can be no compromise."

This seemed to be the recurring refrain of Outsider philosophy. Whenever Auspex said anything about stardust or magic, he repeated the same warning: there can be no compromise. During the rest of their journey, Wren learned that the Outsiders called the planet *Vita*, the Latin word for "life." They survived by growing their own crops of what sounded like legumes and then foraged for berries and other edible plants that they had identified. Auspex was just beginning to explain how young Outsiders' education centered around weapons training when they were suddenly interrupted.

"Get down!" Auspex shouted, shoving Wren behind a particularly dense clump of purplevines. Auspex leaped over to where Simon was walking and tucked him in the hollow of a giant tree trunk. Before Wren had even steadied herself, Auspex had unstrapped some sort of crossbow and crouched down on one knee to take aim. Wren followed his line of sight and nearly lost her footing a second time.

Slinking through the underbrush on silent paws was the largest cat she had ever seen. Its head reminded her of a cougar, with wary almond-shaped eyes fixed on Auspex. Its muscular torso resembled that of a mountain cat, but it was the legs that drew Wren's attention. They were silver plated, as though the cat was armored in some flexible man-made material. Even in the dim light of the forest's cover she could see the glint of metal.

The cat stopped for a moment, sniffing the air and settling in on its hindquarters. Then, in one terrifying heartbeat, it leaped, a huge, un-animal-like lunge across the forest toward Auspex. Wren's scream came out like a squeak as Auspex's crossbow fired, catching the beast in the center of its chest and felling it.

Auspex turned toward her, yanking her up by the elbow, and then grabbed Simon. "Run!" he shouted. "Where there's one hovercat there's more. We must hurry before the whole clowder is upon us."

Wren stumbled over a root, but then she found herself in a full-on sprint. All she could think about was how similar the cat looked to the awful spiders in her dream. Except this wasn't a dream. This was real, and this time she wasn't a silent observer, but the predator's prey. Simon raced next to her, his notebook flapping forgotten in one hand, his jacket streaming out behind him.

Auspex ran with his crossbow loaded, glancing back over his shoulder with a practiced eye. "There are two behind us. Others probably on our flanks. They all are linked with the prime cat, and they hunt us now. Our only hope of safety lies in reaching the island first." He pointed to a dense shadow on the horizon. "Make for that formation there, and split up. It will be harder for them to chase two of you." Auspex sent Simon dashing off to the left and directed Wren straight ahead. "Whatever speed you have in you, girl, use it. Run!"

Wren could hear the clank of metal behind her as the hovercats abandoned stealth and hunted their prey. Her heart was in her throat, her breath coming in gasps. She reached for the pouch around her neck. Would the stardust obey her? Or would it fall flat like it had done before?

Auspex shouted at her again. "Continue on. Don't stop until you reach the island." And then he was falling back, dropping to one knee to aim at the nearest hovercat. Wren didn't wait to watch this time. She made for the hill-like formation Auspex had indicated, and though it seemed only a couple of football fields away, it might have been miles. She saw movement on one side, the metallic glint of unearthly legs, and then the animachine began howling.

Wren braved another look back at Auspex. He had felled a second beast and was sprinting after her, but another hovercat was right behind him. Wren didn't think he saw it coming. She reached for her pouch. She had to try. She didn't stop moving, so her jostling steps sent stardust spilling from her palm, but she began the rhyme. She sped her pace. It was working! The stardust was knitting together, forming into a pulsing ball. She tried something she had once seen in an apprentice lesson, splitting the ball in two. She felt the tightness rattle inside, bottled up emotions threatening to explode all over the place, the loudest of all telling her that she was running out of time. She not only heard the hovercat to her right, she could feel the ground trembling with its approach. The stardust flared hot in her palm. But she didn't need that to know it was working. As on Earth, the weather was changing. The purplevines began to stir, moving in the wind, tangling in front of her. Wren's only hope was that they hindered the progress of the hovercats as well. She ducked behind the nearest clump, peering out to see that the hovercat hunting her was only a few arm lengths away, swatting at the engulfing underbrush.

"Please don't fail me now," Wren whispered to the stardust in her palms. "Not like this. Not when it counts." She aimed a flaming ball at the trapped hovercat, and it howled as the projectile singed its fur, before turning tail and disappearing into the foliage. Echoing yowls answered back, and Wren felt all the hair on her arms stand straight up. She had chased one off, but there weren't only one or two more, there was a whole pack. She hoped Simon had found better luck with his route.

She looked back the way she had come, but there was no sign of Auspex. Just the ominous form of a hovercat batting something between its paws the way housecats do when they've caught a mouse. And then Wren realized.

"Auspex!" she shouted, racing back toward him. The man was unconscious, his limp form rolling back and forth between huge paws, if the animachine's robotic appendages could even be called paws. The beast looked up at Wren, its glinting red eyes narrowing as they found their target. Wren didn't hesitate. She channeled all her emotions into her remaining ball of stardust, sending it straight at the head of the beast. The air around her exploded with sparks. The hovercat screamed in agony, and all the hovercats in the clowder with it. Before her eyes, the half-animal monster crumbled into ash, leaving only a metal shell. *Two down, who knows how many to go.* Wren immediately began working more stardust, but she felt the tension inside dissipate, the rest of her emotions chased away by the growing terror that she was going to die. The purplevines settled back into their listless hanging, and the dust lay flat and lifeless in her palm. Her heart sank. *NO!* Her hands were shaky as she frantically pinched and blew on the stardust, willing it into life. It took her a few minutes to realize that it might not matter. If they had still been around, the hovercats would have devoured her by now, and instead here she was, crouched on the forest floor next to a moaning Auspex.

"Child?" he murmured, his eyes fixing on Wren. "You saved me." He shook his head as though he had been asleep for a long time. "You slew the prime cat and the others with it. How did you—?" and then his eyes rolled back into his head. He was unconscious.

"Auspex!" Wren shouted, shaking his shoulder. He had to wake up!

Just then, she heard the crash of footfalls in the

underbrush, and she reached for Auspex's crossbow. If the stardust wouldn't work, she would have to resort to other measures. The sounds came louder, and Wren pivoted on one heel, aiming the weapon first at one gap between the trees, then another, until the purplevines started shaking, and something burst through them.

Wren didn't wait to see what. She pulled the trigger on the crossbow, which blasted her off her feet and onto her bottom, and sent an arrow shooting skyward.

"Dust and Ashes!" a voice shouted. "Take that thing away from her. Auspex, is that you?" And then there were people there. People dressed in lavenders and grays that matched the forest. People with dirty faces that broke into wide smiles when they saw that she had been trying to protect Auspex. One of them came up to Wren. She looked like a grandmother, but she was lean and strong. She pulled Wren to her feet, eyeing her from head to toe with sharp blue eyes. Her voice was raspy, but it carried loud and clear through the woods. "Take them to the island."

# SIXTEEN

*See a feather, pick it up.*
*Hide it, or you'll have bad luck.*

A dozen or so Outsiders surrounded Wren. A handful of them peeled off to fashion a makeshift carrier for Auspex, and the others fanned out through the forest, watching for predators.

"There was a boy with us," Wren said to the Outsider nearest her, a middle-aged woman with hair cut short to frame her sunburned face. "My friend Simon. Have you seen him?" She dreaded the answer. If a hovercat had gotten to Simon . . .

"No," the woman said, conferring with two of the other Outsiders, who then took off at a sprint. "But if he was in the woods, we will find his trail." After that, Wren didn't feel much like talking. She hoped Simon was somewhere safe.

The trees grew thinner, the purplevines melting into bare branches and slim trunks that looked like bamboo. The clear skies became visible once again. Wren guessed it must be nearing dusk. Near the outermost trees, a pearly lake glistened. As Wren drew near, she saw that it wasn't in fact a lake but a moat. The nearly pink water stretched about twenty feet across. The closer they got, the clearer it became that the mountain she had seen from afar was really an island that sloped upward out of the center of the water.

As they approached, the Outsiders formed a tight circle around Wren and Auspex, the old woman who was clearly their leader at the forefront. Wren looked for a boat or a ferry or some such contrivance, but she was unprepared for what emerged from the water. First a periscope and then a shiny metal rod, followed by a round craft the size of a bus, which bobbed there like a forgotten bath toy. The Outsiders headed directly for it. The round glass window at the top hissed open, and they began to scale an exterior ladder one by one. Wren had plenty of time to watch them maneuver Auspex's litter into the vessel, so when it was her turn she clambered up the ladder and down into the vessel like she had been doing it all her life.

The interior was more spacious than she'd expected. Long benches had been bolted to the metal floor on either side, and the Outsiders took their seats. It was as though entering the submarine had given the Outsiders permission to relax. Their taut expressions melted into smiles, and their bodies lolled against the hard steel walls. Some of them even began laughing at Auspex's predicament.

"Never thought I'd see the day that Auspex fell in the woods," a woman with raccoonlike circles under her eyes was saying.

"Aye." A man with nearly orange hair chuckled. "And to think a Magician girl-apprentice saved his life."

Wren prickled at this. The way he said "Magician girl-apprentice" did not sound like a compliment.

When the submersible jolted to life, bobbing like a cork and then plunging beneath the surface in a stomach-dropping descent, Wren scrambled against the wall, groping for a seat belt or a handhold until Raccoon Eyes laughed at her. Very slowly, very intentionally, Wren folded her arms, trying to act like diving down beneath a pink lake was something she did every day. For fun.

After its initial heart-stopping plunge, the submersible's motion was remarkably smooth, whirring along as the older woman steered it from a command center near one of the regularly spaced round windows. Wren tuned out the joking Outsiders and strained her eyes for her first glimpse of alien aquatic life. Again, she thought of how much Simon would've enjoyed all this and felt a pang of worry for him. If only she could know he was safe! And then, selfishly: *If only he were here with me!*

A large, dark shadow swam by the window. It was close enough that Wren could discern jagged spikes and a tentacled tail, making her feel even more anxious and lonely. She found herself wishing not only for a friend but for something remotely Earthlike. A fish, perhaps, or even an octopus.

"Animachine within range," the gray-haired woman said. "Speed warning." The other Outsiders nonchalantly reached for the handholds that were, after all, neatly tucked into the wall above them. Wren grabbed hers tightly, avoiding the mocking gaze of Raccoon Eyes, as the gray-haired woman turned several knobs and the vessel bolted forward, away from the shadowy creature.

Raccoon Eyes was watching her closely. "There's a spiroshark nearby," she said. "It'll attack the sub if we linger."

Wren couldn't tell if Raccoon Eyes was trying to be nice or not, but she decided that looking out the windows might not be the best idea.

Whatever the gray-haired woman had done was effective. After a few minutes, she announced that they were in the clear, and the vessel slowed, attaching to some unseen dock with a clang. Then the Outsiders were standing, hoisting Auspex's litter, and clambering up and out. Wren lingered, watching Auspex's unmoving form with wistful eyes. She had never thought of the man as friendly, but he at least had been somewhat familiar, and here she was alone once again.

"Coming, child?" the gray-haired woman said. She might have looked like a grandmother, but there was nothing grandmotherly about her. Her attitude demonstrated that she expected Wren to obey her commands. Wren nodded and followed the Outsider wordlessly out of the submarine. They had docked at the shore of an underground lake, and the others moved through a damp cavern to a rusted metal ladder and began to climb.

The world above was as different from the city of Nod as the city's rainy skies were from the clear ones beyond its walls. The ground was covered with the spongy red bushes Wren had seen earlier, and the uneven terrain created a sloping terrace that stretched as far as Wren could see. The island itself must be quite big, and for all the Outsiders' scorn for the city's wall, they themselves were protected by a natural rocky formation that encircled their camp.

They walked down what must have been a thoroughfare, because dwellings flanked it on either side. They resembled earthen huts, but they were more organic, cut out of the terraced ground itself. There were other Earthlike things about the settlement. Clothing had been left flapping on lines to dry, and outside of every hut was an ordinary fire, where Outsiders had gathered for what seemed to be the evening meal. Some of them hailed the party returning from the submersible, and others merely stared at Wren.

A few of their party peeled off to disappear down side routes that hinted at many more dwellings, but Wren was sticking with Auspex. They walked for some time, until the hovels gave way to what looked like farmland, which sprawled out beneath the darkening sky. Beyond that were more dwellings, and some of these had bricks and stone worked into the exterior. In a few she even saw shiny glints of metal. The light was fading, so that by the time the gray-haired woman stopped, Wren couldn't see much about her surroundings, except that they were in front of a long, low hovel. The gray-haired woman rapped firmly on the door, which opened to reveal a wizened old man who grinned toothlessly at them.

"Courage and Honor, Maya," he said with a bow.

"Auspex is hurt," Maya said. "And in need of a Healer."

The ancient man bobbed his head, ushering in the litter-bearers, but Maya blocked Wren's way when she moved to follow.

"No city dwellers here. No compromise," Maya said.

The old man winked at Wren, but he said, "Of course, Maya."

"Can you heal him?" Maya asked, but it sounded more like an order. "Send me status updates on Auspex's recovery." And Maya spun on one booted heel and stalked off into the darkness. The ancient man shut the door in Wren's face, and she stood there for a moment, wondering what exactly she was supposed to do. Until she heard Maya's voice. "Come!" she barked.

Wren followed Maya through the darkness until she stopped in front of a nondescript hut with no fire blazing outside. The woman ushered Wren inside with an expression that brooked no disagreement.

In the dim interior, Wren could see the glowing coals of an untended fire, and the woman knelt, blowing on them and adding bits of the reddish shrubbery. The mantelpiece above held none of the gaslights and gadgets of Nod but was instead sparsely filled with homely, simple-looking things: a few clay dishes, plates, mugs, and a crude candelabra.

"Sit," Maya said, pointing to a stool next to a rough wooden table. She adjusted a rack over the flames to fit a cauldron. As the fire warmed the room, Wren could better make out her surroundings. The hut was rounded like the terraces it was cut from, and the furniture and possessions that dotted its shelves were rudimentary. Some brightly painted pottery. A small stack of very weathered books. A lumpy mattress on the floor in one corner, and several garments hanging on pegs above it. Compared with the crowded halls of the Scavengers' Nest, the Outsider dwelling was positively austere. Except for the wall of weapons. Crossbows of varying heights were hung in order of size next to ordinary bows and clusters of arrows. Swords and daggers hung from nails in between a few other weapons that Wren didn't recognize.

"Do you admire my collection?" Maya said with the closest thing to a smile that Wren had seen from her.

"Um, yes," Wren said. "It must be useful out here." The woman was pouring cups of a steaming liquid that Wren accepted eagerly. The night air here was very cold, and she cupped the clay mug in her hands, soaking up its warmth. She heard the cry of a wild animal and shivered, but this time not from the cold. "Hovercats?" she asked, but the gray-haired woman only shrugged.

"The cries of the animachines are all alike." She turned her unconcerned gaze on Wren. "They may look different, but they all die the same."

"Ah," said Wren, focusing on the tea in front of her. It smelled minty and tasted wonderful. "Will Auspex be okay?"

Maya's face looked just as stern, but Wren noticed the skin around the woman's eyes softening, maybe a sign of tenderness. "The Healer will do what he can. But if the hovercat bit him—" She shook her head. "How did you defeat it, child?"

All softness was gone, and Wren squirmed under her gaze. She instinctively touched the cord that hung around her neck. She could tell Maya about the stardust, but she didn't think that was a good idea. To say that Auspex had seemed anti-stardust was an understatement; who knew what the other Outsiders would think? Wren listened to the cautious little voice inside that told her to take care.

"I'm not sure," Wren said, which was true enough. The creature had basically evaporated into smoke. Even stardust didn't normally do that. "I was so frightened."

"You mastered your fear," Maya said, and Wren detected a faint note of praise. "Admirable for one so young."

"I guess so," Wren said, fiddling with the mug. "I wouldn't like to meet another hovercat, though, that's for sure."

"You might change your mind in time," Maya said evenly. "There is great honor in fighting the animachines."

"I guess. But is there another way to deal with them? With all the resources in Nod, surely something could be done?"

"And interact with those dust-handlers?" Maya

spit on the floor with scorn. "I'd sooner deal with the cursed Alchemists than any stardust-wielding Magician." She spit again at the word *Alchemist*, and Wren shifted uncomfortably in her chair. It was only in that moment that she realized she had expectations. She had expected the Outsiders to be "good guys"; that they would welcome her in and help her. Now she wondered if that was premature.

"I didn't like killing it," Wren said, thinking of how easily the creature had burned with the stardust. Though she was grateful Auspex was okay, she hated using the stardust as a weapon again. Was that how it would be for her from here on out? Stardust failing her unless she was using it to hurt another living thing? She hunched over her mug. Maybe the Outsiders weren't so far off track. Maybe stardust was more of a curse than a gift.

"We might be able to make an Outsider of you, given time." Maya's lips curved fractionally upward, and Wren wondered if that was the closest thing to a smile she was going to get. "Auspex never brings city dwellers with him." She took a sip of her drink, wincing at the heat. "Now. Why are you here?"

Wren wasn't used to such bluntness, or the way in

which Maya offered no smile to gentle her curiosity. She studied the amber liquid in her mug, wishing she knew the right thing to say. Should she mention the prisoners? Or Winter's rally? She wished she knew more about the Outsiders and what their power structure was like.

"I'm looking for my friend. A girl named Robin."

Maya's face tightened imperceptibly at the name, which, given her stoicism, was probably the same as if anyone else had gasped out loud and fainted. "I know Robin," Maya said.

"Is she here?" Wren half stood. "Somewhere in the village?"

"Sit down, child," Maya said. "Robin hasn't been to the village for six months or longer. She left to try to find allies among the city dwellers." Maya's scornful look showed what she thought of that. "If you were hoping for more," she said, and shrugged, "I'm sorry. You've wasted your journey and risked your life in the forest for nothing."

Wren sat back down heavily. Was that really it? Was this another dead end?

Maya stood and worked a pump at a washbasin, rinsing her mug and setting it to dry on a wooden frame. "You may stay with us and return to Nod with the next expedition. We have no use for curious bystanders. You're either one of us or one of them. No compromise."

Wren was tired enough to fall asleep, even on the hard, unwelcoming pallet Maya prepared for her by the fire. She burrowed under the fur blankets and shut her eyes tight. She was all alone. Cole and Mary were locked up in the House of Never. Jack, despite his heroic effort to give himself up to save her, might as well be dead for all that she knew. And Simon . . . her heart gave a throb of pain. She flipped over onto her other side. She wouldn't think about Simon.

She woke several hours later, the pelts twisted around her frame and her face clammy with sweat. It had been another nightmare. A repeat of the one with the wall of water, only this time she didn't wake until it crashed over her. She lay very still on her pallet, trying to calm her panicking body. *You are in Maya's hut,* she reminded herself. *In the Outsiders' camp.* The ominous wall of water wasn't real, and the city of Nod was miles away. She studied the ceiling and the sparse shelves, waiting for her breathing to return to normal.

The fire had burned low, only a few embers glowing in the small room. Suddenly, Wren shot up with a jolt, barking a quick cry of fear. That wasn't just a shadow on the stool by the fire. It was a person. Watching her.

"Peace, child." Maya's voice came from the darkness. "And Courage."

Wren gathered her jacket more tightly around her. "You were *watching* me?" Even though the room was warm, she felt a sudden chill.

"Keeping watch, you might say." Maya fanned the embers into life and added a few twigs. "The night hag has been to call on you."

"The *what* has done WHAT?" Wren didn't feel any better at that pronouncement.

"The witch who brings the nightmares." There was no empathy in Maya's voice, only observation. "You were whimpering in your sleep. Tossing and turning like one flogged by Craven Fear herself." The fire was stirring back to life, and its welcome, Earthlike warmth made Wren feel a bit calmer.

"The nightmares?" Wren thought the idea of a witch bringing them sounded more like folklore than fact.

"Have you not seen the taint of stardust?" Maya's face was half cloaked in shadows. "Evil things cause evil deeds, and the nightmares are yet another injury we can attribute to the city dwellers' use of stardust."

"Everyone in the city is having nightmares as well," Wren said. "Why would they use stardust to hurt themselves?"

"I didn't say they were doing it on purpose," Maya said impatiently. "I said it was a side effect of stardust use." She peered closer, her angular face jutting into the light of the fire. "*You* use stardust."

Wren let out a wildly inappropriate nervous laugh. All she could think of was how fishlike Maya's stern face seemed in that moment. "I've worked the stardust," she admitted. "Though not very well. And lately not at all," she added as an afterthought.

"A wise choice." Maya's face relaxed a bit at that. "Though the night hag haunts you yet. Take care, child. It is better to be done with stardust altogether. No compromise." She got to her feet. "Not to worry. While you're with us, we'll train the desire out of you."

"What?"

"Get up. Training began at dawn." Maya drew aside an animal pelt that had been tacked over a hole in the dirt wall. Beyond, Wren could see the pale colors of the lightening sky.

★ ★ ★

Wren's first full day among the Outsiders was long and hard, with little room to discover much about the Outsider plans to rescue the research subjects, let alone what had happened to Simon. There had been no word from him, and the Outsiders hadn't found his trail in the woods. In the morning, when Wren pressed to go out and look for him herself, Maya scowled at her.

"Don't be an idiot, child. The scouts will find his trail without the help of an ignorant city dweller."

When Wren began to argue, Maya slammed her fist down on the table.

"And how will you survive out there in the forest alone? I don't know how you managed to slay that prime cat, but it was not because of your skill. If I let you loose in the woods, the only thing that will come of it is my scouts will have to search for two ignorant city dwellers instead of one."

"Simon's not ignorant," Wren mumbled under her breath, but she saw Maya's point. She hadn't the first clue where to look for Simon. She felt like banging her fists on the table as well. Nothing was working out like it was supposed to, and more frustrating than that, her friend might be in serious danger. If not worse. But Wren pushed that thought out of her mind. She had to hope for the best for Simon, at least until she could find a way to help him. And all the others depending on her. *And* figure out a way to get back to Earth. Oh, and cleanse the tainted stardust while she was at it, too. *No problem!* She shook her head, struggling for clarity. For now, she had to focus her physical and mental energies on trying to keep up with the training exercises required of all Outsiders. Maybe if she could prove herself to them by the time Auspex awoke, they would think better of Alchemists.

The young people among the Outsiders weren't at all like apprentice Fiddlers, which, upon reflection, made sense to Wren. There was no need for stardust or spell work or rhymes. But they weren't educated like children on Earth either. No reading, no writing, no mathematics—in fact, after her first day of training, Wren realized that more than half of them were illiterate. She supposed they didn't need to read, not when it took all their energy to survive long enough to grow to adulthood. The day was filled with physical challenges. Running. Throwing huge stones, to build muscle, the trainer told her. And then more running. And more throwing. And that was all before breakfast.

After that was weapons training, and Wren was

put through a whirlwind crash course in how to use a crossbow, followed by archery practice and then sword fighting. There was a short reprieve for what the Outsiders called a Naturalist lesson, which, from Wren's perspective, would better be called a How Each of the Plants and Animals in This Region Can Kill You lesson. By the time the midday break came around, she could barely hobble back to Maya's hovel.

"Good," the woman said, shoving a cloth-wrapped piece of bread and some kind of cheese at her. "You can tell me about the politics of Nod while we tend the garden." Which meant that most of the afternoon was spent pulling weeds and being interrogated by Maya. It was almost a relief for Wren to return to training, except when she saw that it was time for hand-to-hand combat, which meant being completely bested by every single other student. After a while, they stopped even trying, out of pity, and the instructor let Wren sit on the sidelines and bring water to the thirsty contestants.

They were all amazingly deft, able to maneuver their bodies and wooden practice weapons in a blur of energy. Just watching the pair nearest her made Wren feel tired.

A girl with a long blond braid was fighting another

girl much smaller than her. A wide chalk line across the dirt separated them, and to win, one would have to push her way onto the other's side. Wren didn't like the way the bigger girl seemed to mock the smaller one's weakness. She couldn't hear what they were saying, but the blond one was whispering what looked like taunts. The younger girl redoubled her efforts, attacking her opponent with a fierce cry until the blond girl finally clobbered her on the head with her weapon. Instead of congratulating her opponent like the other pairs had done, the blonde raised both arms in gloating victory.

"She used an illegal move," a boy next to them said. "She shouldn't have won." Wren silently agreed. She hadn't learned much about the rules of the weapons ring, but she did know that you weren't supposed to hit anyone on the head.

"And you think the animachines will play by the weapons ring's rules?" The white-haired instructor shook his head. "Get up, girl, and get back to work. No compromise."

Wren brought the smaller girl extra water, but she refused it, her face hardening with determination. The Outsider kids continued their practice until long after nightfall. By the time Wren tucked into her pallet that night, she didn't care if the night hag visited again. Nothing could keep her from sleep. The next day was much the same, and though Wren was less sore by the end of it, she was no closer to figuring out how to help Simon or the other captives. If only Auspex would wake up! At least he had some sort of plan and would be able to get through to these people. "Do you think Auspex will be better soon?" she asked Maya one night at dinner.

"Don't get your hopes up," Maya said in an emotionless voice, mopping up salty broth with a hunk of bread. "Wounds given by hovercats are no minor injury. He'll be lucky to wake at all."

Wren gnawed on her piece of bread and tried not to cry. Even the food the Outsiders ate was tough as nails.

The next day Wren completed her training exercises slightly better than the day before, and that night she made her way to the Healer's hut to visit the still-unconscious Auspex. The Healer had been the one Outsider who had made her feel even the teensiest bit welcome. The other students looked at her fondly, almost as though she were a fun pet, but none of them ever really spoke to her. And though Maya talked to her, talked too much, actually, with her endless questions and unsmiling responses, none of it was friendly. Only the Healer seemed to recognize that courage and bravery might also coexist beside compassion and friendliness. Only the Healer seemed to think there might be space for some compromise.

"Courage and Honor, my friend," the Healer said in his reedy voice when Wren rapped on his door that evening, a bundle of the root vegetables she and Maya had harvested that afternoon under one arm. He darted quick glances to each side to make sure no one was watching. "Come in! Come in!"

Behind him, a birdlike creature squawked its greeting, giving Wren a pang of longing for Coeur. She hoped Vulcan was taking good care of her.

The Healer was humming a tune as he limped around the crowded hut, sending his wispy white hair dancing around his ears.

Auspex lay on a bed on one side of the room, the rest of which housed a long wooden table covered with jars of potions and herbs of all shapes and sizes. Wren knew that the Outsiders scorned the use of stardust, but for all their distaste, the Healer's hut looked very similar to many rooms she had seen back at the Crooked House.

"How is he today?" she asked, peering down at Auspex's gray face.

"Middling," the Healer sang. "Middling, middling me." He seemed to speak only in poems, and Wren didn't know whether to demand a straight answer or laugh outright. She settled on a smile and tried to enjoy the fact that this was one Outsider, at least, whom she didn't need to impress.

The Healer held up some bright red feathers. "Another bird is nearby. Near, near, nothing to fear," he chanted.

Wren had to work to keep her amused smile on her face. She recognized them. They were the exact same shade as Coeur's tail feathers. She looked sharply at the Healer, but he was busy weaving them together to make what looked like a feather duster. Surely he didn't know about her falcon. It took everything Wren had not to run out of the hut and start calling for Coeur. What would the Outsiders do to an Alchemist's falcon?

"Healer," she said. "I've heard about Alchemists on Earth. Ones who ride birds with feathers like these." She watched him carefully out of the corner of one eye.

"Yes! Yes! The Alchemists on Earth." He clapped his hands and grinned; then he skip-hobbled over to a little corner cupboard and retrieved a book from under a pile of dried herbs. "Not for all to know, though, you see." He put a finger up to his lips and gave her a sly look. "Secrets make friends."

Wren nodded. "I won't tell anyone." The book was weathered with age, but Wren recognized the title. She had seen its twin back at the Crooked House. She eagerly flipped through the pages, examining the illuminated drawings. She wondered if her copy was still stacked on her nightstand table in her old room. She found the Weather Changer chapter, and then leaned forward, giving it her full attention. She had completely forgotten! Her copy had been missing several pages, but this one was complete, and the intact pages had to do with Dreamopathy.

There was an explanation of the various ways one could communicate in dreams. How to control someone's thoughts, how to communicate with others, even how to communicate with multiple people at once.

"Where did you get this?" Wren asked.

"The bird girl." The Healer placed one finger alongside his nose mischievously. "She left it here. Should be in her lab, it should. Robins should stay close to their nests, after all."

"Robin!" Wren exclaimed. "You know her?" She then realized what the Healer had said. "Her lab. Where is it?"

"Birds keep their nests to themselves, that they do." The Healer shrugged. "The bird girl would have liked you, I think," he said, turning back to his work.

Wren swallowed her disappointment. The Healer couldn't direct her to Robin's lab, but at least she knew it was out there somewhere.

"Healer!" Wren said, trying to keep her voice even. "Might I borrow this?"

"Eh?" The Healer was casting something that looked like dice into a ring of concentric circles. He looked up, confused. "Ah, yes, my friend. But keep our secret." He turned to the crowded shelf, taking down an ancient-looking compass and blowing the dust off the top. "The bird girl also left this. You should have it as well."

Wren clasped it eagerly with both hands. It was slightly different in appearance from the one Cole had given Astrid, but Wren recognized it as the apparatus needed to contact other Fiddlers through their dreams. Her new acquisitions gave her much to think about, and they also gave her the tiniest sliver of hope.

★ ★ ★

It was well past the middle of the night when Wren eased off her blankets and rose from the pallet. The hovel was cloaked in shadows, and Maya was snoring softly in her chair by the fire. Wren grabbed her boots and tiptoed toward the opening. One good thing about dirt floors was that there were no creaky planks to worry about. Once she was out in the main street, she tugged on her boots and let herself begin to breathe normally again. The Outsiders in this part of the settlement were all abed, and she was not going near the watch posts where sentinels kept vigil. Instead, she crept past the dying embers of their neighbor's fire and circled around to the open farm field.

"Coeur?" she whisper-called. "Are you out there?" Had she been mistaken? The Healer *had* to have seen Coeur, unless there were other birds with red tail feathers outside the city? Why couldn't they have talked about that in Naturalist class instead of how deadly everything was? "It's me, Coeur," Wren tried again, but there was no familiar flapping, no brush of feathers in response, not even a hostile screech. Wren dug in her pocket for the piece of dried fish she had brought and set it down in case Coeur was out there somewhere.

The realization that she was still all by herself should have made her sad, but instead it made Wren more determined to do what she needed to do.

There was no starlight, no sliver of a moon to see by, so Wren pulled the matchstick she had taken from Maya's mantel from her vest pocket and struck it on the nearby rock. She winced against the brightness of the tiny flame, and crouched low as though she could hide its light with her body. She flipped the Healer's book open to the section she had read earlier. *How to communicate with other Dreamers* was emblazoned across the page. It explained how Dreamers could learn to speak to other Fiddlers in their dreams, and Wren recognized that this what Boggen had done with her and Jack. If Boggen could talk to Jack in his dreams, maybe she could as well. She started to read again until she nearly dropped the book when a second realization struck her. Boggen wasn't the only one who had contacted her in dreams. *Robin had, too!* If she could figure out how to work the rhyme, she might also be able to find Robin. *Robin or Jack.* Who to contact first?

Wren's fingers were shaking with excitement as she ran her finger down the simple instructions. *Pinch a half thimble of stardust,* which she had, if only just. *Fiddle the rhyme according to the pattern above, but work it only in tandem with sleeping night.* She glanced back at the quiet village. It would have to do. *The Weather Changer must add to this a heart of courage and a will of iron.* Wren sped past that part. The oldest rhymes always had those bits, but the newer copies she had studied in the Crooked House relegated them to footnotes. Her teachers had explained that it was superstition more than alchemy. Wren hoped they were right. Or that maybe her time with the Outsiders and all their Courage and Honor nonsense had rubbed off on her. She was out of luck if it required something more. Spreading the book before her, she began the rhyme.

Now, to think of Jack. She had only enough stardust to do this once, and Jack was the surer bet. She wished she knew if he was sleeping or not. The description in the book said that it was easiest to make contact with a sleeping Dreamer, and the two needed to have a strong connection. She hoped that saving his life was a strong enough connection. It was certainly more than she had with Robin. She fixed his countenance firmly in her mind and pinched the correct amount of stardust. Nothing happened. The dust didn't even flare with its usual light. *Not now. It can't fail now.* She carefully cupped the dust in her palm and tried again. Maybe if she focused harder. But the little pile in her hands might as well have been a thimbleful of dirt. "Come on!" Wren hissed at it. Maybe she needed to feel threatened. Maybe she needed an animachine to attack her and *then* she could finally get the stupid stuff to work. She flipped back a page. Or perhaps she was reading the spell wrong. She peered closer, willing her nearly numb fingers to work, when the stardust flared to life. Carefully, painstakingly, she worked the rhyme, watching the dust spiral outward and gather into a shimmering circular disk that hung in the air much like a mirror.

Inside it, tendrils of fog swirled until a pale-looking Jack appeared in front of her, squinting into the distance. "Wren?" His voice was hoarse. "Is that you? Really you?"

"It's me, Jack!" Wren laughed, tears of relief filling her eyes. Her friend was all right. "I've found a Dreamopathy rhyme. It's how Boggen was—"

Jack waved her explanation away. "I know what Dreamopathy is . . . but where *are* you? Are you back on Earth?"

Wren gave a weary laugh. "I'm in the Outsiders'

camp." She told him all that had occurred since they'd parted ways. "I'm coming to rescue you, Jack. Not long now, I think. I only need a little more time to gather some support."

The hopeful look that had bloomed on Jack's face when Wren said *rescue* deflated, and Wren noticed for the first time that a bruise purpled one of his cheeks.

"There isn't much time," he said in a low voice. "Boggen has me acting as his errand boy for now, and I'm piecing things together. He's accelerating his research and moving more captives to his hidden stronghold." He frowned. "And Mary and Cole were sent there several days ago."

"Where is the stronghold?" Wren asked. It wouldn't do much good to rally support and lead an attack on an abandoned House of Never.

Jack winced. "I can try and find out. It won't be easy, though. Boggen isn't the most forgiving of people."

"He's hurting you," Wren said hollowly. "Isn't he?"

"Small price to pay if we can beat him." Jack gave her a wan smile. "You put together the rescue team. I'll figure out where you have to go."

Wren nodded. Tears were making Jack's form go all blurry. She scrubbed at her eyes and then realized it wasn't her crying at all. The stardust was fading.

"Just make sure you don't—" Jack started to say, but his voice cut out.

Wren raced to the compass, shaking it. "What did you say? Jack? *Jack!*" But she was too late. She hadn't kept a steady supply of stardust on the compass, and the dream had winked out. She reached for the pouch around her neck. Maybe if she hurried . . . maybe if she was fast enough, she could find Jack again. She peered closer, so absorbed in what she was reading that she let out a shout when someone approached her.

"Having trouble?" Maya spoke without a hint of sleepiness in her voice. "Perhaps I can help."

"Maya!" Wren couldn't keep the scolding tone out of her voice. "What are you doing awake?"

Maya raised one eyebrow. "Something I could easily ask you myself. What are you doing out of bed, child?"

Wren gathered her wits. Maya mustn't see the stardust. But there wasn't time to put it back in the pouch, which still lay spread out with the other things in front of the book. With only a moment's hesitation, Wren let the dust slip out of her fingers to join the dirt on the ground. Now Wren only had to hide the pouch without drawing attention to it. But it was too late.

Maya's gaze followed Wren's and she pounced like a cat. Before Wren could even move, the other woman had reached the book, turning to glare at Wren with accusation written all over her face.

"Magic?" She hissed the word. "Magic? Here? Within our very own camp?"

"I—" Wren started, but she couldn't even begin to think of what to say.

The other Outsiders might be illiterate, but Maya certainly wasn't. She grabbed the book. "Dreamopathy?" Her voice was equal parts incredulity and anger. In two strides she had crossed the clearing, and she struck Wren hard across the face. "Stupid girl. Did Boggen send you to spy on us?"

Wren closed her eyes and shook her head. Her cheek stung where Maya had hit her. "What I said was true. I'm Robin's friend."

Maya snorted. "What else have you been hiding? Who are you really?" She picked up Wren's pouch and hurled it and the book into the darkness. "You brought your filthy stardust here!"

Wren half expected Maya to unsheathe the dagger at her waist and attack her right then and there. She had to do something. She watched the arc of the pouch as it disappeared into the darkness, taking her last grains of stardust with it. Without it and the book, there was no hope of contacting Jack. Or Robin. She sighed. "I'm an Alchemist," she said quietly. "From Earth." There was no use hiding it now. "The Crooked House sent me to cleanse the gateway, but we were betrayed by one of our own and brought to Nod by someone who's now working with Boggen. My friends are all imprisoned." She shrugged. "But not me." She didn't tell Maya everything. Only the bits she thought might sway her. About helping Auspex escape and wanting to help the other captives. "I've told you the truth. Things aren't peaceful in Nod. Some of the 'city dwellers' don't want Boggen in charge either. Auspex was going to explain all of this. He said you'd have a hard time believing." She reached out to the older woman, then immediately withdrew her hands when she saw the calculating look on the other woman's face. "We were hoping you would help."

Maya stood staring at her for several heartbeats. Wren wondered what the Outsiders did to punish liars and Magicians, or if they even cared to hear both sides of the story. She thought of what she had seen over the past days, the brutal punishments she had witnessed in the practice yard, and the way everything was a life-or-death decision for these people. She did knew there wouldn't be any room for compromise.

Wren heard the unmistakable sound of feathers ruffling over where she'd left the fish, and her heart leaped. She willed Coeur to stay away. *Fly,* she thought, as though the falcon were telepathic. Maya didn't seem to notice, and Wren hoped the bird would have sense enough to return to the city. The sounds stilled.

"We don't help Magicians. Or Alchemists. No compromise." Maya clenched her jaw. "What I should do is call the leaders together and hold a judgment against you right now." She stared at Wren in silence for what felt like a long time, before jutting her chin forward as if coming to some kind of internal decision. "But I have a better idea." She grabbed Wren's elbow. "Come with me."

# SEVENTEEN

*Dickory dickory dare,*
*The girl walked through the air.*
*The horrible sound*
*Soon brought her down,*
*Dickory dickory dare.*

Maya didn't take Wren back to the camp. Instead she led her through the farmland and to a side of the island Wren hadn't yet seen. The path soon gave way to rugged terrain that Maya easily navigated. The vegetation had overtaken what might have once been terraces. Now, the ground had collapsed in on itself, leaving a slew of precarious tunnels and caverns. Maya hardly slowed. She had obviously been this way before. And more than once. "Faster, girl" was the only thing she said whenever Wren stumbled over a particularly cumbersome boulder. "The night wanes."

Wren laughed weakly at that. She was still sore from the days of training sessions, and the thought of another sleepless night tripled her exhaustion. She scrabbled over a rock that rested precariously against another, trying to catch her breath. Maya wasn't even winded. Wren didn't think the woman was leading her to her death, but that was only because she knew that if Maya wanted to kill her, she'd have done it already.

Maya disappeared into the tunnel in front of her, and Wren plunged after. As suddenly as they had started, they had arrived at the last place Wren had expected to find on the Outsiders' island.

"A laboratory?" she said, scanning the hidden room. Wren wasn't familiar enough with the technology of Nod to know if these were new or old machines, but their weathered faces and the makeshift way some of them had been patched together led her to believe the latter. "I thought you despised everything having to do with Nod. I thought the Outsiders never compromised."

"We don't." Maya's face twisted. "And I do despise everything to do with Nod." She reached over and began flipping gears, sending the machines whirring to life. The cool glow of gas burst into flame next to Wren, and she jumped aside to keep her shirt from getting singed. "But I despise Boggen's evil use of stardust even more."

Wren moved around the room. She didn't recognize most of the equipment, but the different devices seemed to be connected by corkscrew wiring to a wide shallow bowl in the center. Indeed, Maya was directing most of her attention that way. She took a gauge and inserted it into the steaming liquid in the bowl, peering at the meter and scribbling a temperature in a leatherbound book.

"What does all of this have to do with Boggen's experiments?" Wren asked. Her unease about Maya's intentions was overcome by her desire to help.

Maya peered at her over the edge of the book, but she didn't stop scribbling. "You know about Boggen's plans?"

"I know the stardust is tainted." Wren looked up from the map she had been studying. "And that Boggen is conducting human experiments to try to minimize the damage."

"Oh, yes, his 'research.'" Maya's lips curved into a hard smile. "Well, he won't be able to continue that without any stardust." She glanced up at Wren again, a glint in her blue eyes. "I've been draining the wells."

"You?" Wren stared at the woman. "The Outsiders are the ones taking the stardust?"

"Not taking it." Maya looked horrified. "Destroying it." She put her pencil in the book to mark her place and folded the cover closed, giving Wren her full attention. "I have made it my mission to stop Boggen's drilling. Call it a"—she squinted up at the ceiling as though looking for the right word—"personal passion of mine." She crossed the room and riffled through the maps spread over the table in front of Wren. "We've now found six of the seven wells." She pulled out a detailed map with several Xs across the surface. "But not the last. Or Boggen's stronghold."

Maya ran a finger over the map. "We're at a disadvantage, you see, because for every search party sent out, the Outsiders don't only have to hunt for the secret wells; we also have to contend with surprise ambushes by the animachines. And now you've come." She was eyeing Wren unsettlingly.

"Me?" Wren echoed. "I think there must be some misunderstanding. I don't know anything about Boggen's wells, and I haven't the first idea how to destroy stardust." Wren didn't add that she wasn't exactly sure she *would* destroy stardust even if she could.

"You are a Weather Changer, are you not?" Maya was back to shuffling around in the stack of papers.

In the second Wren took to deliberate, she realized that lying would do her no good. At least if Maya thought she was useful, she might not go all Outsider discipline on her.

"I am," Wren said. "But how did you know?"

"Does it matter?" Maya knelt down and began rooting through a cupboard. "A Weather Changer is precisely what I need."

Wren felt a flicker of unease. Should she tell Maya she wasn't always able to work the magic? Or would that make her no longer useful? "I'm only an apprentice Alchemist," she began.

"It would be better if you talked less," Maya said dismissively. "I have little love for the Alchemists," she said, enunciating the word with stinging precision. "But they are the lesser of two evils. Perhaps"—she looked up at Wren again, calculatingly—"perhaps you will prove useful even after you help me find the wells."

Wren instinctively took a step back. The glint in Maya's eyes looked positively malevolent. Still. She had to do something. "No," Wren said in a quiet voice, and Maya's eyes widened.

"No?"

"First, you agree to help me. Then I'll help you."

Bargaining with Maya wasn't easy, and Wren's shoulders were knotted from the stiff posture she had held while going back and forth with the woman. But in the end, it had been worth it. At least she hoped so. She was going to help Maya. "I'll do what you ask," she had said. "And then you will help me free my friends." Wren was taking the risk that Maya might go back on her word, and the edge in Maya's gaze still made her nervous, but she had given it her best shot. Hopefully, the rest of the Outsiders would come through. She shook her head. She should be focusing. She would need all her attention to get the stardust to work, and bartering or no bartering, Maya wouldn't help her unless she found the well. The older woman stood on the other side of the steaming bowl, checking the temperature and pressure gauges one last time.

"It's ready," she said. "Are you?"

Wren gave her a tense nod. She was as ready as she was ever going to be.

Maya moved to a hidden niche in the rock and took out a carved wooden box before returning to stand next to Wren. Wren couldn't make out the design etched into the metallic inset on the lid. Maya swept her fingers reverently over the pattern before opening the lid to reveal a faded velvet lining filled to the brim with glittering jewels. Maya ran her knobby fingers through them, sifting and pawing until she found the ones she was looking for. First, a silver gem cut into a diamond. Then a golden pear-shaped one. A glistening green orb. And finally a clear oblong streaked with yellow.

"What are those?" Wren asked.

Wren's words seemed to snap Maya out of her reverie. "We're not here for a lesson, girl," she said. "But to find a well. Ready yourself."

Wren wondered what exactly Maya was expecting her to do. The bowl in front of them was heating up as though it could sense that something was about to happen. The liquid bubbled and boiled, sending up clouds of steam that rolled over Maya's hands and turned the hair around Wren's forehead into damp curls. Maya pinched the green stone between two fingers, mumbling something under her breath as she held it above the scalding liquid. It was then that Wren saw what she hadn't noticed before. The jewels weren't jewels at all. She took an instinctive step back.

"Are those—"

"Eyes?" Maya asked, tossing the first glittering green eye into the liquid. "How else to see his wells?"

The potion hissed and bubbled even higher once the eye disappeared. Little pink clouds of mist arced above the surface like a fleet of invisible dolphins. Wren felt hard rock behind her and realized she had been steadily backing away from the cauldron. Was this some kind of dark magic?

Maya had thrown in the other eyes now, and rainbow arcs of green and orange and gold leaped higher, reaching almost to the ceiling of the cavern.

"Girl!" Maya shouted, noticing for the first time that Wren wasn't beside her. She darted lizardlike across the room and grabbed Wren's elbow, her piercing blue gaze pinning Wren in place.

"Frightened, girl?" She set her mouth in a thin line. "You should be. We all should be wary of the magic."

Wren swallowed the squeak that started to come out of her mouth. "I won't do dark magic," she managed. "Not for you. Not for anyone."

"Dark magic?" Maya's face looked like a thunder-cloud. "You think I would ask you to do *dark magic*?" She yanked Wren forward, and Wren winced. Surely a bruise was forming on her elbow by now, the way the woman liked to haul her around by it. "They're not real eyes, foolish girl." She hauled Wren over to the water, which had settled down to a more moderate simmer, the colors congealing to make blobs of solid greens and blues and browns separated by the pearly pink liquid, which was reminiscent of the water in the moat around the island.

"They are gemstones taken from different regions surrounding Nod," Maya explained. "I think these four most likely"—she tapped the map—"but we'll only know for sure once you work your rhyme." She let go of Wren's elbow and turned to look at Wren, her face contorted in a painful expression. Wren watched her, perplexed, until she realized that Maya was trying to smile at her.

"You mustn't tell anyone," Maya said. "We can tell the others you found the well, but we must not tell them about the stardust." She worked hard for another smile. "This lab was one of Malcolm's from the early days. He was adept at playing the stardust. I only know it is here because of my respect for him."

Wren realized what Maya meant. "The others don't know," she breathed. "About what you're doing." She thought of how Auspex had scorned stardust use, how the others used the word *stardust* as a curse. "All this business about *no compromise*." She stared at Maya. "And here you are making the biggest one of all."

The smile vanished from Maya's face and the familiar hard-as-nails, no-nonsense expression was back in place. "You will not tell anyone." She set her jaw, as though she was fighting a war within herself. "Evil must be stopped." She shook her head. "I'm only using the magic to fight the magic. Sometimes one must compromise." She gave Wren an expectant look. "Well? Get out the accursed stardust. We have work to do."

Wren had to admire the woman's tenacity, whatever else she thought about her methods. She almost hated to disappoint her. Almost.

"Maybe you won't have to compromise after all," Wren said quietly, avoiding the woman's sharp gaze. "I'm sorry, but I don't have any more stardust." She shrugged. "The last of it was in that pouch you threw away."

Maya's eyes widened at this revelation, but only for a moment. She hastily checked the temperature gauge on the potion. "It will be all right," she said. "Wait here."

She disappeared the way they had come, but Wren barely had time to wonder where she had gone when the woman was back, a small stoppered jar cupped in one hand.

"Use this instead," she said, handing it to Wren. "You will have to work the rhyme."

Wren looked at it dubiously. The jar held a dark liquid that looked nearly black. She swirled the bottle to get a closer look, and tiny pinpricks of neon light blossomed inside it. "What is it?" she breathed, transfixed by the display.

Maya unclenched her jaw. "Starmilk. Preserved from before the plague. Take care, as it's not very stable."

Working the starmilk was very different from working the stardust. Maya had only the vaguest idea of what to do, and Wren found herself fumbling through the first rhyme. She poured out several drops of starmilk into her hands, and it clumped there, thick and gluelike. Maya read the rhyme instructions from an ancient-looking book, and the archaic language was hard to follow. Wren traced her fingers through the starmilk. Five vertical lines, crossed by five horizontal. Then again from the opposite direction. Nothing happened the first two times she tried it. Fortunately, Maya seemed to think this had more to do with the cursed magic than any fault of Wren herself, and she hovered over Wren's shoulder with her painful-looking smile in place. Wren guessed Maya meant to be encouraging.

"Try again," Maya said. "But this time perhaps you should start the vertical lines from bottom to top."

Wren humored her. She wondered if Maya would be as encouraging if it turned out that Wren couldn't help her after all. Wren pushed all thoughts of failure aside when the liquid flared with light, sending a warm pulse of energy across her palm.

This time it was Maya who took several steps back, her face tight with worry as she eyed the magic the Outsiders loathed so much.

"It won't hurt you," Wren said, buoyed by the feeling of light and life in her hands. And for once she wasn't going to use it to hurt anyone, but to help them. How she had missed this! "What next?" she prompted, moving toward the bowl. Following Maya's instructions,

Wren sprinkled the starmilk over the bowl, reciting the words of the rhyme:

*All night long my nets I throw*
*To the stars in the twinkling foam.*
*Then up from the waves comes the light I know,*
*to take me where I want to go.*

As she did so, the landscape in the bowl shifted. The starmilk hovered above it, pulsing with brightness, and then fell into an unmistakable dome over the orange-hued hill near the western edge of the bowl.

"The Old City," Maya whispered. "Only Boggen would put a well there." The starmilk arced out, creating a maplike effect that pinpointed one location. Maya marked this all carefully on her map, muttering curses at Boggen all the while. While she did so, Wren slipped the little glass bottle of starmilk in her pocket. After all, Maya had thrown away the rest of Wren's stardust. Finally, Maya was done, and she looked up at Wren, a feverish light in her eyes. "Well done. Now we drain it."

They were back at the Outsider village by dawn. The bright glare of the sun was muffled by the smoke from the morning campfires. Maya, her expression blazing with purpose, strode down the main street of the settlement, clanging an old bell. Whispers and stares followed Maya and Wren as they wound their way past side roads where Outsiders gathered to gawk. Wren wondered whether their speculation matched the reality.

"We've located another of Boggen's wells," Maya announced when the others had clustered around the village green. "And a crew leaves this morning to deal with it."

There was a rustle of movement: not the wide-eyed stares Wren had expected, but the purposeful strapping on of weapons, the whispering of good-byes between very young children and their parents.

"Not all of us will be able to go." Maya pointed at a few of the fiercest and most scarred Outsiders. "Captains," she barked. "Choose your crew. We leave in a quarter hour."

The movement intensified. Some Outsiders were arguing. Others were making ready to fight. None was reconciled to staying behind. Even the younger Outsiders were begging their trainers to take them. Wren sat down on a nearby stump. Maya had seemed distracted by all the preparations. With any luck, she would forget Wren altogether. Wren yawned. Perhaps she could spend the day asleep in the hovel. Then when the Outsiders returned from emptying the well, they could plan the rescue. Every bone in her body felt tired. It was as if the night's work was only now hitting her. She leaned her back against the side of a nearby hut and let her body relax. Perhaps if she just rested her eyes for a moment.

"Girl!" Maya's sharp words jolted Wren to attention. She sat up, stifling a groan at the stiffness in her neck. How long had she dozed? The Outsiders had finished their preparations and were standing in a loose semicircle, packs strapped to their backs and weapons at the ready.

"Girl! Where is your gear?"

Wren rubbed her eyes. "Gear?"

But Maya ignored her. She flicked a finger impatiently at a sour-faced boy, pointing toward the weapon house. By the time Wren was on her feet and had gathered her wits, the boy had returned, an extra pack in hand and a hopeful expression on his face.

"Well done," Maya said, taking the pack, then dismissing him and dashing his hopes.

Wren watched the boy go, wishing more than

anything that she could swap places with him. "You want me to come with you?" she asked, the meaning of Maya's impatience becoming clear. "But why? I can't fight."

"No," Maya began, giving her a hard look. "But you can do *other* things. We have a bargain, and your part isn't done yet."

Wren supposed she meant something to do with the stardust, but Wren was too rattled by the cool stares of the Outsiders to argue her way out of this one. She had been able to work the magic last night; Maya probably wouldn't believe her if she told her otherwise this morning. Shouldering her pack, she reached for the crossbow, hoping that her few days of lessons might pay off if a hovercat decided to stalk them. "This is it, though, Maya," Wren said in a quiet voice. "One well. And then you fulfill your part of the bargain."

Maya's mouth twisted into a hard line, but she nodded her agreement. "Move out!" Maya called. Scouts skirted the clearing warily, as though they expected an animachine to pop out from behind the toddlers who stood in a doorway cheering for them.

Maya leaned in toward Wren. "Remember. No one must know about the starmilk."

Wren studied the old woman's implacable face. If she didn't know better, she would think that Maya sounded anxious.

Wren thought of how she had seen one of the Outsider students disciplined merely for mentioning stardust. Maybe Maya was afraid of revolt. Or worse. "Don't worry, Maya," she said. "As long as you fulfill your part of the bargain, your secret is safe with me."

Maya's right eye twitched, but she didn't reference the starmilk again. Instead, she was back to giving orders. "Stay close to me. And stay alive."

The search party did not depart via the underground lake. Apparently, the well they were looking for was located on the opposite side of the island.

"Out near the ruined caves," a boy Wren vaguely recognized said half ominously, half eagerly. Wren watched him move easily with the scouts, wondering what it would have been like to have grown up among the Outsiders, learning that courage and honor were the highest goals. She wished she felt that they were more worthwhile right now. If she wasn't so exhausted, she would be terrified.

The group she was traveling with wasn't large—two

dozen or so. Most of them were grown-up Outsiders, both men and women, with a few older kids sprinkled in the mix.

She fell in beside a girl whose blond hair had been plaited into a long braid. She was a good bit older than Wren, but Wren remembered watching her in the weapons ring. She was the one who had clobbered the other girl on the head. An Outsider A-student. She walked deftly across the uneven terrain, an arrow nocked into her bow. She swiveled alertly with each footstep, but she also watched her elders, mimicking their movements.

"So what happens when we get to the well?" Wren asked her.

The girl let her bow fall to one side. "Does it matter?"

"Kind of," Wren said. "Don't you care what happens if all the stardust is gone?"

The girl spun, and Wren found herself looking down her nose at a very sharp arrow tip.

"What did you say?" the girl hissed.

"Never mind." Wren waved her hands in front of her face. She was letting her exhaustion get to her. She knew better than to try and brave conversation with Outsiders. She had been fooled by the fact that the girl seemed to be around her own age. Wren tried for an apologetic smile. "Nothing. I said nothing."

"That's better," the girl said, letting her attention return to the dense woods, and Wren thought twice about asking any more questions. She was beginning to suspect that the Outsiders didn't ever ask questions. Courage and honor were all well enough, but without knowing what they served? She scanned the weathered faces around her. How many of them had even been to Nod? Or knew a Magician?

Wren wondered if she could do as they were doing. Follow orders that might mean her own death simply because she'd been told it was the honorable thing to do. She tripped over a sharp stone in the path and barely caught herself before falling, winning a scornful glance from the girl with the blond braid. It was just as well Wren wasn't an Outsider. Between wanting to know the reason for things and her inability to stalk, she probably wouldn't have lasted past her fifth birthday. The forest emptied out onto a high cliffside that bordered the island to one side. The Outsiders had spread out into a V-like formation, with some scouts fixing their weapons on the skies and others aiming theirs across the ravine that lay in front of them. Wren adjusted the crossbow strap across her shoulder.

Maya held up a fist to signal a halt, and the company drew in close together. A few of the men busied themselves at the cliff's edge, pulling on a rope that seemed to be attached to a pole. The younger Outsiders had gathered around Maya, their weapons momentarily forgotten. Wren watched them, though she couldn't hear their conversation. From this distance they looked like a pack of puppies, fawning over their owner for a dog treat. And it seemed that Blond Braid had won it. With a gloating smile on her face, she clasped forearms with Maya and then circled around the other kids.

Suddenly the blond girl sprinted back toward Wren, her face set in stone, tugging a rope behind her. Just in time Wren leaped out of the way, stumbling and falling gracelessly into a spongy bush, and by the time she righted herself, the girl had turned around and was sprinting just as hard toward the cliff's edge. Now Wren could see that she had the rope tied around her waist, and the rope was attached to a towering tree. Wren stifled a squeak as the girl swung out over the gorge, her body hanging in the air for one long moment, before she landed sure-footed on the other side. She attached the rope to some sort of post, and then turned to face her friends.

A cheer erupted from the Outsiders, and even the kids who had been passed over looked pleased. Blond Braid stood on the other side with her hands raised in victory for a moment too long.

A cry of alarm came from someone on Wren's left, and then arrows were in bows, shooting their way across the ravine, but it was too late for Blond Braid. Something had descended from the sky. It was the size of a fully grown Fiddler falcon, with claws like steel daggers. Its wings thumped the air with a metallic sound, and its war cry sounded like scrap metal being crushed at a junkyard.

Everything after that happened very fast. Crossbow bolts and arrows flew across the gorge. Some struck the initial animachine; others flew toward the second, which had just joined its mate. There were other weapons, ones that shot fiery bolts that seemed to maximize damage with each blow. Before Wren had even found her feet, the whole thing was over. The first animachine fell from the air, spiraling down and out of sight, while the second gave an ear-piercing screech. It scooped up the blond-haired girl's body and flew off toward a mountain on the horizon. The group of Outsiders grew suddenly still at the escape of their enemy.

"They'll be back," Maya finally said in a hard voice. "Best we be across the gorge before they return."

Wren was speechless. She looked around at the others, who were matter-of-factly packing up their gear and stowing away weapons. "What about the girl?" she asked Maya, who cut her off with an icy stare.

"You think you care more for one of our own than we do?" was all she said, and Wren didn't dare ask any more questions. Even if she had wanted to, she needed her full attention for what came next. Apparently, the blond-haired girl's task had been to connect the rope to a pulley. Once attached, Outsiders on this side could pull up a threadbare woven bridge that hung between the two cliffs. Wren realized with a sinking sensation that they all intended to cross it. She instinctively felt for the pouch around her neck and cursed the stupid Outsider fear of stardust. If she hadn't spent her time back at camp snoozing, perhaps she could have gone looking for it. She had no idea how the unpredictable stardust could help her across the dizzying gorge, but she wished she had the security of it nonetheless. Instead she had to settle for the few drops of starmilk left in the bottle she had taken.

"Girl," Maya said. "You're next on the bridge."

Wren gave her a blank look. Calling it that was generous. Two ropes, one strung above the other, did not make a bridge. Several of the Outsiders were already halfway across, hands shuffling quickly over the top rope and feet moving easily across the bottom.

"You've got to be kidding," Wren mumbled under her breath. Surely she could go back to the village. Help the Healer with Auspex. Do more training. Anything else.

"I never joke," Maya said, and even if Wren doubted the woman, which she didn't, the hard edge to her jaw made her intent clear.

"Perhaps I could—" Wren began, but Maya didn't even let her finish.

"You will find your courage in the doing," she said, piloting Wren by her sore elbow until she was teetering on the edge of the cliff. "You want the Outsiders to help you?" She nodded toward the ones who had reached the other side and were assisting their companions through the final stretch. "Act like an Outsider."

Wren swallowed all her protests. Stopping Boggen and rescuing the others was too important. She gulped down her fear and edged her first foot out onto the rope. Her gloves slid smoothly over the top rope, and they kept her hands warm. This high up, the wind whipped cold around her cheeks, sending loose tendrils of hair stinging her forehead. Wren tried to keep her gaze forward, out through the gully and toward the high wall of the city of Nod. From this perspective, the Outsider island wasn't an island at all. It was more of a peninsula surrounded by the pinkish lake. The fourth side merely ended in a cliff wall that dropped straight down into a heavily wooded area. The landscape seemed to repeat in this fashion, for she could see similar gullies and crevasses out toward the horizon. This was the rippled pattern she had seen on her initial descent into Nod. What had looked so peaceful now only kindled her fear.

She tried to keep her mind on the task in front of her. "One step at a time," she told herself, moving first her right foot, then the left. It was about halfway across that she made the mistake of looking down. The ground far below was a carpet of treetops, and her shifting body weight caused the ropes to sway. Wren lost her nerve, clinging tightly to the ropes, which made them twist and buckle even more.

"Keep your head, girl" came Maya's voice from the other side of her.

Wren peeked over and saw the stern-faced woman

moving across the rope bridge toward her with an ease that indicated she had done this many, many times. Wren stared at Maya, willing her body to calm down, but she was paralyzed. The tiniest bit of fear had escaped from her shut-tight box of emotions, and she was captive to it. She didn't dare release the rope and move her hands; she couldn't even inch her foot a minuscule step forward. She loathed the thought that even once she got across the stupid bridge, she'd somehow have to cross it again on the return trip.

"Don't look down," Maya said, and her words were a hint softer this time. "Keep your eyes on your destination."

Wren tore her gaze from Maya's approaching form, and ever so carefully shifted her head a fraction of an inch. Something inside her was sure that talking, moving her head, even breathing would send the bridge swaying again. She saw the horizon, the faraway turrets of Nod, and then she looked opposite, to her destination. Why, it wasn't much farther at all. She was more than halfway across the gully. She saw the Outsiders there, a few of them watching her appraisingly, others already spreading out into the forestlike vegetation beyond.

From somewhere else she heard the distant cry of an animachine, and fear jolted through her again. But this time it spurred her to action. She slid her feet forward, shutting out the swaying of the ropes, pulling herself along until the cliff's edge was in sight. With one final leap, she was over, crouched on the spongy ground, her breath coming in sharp, relieved gasps. She could feel the dirt beneath her fingers, smell the mineral scent of it.

"Well done, girl," Maya said gruffly from where she stood, disconnecting the rope and ensuring that no one could cross back over to the island.

Embarrassment enveloped Wren. Kind words from Maya equaled a standing ovation from just about anyone else. No more praise was forthcoming, but the old woman seemed to look at Wren less as an alien creature and more as a fellow Outsider. *I might as well act like one, then.* She got to her feet and brushed the dirt off.

The Outsiders were circled up near the cliff's edge, and Wren realized it was the place where Blond Braid had first fallen. There were no speeches. No tears. Instead, one of the crew captains held a fist up to his chest in a gesture of respect. "Courage and Honor," he said, and then he dropped to one knee. "May Hawthorne find peace."

A little murmur of echoes ran around the group. Wren whispered it under her breath. "May Hawthorne find peace." She hadn't even known the girl's name, and she felt tears welling up in her eyes. What had happened to her? What did the animachines do with their prey? She watched the other Outsiders' stony faces as they prepared to journey on. Even the kids seemed to accept it as a matter of course. She wondered how many such ceremonies they had witnessed. The search party began to move, and Wren shouldered her crossbow like the Outsiders in front of her and followed stoically behind.

It was hard work keeping up with the others as they hiked easily through the rubbery undergrowth, but the adrenaline kept Wren's exhaustion at bay for a time. Even so, she was more than grateful when someone decided it was time for a water break. The group passed canteens around but said little. They rested in shifts. Ever-alert Outsiders stalked the clearing, looking for enemies, while others leaned up against trees in what would be very dangerous to mistake for a relaxed pose.

They journeyed and rested twice more, a stretch of time that was as hazy as a dream to exhausted Wren.

No one spoke. No one told tales. No one did anything to pass the time. Wren carried her crossbow as Maya had instructed her, but she hardly thought she'd be able to shoot. Her arms ached with the weight of it. Maya must have noticed, because some time later she positioned Wren in the center of the group. "Don't stray, girl," she said, and disappeared with the others. Wren had given up hope of impressing them. They'd either have to help her out of the goodness of their hearts or not, because she couldn't act like an Outsider any longer. She could barely walk without tripping all over herself. She stumbled yet again into a bank of shrubbery and got to her feet, but this time she didn't keep moving. It wasn't because she was tired. It was because she recognized the scene in front of her.

"What is this place?" she whispered, and then louder, in Maya's direction. "Where are we?"

The scorched ground in front of them lay in a shallow bowl, and the knobby outlines of trees marked its rim. Wren felt goose bumps up and down her arms.

"The Old City," Maya said in a weary voice.

Wren already knew this eerie landscape from the dream she had experienced back on Earth, but that didn't make it any less creepy to see it in front of her while she was awake. When she had come here in her dream, there had been a bird that attempted to tell her something. She tried to gather her scattered wits. Had Robin brought her here? No. She scanned the horizon. She had come here on her own. In a reckless attempt to escape from Boggen's hold in the dream. Somehow she had ended up here.

Maya's mouth was pinched tight in a firm line. "You can see what comes of using magic." She nodded sternly toward the desolate landscape. "So much loss."

They walked single file, a stretched-out line of silhouettes against the deadened landscape. Wren had the uncanny feeling that they were being watched, but each time she glanced back over her shoulder, she saw that no one else was there. When she passed a gnarled tree a little shiver ran through her. She recognized the spot. It was where the bird had first crowed at her. But the air remained silent, without even a whisper of wind to break the quiet. The soft crunch of boots against dirt followed Wren as she caught up with Maya.

The group was entering the ruins of a settlement. Buildings must have once stood here, but now there was only rubble. Clay bricks lay in piles of ashes. Everywhere she looked was ruin and destruction.

"What happened here?" Wren matched her pace with the other woman's, sending up little puffs of dirt as she walked.

Maya didn't say anything, and at first Wren thought she simply wasn't going to answer. Then, without breaking stride, she began to talk. "This was an outpost—a research station designed to study and improve upon the biological life native to this planet—but the Magicians here ended up creating the animachines." She shook her head. "They should have known better, but they used stardust to tamper with things better left alone. The station was destroyed after the plague." Her feet stumbled a bit when she said this. Wren wouldn't have noticed if she hadn't been trying so hard to match Maya's stride. "Would that all the stardust would have been destroyed along with it."

"Did you . . ." Wren paused, wondering if there was a polite way to say this. "Did you lose someone in the plague?" Maybe that was why Maya was so hard and emotionless.

Maya's eyelid twitched. "Yes."

Nothing else was said, and Wren was wondering how she could delicately ask for details, when a strange whistle came from somewhere far ahead of them. In an instant Maya crouched down, shoving Wren up against the nearest half wall.

"The animachines are coming," Maya hissed. "We won't have much time." She reached into her pocket and pulled out one of the gems they had used to work the spell. It was glowing dully, pulsing with an internal light. "We're getting closer to the well. With luck, we can drain it before the animachines find us."

Wren knew better than to ask questions. The air was taut with tension. All the Outsiders had melted away into the ruins. Wren eased her crossbow out and waited. Maya crept forward, beckoning behind her for Wren to follow. Another whistle came. And then the haunting cry of an animachine. Wren scanned the skies as if one of the swooping creatures from earlier might snatch her up next, but Maya grunted. "Not that kind, girl. These ones come from the ground."

They turned another corner, and then Wren understood. The barren, burned-out field wasn't the only place she had visited in her dreams. She felt her skin turn to ice. She had been in this city before, too. She recognized the desolate, orderly rows of houses and the way they stopped before a wall of spikes. And a door in it that she was confident led to a deep underground pit.

"The spiders?" she whispered in a shaky voice.

Maya looked at her with piercing eyes. "Yes. They live in the research station itself. The first animachines. How did you know?"

Wren sighed. "Lucky guess." She counted her crossbow bolts. She had five in the pouch that hung from her back. She wondered what they would do to one of the spiders from her nightmares.

"Hurry!" Maya ordered, waving Wren through the crossroads. There was no motion from the edge of the research station, and Wren hoped that meant the spiders were gone. Or sleeping. Or pretty much anywhere else. And then came another heart-stopping cry. This one was followed by human shouts and the sound of the firebolt weapon.

But Maya wasn't distracted by that. "Come here, girl," she said. "Hold the stone."

She handed Wren the eyeball-shaped gem, which, though it glowed with light, was cool to the touch. As Wren closed her palm around it, a piercing green light burst forth, shooting through her fingers. She could see a matching signal flare up several streets over.

"There!" Maya said. "To the well. Before the animachines notice."

Wren didn't think that was likely. Unless the spiders were somehow blind. The stone was like a giant spotlight for any living thing with eyes. But she didn't argue. Maya was running now, her weapon perched on her shoulder as she skidded around corners, scanning the scene. Wren followed, trying to manage her crossbow and hide the stone as much as possible. Neither was very effective, but it didn't seem to matter. More animachine cries had sounded across the city, but Maya seemed wholly concerned with reaching their destination.

They ducked down another alley, and then they had reached the source. A circular panel that reminded Wren of a city manhole cover was set in the dusty ground. Maya stood looking down at it. "Excellent. Now open it."

"Me?"

"Who else?" Maya said mildly. "You are the Weather Changer. You have the starmilk; I saw you steal it."

"What do I do with it?" Wren asked, too tired to be ashamed. Even if the magic worked for her, it wasn't like she knew the spell.

"The locator rhyme you used before will open the well," Maya said with a determined expression on her face. "I'll do the rest."

There wasn't time to argue. The commotion of the fighting was increasing, and given the volume, the spiders were on the move and headed in their direction.

Wren crouched down over the panel, which was labeled with an unreadable formula. But one thing was obvious. There was a gem-sized hole in the center, and Wren dropped the green stone into it. The light from the stone now burst forth from the well itself, sending brilliant green through the cracks around the panel. Along with the light came a fierce wind that nearly pushed Wren back on her heels.

"Work the rhyme!" Maya called.

Wren fumbled in her vest pocket for the near-empty bottle of starmilk. Fighting to hold her hand steady in the wind, she dumped the liquid into her palm and whispered the rhyme. Instantly, the magic flared to life, sending a rushing sense of well-being throughout Wren's body. The panel in front of her began to move, swiveling up and out, hovering over the hole in the mighty current of green air. Despite the increasing volume of the spiders' cries and the buffeting storm, Wren felt like laughing. Maya was laughing. She stood, weapon at one side, laughing in the warm flood of the magic, her tightly cropped gray hair ruffling in the wind and the unearthly green glow reflected in her eyes.

Wren did laugh then, forgetting for a moment that she was on a strange planet. Forgetting the threat of the animachines. Forgetting everything but the feeling of being alive, of having gotten through everything to be here with Maya. The magic was shooting up and out of the well, and for a moment it looked like the horizon of Nod was visited by an aurora. But then it dissipated into the atmosphere, the brilliant greens and blues fading into a smoky cloud that swirled around her, blocking Maya from sight and paralyzing Wren with chains of fear.

Jagged bolts of light shot through the dimness, sending matching pangs of pain through the base of Wren's neck, and then *he* was there. Boggen, his face shiny with perspiration and framed by a strange otherworldly helmet, stared at her through overly bright, insane eyes. He was standing on a rocky precipice, surrounded by walls of obsidian. A neon glow pulsed from somewhere above him.

"My missing apprentice," he said in a controlled, quiet voice. "I should have known."

Wren was frozen in place. He had come to her in

waking dreams on Earth, but then a whole galaxy had separated them. What would he do now that she was here on Nod? Could those awful spiked gauntlets reach through and grab her? Somehow his presence ushered in a terror so compelling, so complete, that it held her captive and unable to move.

"I was prepared to thank you for delivering Jack to me." He gave her a wicked smile. "And now I find that you are aiding my enemies. Emptying my wells. Thwarting all I am working for." His face became a mask of anger. "Why? Why do you fail me?" he screamed, and the sudden change in volume from near-whisper to raging cry took Wren's breath away.

"I hate those who fail me, Apprentice." The icy calm was back. "Now I will destroy you. And those you love."

Wren willed her body to work, ordered her mouth to speak, to shout, to scream, "Never! Get away! Help!" Anything! But no words came. She fought her paralyzed legs and with a great effort forced herself to take a step backward. At first her muscles didn't respond, but then she felt the slightest movement. She worked harder, fighting the pull of Boggen's dream spell and its accompanying crippling fear, but instead of moving away from him, she fell to her knees, cowering before him.

Boggen's pleased laugh sent spirals of shame coursing through Wren. Some Fiddler she was. Her friends were depending on her to rescue them. All of Earth was waiting for her to cleanse the stardust. Even the Outsiders thought she could help them put a stop to Boggen's research. And here, when she was confronted with Boggen, she was powerless to do anything except bow before her cruel master. Maybe she did belong to him.

Boggen's form towered over her, the pulsing neon cloud casting everything in an eerie glow. "You will come to me, Apprentice," he said gloatingly. "A Weather Changer for a pet. I wonder what effects the tainted stardust will have on you." He reached out with one arm, beckoning her, as if he could draw her to himself through the dream. As he did so, Wren felt a magnetic pull, a strong sense that Boggen was somewhere to the east. Everything inside her compelled her to go to him, as though she had a powerful itch that could only be scratched once she arrived. And somehow, Wren knew that she would go to him. Whatever magic he had worked, whatever he had done, held her captive to his will. She could fight it no more than she could fight the powerful fear that kept her paralyzed.

"You belong to me," Boggen said with a leer. "And I will see you soon." His words hammered nails into Wren's soul. She knew it was inevitable. Her fate was inextricably tied to Boggen's. Perhaps it would take one day, perhaps twenty, but he would have her. With a wave of his gauntleted arms, the cloud disappeared, and with it some of Wren's dread. She could move her body again, and she worked her jaw carefully, but she still felt the powerful pull to the east, the inexorable draw of the reunion that must happen.

"We did it. The well is empty," Maya was saying. The air had gone still around them. All the colors of the aurora had dissipated. It seemed that Maya knew nothing of Boggen's encounter with Wren, which was likely a good thing. Maya might just kill her on the spot if she knew that Boggen had marked her in such a way.

Maya gave her a rare genuine smile, and Wren forced something like it onto her own trembling lips, until a screeching sound broke the moment. From the end of the street a gigantic silver shape stumbled into sight. The spider was even larger in real life, and it came crashing toward them, crushing the last walls of the ruins as it moved.

Wren dropped the starmilk bottle, fumbling at her shoulder for her crossbow, but Maya stepped in front of her, turning her around and shoving her back the way they had come.

"Go!" Maya barked. "Back to the rope bridge. Get to the island." Maya was already unstrapping her weapon, sending a bolt straight at the spider's metal underbelly. It struck dead center, sending the beast stumbling for a moment, but then it came implacably on. Wren saw the spindly legs of another spider cresting the top of a building.

"There's no courage in getting killed needlessly." Maya was moving toward the animachine, throwing a dagger into the thing's eye. "I can fight better without tending to you, girl. We're done here. Now go! Back to the island."

Wren didn't wait any longer. One of the first lessons she had learned in the weaponry ring was that distractions could be deadly. Maya was right. Maya would fare much better not having to watch out for Wren. She sped back the way they had come without turning to see if she was followed. She tore down the city streets, not remembering which ones they had taken at first, but knowing that the desolate field was behind the Old City. She dodged down one street only to see a smaller, human-sized spider scuttling through a crossway. Wren doubled through an empty building to escape it, racing past burned-out rooms and forgotten rubbish. Her right side ached, and her chest felt tight from the running, but she pressed on, driven by the cords of fear that bound her to Boggen and her increasing terror of the animachines.

She heard screeches in the distance and wondered how Maya was faring. How many spiders were there? She fought against the eastward pull of Boggen and pumped her legs faster. Now that she was in control of her own body again, she felt a glimmer of hope. Perhaps there was a way to fight Boggen's magnetism. Perhaps the Outsiders or Winter or the Scavengers would know a cure for being marked as his.

As if she could outrun her connection with Boggen, she sprinted on. She was halfway through the field now, but she didn't stop running. She barreled through the forest, crashing through the underbrush in what felt like an endless sprint. Twice she had to slow to a walk to catch her breath, but then the distant echo of an animachine's cry spurred her on. She knew very well the spiders weren't the only threat. What if a hovercat was in these woods? Or one of the flying ones? She had to be getting close. She recognized the ground here, the way it sloped down toward the flat outcropping where the rope was tied. She heard human voices ahead. Could it be that some of the Outsiders had already reached the ravine? She hoped so. She had been so busy sprinting she hadn't even considered what would happen if she had to swing across the chasm on her own. She was almost there. Yes, those were definitely human voices, shouts, and cries. She wondered how many Outsiders had made it to safety. Then as she burst through the underbrush, she heard a scream and saw in unforgettable clarity the silhouette of an Outsider being snatched up by an animachine. Too late, she heard the thump of mechanical wings behind her. Wren screamed and dropped to the ground, narrowly dodging the outstretched claws of the flying animachine that tore through the air where she had been moments before. Now she realized what the cries had been. Battle was being waged here, too. Whichever Outsiders had escaped the spiders had made it through the forest only to discover the flying monsters on the other side.

"When it next circles around, I will draw it away. You get to the bridge," said a gruff Outsider, who stood at attention at the edge of the woods. He pointed to the animachine, which was circling around and preparing to dive-bomb them again. "Our only hope is to get across before more come. The spiders are hunting through the woods, and soon they'll have us all pinned."

Wren couldn't even find the words to answer him. Her breath was coming in ragged gasps, and every muscle in her body screamed in protest. She leaned forward and rested her palms on her knees. Black spots swam before her eyes. How was she supposed to get across the bridge if she could barely catch her breath?

The Outsider was moving, expertly drawing a steel-plated arrow and aiming at the animachine. "Now!" he called, and Wren willed her exhausted body forward. She jogged to the bridge, grasping the top rope with trembling hands. The spots swam in front of her eyes again, this time not from exhaustion but from fear. She had thought the threat of the animachines would trump the agony of the bridge, but the dizzying depth below sent panic coursing through her body. She breathed deeply, willing herself to find courage. She had to do this.

She eased herself out onto the rope, and all her senses focused inward. She could hear the screeching cry of the animachine stalking the ledge, hear the twang of the bow as the Outsider shot his arrow. She heard calls from the other side as Outsiders who were already on the island tried to lend her their courage and distract the beast.

"Halfway done," one of the other kids called. Wren felt the cold air against her cheek. Saw the blue sky with nearly painful brightness. Every sense was alive. Which was how she knew the moment another animachine had found her.

The cranking sound of its wings came from behind her, the mechanical chop of a machine coupled with the screech of a beast. In that moment, Wren wasn't afraid. She held on to the rope with one hand and, trancelike, reached for her crossbow, pivoting to aim one final shot at the all-too-living eye that was examining her from several arms' lengths away. The animachine was hovering there, not even fighting. Wren realized that it was waiting. It was so sure of its prey.

She glanced across to the island and saw the other Outsiders there, kneeling with their hands clasped in the gesture of respect. They knew she was already dead.

Wren shot the crossbow straight at the bird, which easily evaded it. It rose up, higher and higher, until for one
brief moment Wren thought that perhaps it would leave
and she might escape after all, but then it gave a crow-
ing sound and came racing toward her in a hunter's
dive that ended with a tight mechanical grasp around
her waist. Wren struggled and kicked, tugging hard
at the metal trap around her waist, but she knew it
didn't matter. Even if she could escape, only death lay
at the bottom of the deep chasm, or worse, at the hands
of Boggen. As it flew higher, she gave a bitter laugh.
Her only consolation was that Boggen wouldn't have
the satisfaction of experimenting on her after all. The
Outsiders' kneeling forms were distant specks on the
edge of the island when suddenly the bird slammed
into something, sending a jolt through its body that
Wren felt reverberating through its claws.

The animachine screeched, circling around to scan
the area for enemies. Wren scoured the ground below
them, hoping for a sign of rescue, pleading for a hint at
a happy ending, but there was nothing. They were too
high up, and the land below them looked desolate, bare
of any living creatures. The invisible force hit again,
this time spinning the animachine in a circle. The

claws around Wren clenched tight and then loosened. Wren squirmed in her prison. If only the animachine was over water, then when Wren fell it wouldn't be so bad—but she didn't have more time to think about it, because the next jolt sent the animachine reeling, and its claws opened, dropping Wren into a free fall through empty air.

# EIGHTEEN

*Sugar and spice*
*And everything nice*
*Are not what Fiddlers are made of.*

W ren was surprisingly calm as she fell. Cold air whistled past her ears, drowning out the screech of the animachine. Down she fell. On one side she could see the edge of the cliff. She plummeted into the gorge, down and down, the hard ground rushing up to meet her. She spread out her arms to either side. This was really happening. She was about to die.

With a jolt, she landed on something soft but firm. It wasn't the ground, for she was still several hundred feet up in the air. She was no longer falling but moving forward, coasting as though she really was flying. She felt movement, the recognizable sensation of wings flapping. But not animachine wings. A familiar squawk welcomed her.

"Coeur!" Wren cried, flipping over to plaster herself across the falcon's invisible body in a hug. "You saved me!"

Coeur screeched back. Wren felt hot tears sting her eyes. She wasn't going to die. She gave a weak laugh. She was alive! She pushed herself up into a seated position, feeling carefully for the edges of the bird's back to orient herself. The animachines might still be out there, and even if Coeur was invisible, Wren wasn't. Her silhouette against the very blue sky was likely enticing prey. Wren tugged hard on the lead feathers that would turn Coeur toward the city. "Fly back to Nod."

There were no more animachine attacks. The falcon flew steadily and surely, circling around the Outsiders' island. It took Wren a moment to realize that she knew the area well. "Have you been exploring?" she whispered to her bird. "It *was* you who came that night, wasn't it?" But Coeur flew silently on. Wren was still whispering quiet thank-yous when she began to realize there was a problem. Nod was on the horizon, but Coeur wasn't flying toward it. Instead, the bird was angling across the gullied ravines and toward a place where rock formations poked upward like thin needles reaching to the sky.

Wren tucked in closer to the falcon's body, shutting her eyes at a narrow miss with one of the spires. Coeur ducked and dodged, cleverly navigating the spindly towers until they reached a wide valley. Wren peered down, noticing that in one area, a cluster of animals grazed, tiny dots that became recognizable as the bird prepared to land.

"Coeur! What are you doing?" Wren shouted when she saw the metal plating on their flanks. "Those are *animachines*! Get out of here!"

Coeur ignored her, despite Wren's frantic kicking and pulling on her lead feathers. Instead, she calmly lit on the spongy earth and waited patiently for Wren to dismount.

Wren shut her eyes tight. How long before the animachines attacked? And when they did, would Coeur finally see what was going on and fly out of here? Even if Wren could work the stardust, she didn't have any more, and all of a sudden she felt completely vulnerable. What use were her hands and feet against monstrous machines?

Wren spent several seconds imagining a horrible

death before she realized something. If the animachines were going to attack, they would have done so already. She began to hope that perhaps she and Coeur had somehow miraculously escaped their notice, because nothing was happening. There wasn't any awful metallic attack cry. There wasn't the sound of huge paws crashing toward them. Instead there was quiet and the trickle of running water, and then the last sound Wren had expected to hear.

"Wren?"

"Simon?" she squeaked in the direction of the familiar voice. "Is that you?"

"Excellent job, Coeur," Simon was saying to the falcon in the crooning way he had with all animals. "Very well done." Wren stared. Her ears weren't deceiving her. Simon was standing there, a Simon who looked remarkably ragged with his grubby clothes and dirty face, but it was definitely Simon, and he had a handful of treats, as if this were a perfectly ordinary day back at the Crooked House falcon mews.

"Simon!" she said as her wits came back to her. She didn't have any idea what her friend was doing all the way out here, but it didn't matter. They were in danger. "There are animachines! Very close!" She scooted forward on the bird. "Hop on, and will you please tell Coeur to get out of here?"

"Coeur knows what she's doing." Simon grinned and laid a hand on Wren's arm. "Climb down, and I'll show you."

"Didn't you hear what I said? *Animachines!*"

"I know," Simon said distractedly. "And they're probably ready for their evening meal. If you hurry, you can help feed them."

Wren gaped at him. "Are you crazy? If we get close to those things we'll *be* their evening meal."

Simon rubbed his forehead as though working out a puzzle; then his eyes widened as he landed on the solution. "You think—?" he laughed. "No, Wren, you've got it all wrong. Those are *my* animachines; they won't hurt you. Come here, and I'll show you."

With much persuasion, he led Wren around one of the rocky outcroppings and closer to the animals. "The Magicians are mistaken," he said. "The animachines aren't interested in attacking people; they're only trying to defend themselves." He whistled and one of the giant creatures loped toward them.

"A hovercat?" Wren gasped. "Simon, you saw what one of those did to Auspex."

"I did," Simon said gravely. "And I saw what you did to the prime cat." He offered his hand, palm up, to greet the beast, and then began scratching behind its ears. The cat gave off a huge rumbling purr that sounded like a car engine. "The animachines would rather live in peace with humans than be hunted by them."

"The animachines think the people are the ones hunting *them*?"

"What else would you call it?" Simon moved over to a thick pile of what looked like palm leaves. "People attack their habitat and hunt them in the forest. You know the rain shield over the city of Nod? When an animachine flies into it, it gets electrocuted." Simon began throwing the leaves toward the herd, and the animachines came over, pulling the fronds between their paws and gnawing on the ends contentedly. "There are hostile animachines, of course, but humans are not their natural prey. It is possible for us to coexist in peace, especially once we understand one another."

While Simon tended to the animals, Wren thought about this new perspective. Even if she didn't quite believe it, here was proof before her very eyes. Simon showed her several herds of different species, all equally content to leave them alone.

Later that night, Simon started a fire. Wren noticed that he didn't use stardust. Instead he gathered kindling and dry grasses, rubbing sticks against each other as a Boy Scout might. The growing twilight was calm, filled with a gentle breeze and the soft sound of contented animachines, but Wren felt increasingly agitated inside. Now that the terror of being hunted by the animachines had faded, the thrumming of Boggen's summons was growing loud again, drawing her eastward. Wren tried to block it out, but every effort only increased her anxiety. Talking seemed to help. "You've been living here, Simon?" she asked. One of the rocky spires had a cave at its base, and Simon had created a shelter there. He had fashioned a few rotting tree stumps into stools, woven a thick pallet of palm fronds for a bed, and neatly wedged his brightly colored notebooks against the rocky wall. "For how long?"

"Since we got separated in the forest. While you fought the prime cat, I began talking to one of the subordinates."

"*Talking* to it?"

Simon nodded matter-of-factly. "How else do you think I know their side of things? It's actually more

telepathy than it is talking, though." He flushed a little when he saw Wren gaping at him. "Mary did say
once that my Fiddler talent might be an affinity with
animals."

Wren shook her head, stupefied. She wasn't sure
what was more surprising: that Simon was claiming to
be able to telepathically communicate with alien creatures or that he had survived this long on his own.
"Where did the food come from?" She pointed to the
collection of dried fruits and hard bread heaped in a
mound on one of the stumps.

"Oh, are you hungry?" Simon asked, offering her
some. "Vulcan brought these." Simon explained that
he had summoned his falcon, Leo, and used him to
send messages requesting supplies to Vulcan. "Most
days Vulcan himself comes to make deliveries. He says
that I'm his responsibility, as a sort of honorary Scavenger, but I think he really likes flying on the falcon."
Simon smiled conspiratorially.

"Wait just a minute," Wren said. "So you guys have
all been one happy family visiting back and forth, and
I've been stuck on my own in the Outsiders' camp,
which wasn't easy for your information, trying to figure out a way to get back to all of you? I risked my

life trying to do a Dreamopathy rhyme so I could talk to Jack." Wren knew that was a slight exaggeration, but Maya *had* been very angry. "I—" Wren stumbled over the words. Surely she could tell Simon about the encounter with Boggen. She had told him everything else all along, hadn't she? Simon was her best friend! But shame held her tongue. She hadn't been strong enough to fight Boggen off. She had knelt before him. She hadn't even been able to say a word in his presence. Wren slumped under a cloud of defeat.

"I knew you were okay," Simon was saying. "I concluded that you were making valuable alliances with the Outsiders and should be left to it." He rearranged the palm leaves so that there were two pallets near the fire. "Coeur was watching you the whole time. How else do you think she was right there when you needed saving?"

This made Wren feel a little bit better, but only a little. "Well, that would have been nice to know," she said grumpily as he prepared her makeshift bed. She knew it was wrong to be upset with Simon. It wasn't his fault Boggen had overpowered her. If only there was someone who *could* save her. She lay back and looked up at the starscape of Nod in all its glory. "I

would do anything to be free of him," she whispered
to the unfamiliar stars. If only Simon or Coeur could
have somehow been there when Boggen had come for
her. She knew Simon would have tried to help. Simon
always looked out for her. The leaves were surprisingly
comfortable, and their faint herbal scent made her even
sleepier than she'd been before. "Simon," she said after
a few minutes. "Thank you for saving my life."

"Any time, Wren. Any time."

Wren opened her eyes and sat up. The air smelled different, spicy-warm this time, and the space around her
swirled with infinite shadows. Purples, blacks, and
grays blended together in a smoky cloud. She gasped.
Had Boggen found her again? She braced herself for
a nightmare, but instead the shadows grew more dis-
tinct, coming together to form a familiar shape until
they loomed large, and Wren recognized them.

*Wren.* The Ashes didn't speak, but somehow Wren
perceived their intent. It had always been that way when
they communicated with her—their thoughts reso-
nated someplace deep inside her being. Maybe Simon
talked to the animachines the same way. The Ashes'
wings rippled in shadows that shifted and swayed with

the movement of their flight. *Wren. The Crooked Man waits.*

"The Crooked Man?" Wren asked feebly. The Scavengers thought he meant to destroy Nod. The Outsiders seemed sure of it. Wasn't it enough that Boggen had control of her? What could this other powerful Magician possibly want with her now?

*It is time. He summons you.* The Ashes spread their massive wings, and then they were carrying her in what must be their claws, though they, too, were covered with feathers, propelling Wren forward into a warm amber light. It was not the cool blue-green of stardust, but the effect was very similar to her flight in the aurora. Yellow and gold and orange leaped and played about her, swirling thicker and brighter until she had to shut her eyes against the brilliance. A part of her brain told her she should be worried—that energy this powerful could consume her like fire—but the rest of her knew deep inside that she would be okay. As they carried her farther in, the panicked beat of Boggen's mark flared to life. She felt as though danger was all around, and Boggen's chains of fear pulled tighter.

Below, a sea of sapphire spread out smooth as glass. In the center was an island of sorts, a constantly moving spot of energy where the amber liquid leaped and danced in infinite loops. The Ashes made for a wide outcropping of jagged shale that was the color of their feathers. Cool, solid rock met the ephemeral light that danced around them, and in the center of it all was the Crooked Man.

The moment she saw him Wren realized that she had been expecting some kind of alien creature, or at least a superhuman being. Instead, an ordinary man moved toward her. There was nothing remarkable about his appearance. He didn't seem to be old, but his face looked wise. He was dressed in rough grays and browns, and he came toward Wren with his hands stretched out in welcome.

The Ashes gently released her, and Wren stumbled forward onto all fours. The Crooked Man reached down and helped her up.

*Come.* His words came like those of the Ashes. Internally. *Rest by my starfire.*

He led her to what, for lack of a better word, Wren thought of as a waterfall. The amber liquid spilled and leaped over the rocky terrain like a river of fire, orange and red and crimson shooting out like droplets from a rainbow. The Crooked Man beckoned for her to sit in a shallow bowl cut into the rock to form a seat.

"Is that starfire?" She thought of all the legends she had heard. "Do you mean to destroy Nod with it? The legends say you will."

*The legends are right, but the great fear they bring is misplaced. That is not the starfire. I am.*

Wren pondered this but could make little sense of it. Was Starfire the Crooked Man's name? "Why have you brought me here?" she finally asked.

*To make things well.* The pulse of his thoughts changed, warmed with fondness and favor. *I am the guardian of the pathways through space, a friend to all Fiddlers—Alchemists and Magicians alike. Once, they knew me well, but most have long forgotten my existence.*

"I think they know you by another name," Wren said, recalling all she had heard of the legends. "Everyone I've talked to calls you the Crooked Man."

*Perhaps it is you who are crooked, and I am unbent,* the Crooked Man said, and his voice was like the beating of a thousand Ashes' wings. He stood and beckoned her over to the living river of fire. *The Alchemists and Fiddlers are always on my mind. I have seen how they have taken the gift of stardust and used it to crooked ends. Wars and divisions, slavery and injustice, monstrous destruction of living things. I have seen their suffering and their many troubles. You, also, seem troubled.*

In the Crooked Man's presence, Wren felt shame and regret fall on her like a heavy blanket. He had once intended her to help cleanse the stardust, and now here she was, captive to Boggen and unable to do anything. She didn't dare look into that wise face.

*You are weighed down by fears, Little Bird. Why is that?*

His words gave Wren the courage to look up. Her father had called her *Little Bird* when she was very young and still did sometimes, and the sound of that familiar nickname was so solid in the midst of all the uncertainty of being on Nod and Dreamopathy and whatever it was Boggen had done.

And like a young child, Wren poured her story out. How afraid she felt—first, when she began to lose her control of the stardust, and then when everything had gone wrong at the gateway, and here on Nod where all her friends were prisoners, and . . . she forced the words out. "Boggen marked me. I belong to him now."

The Crooked Man looked at her with kindness. *Only if you choose. Boggen's spell can be broken if you wish it.*

Wren's heart began pounding. "How?"

*You cannot belong to him if you belong to another.* The

Crooked Man knelt and cupped his hands, scooping up some of the starfire, which danced in his palms like a living thing. *Starfire cleanses. Refines. Purifies. Consumes.* He looked at her solemnly. *And, yes, destroys.* He got to his feet and beckoned toward the river of fire. *If you step into my starfire, you will no longer belong to Boggen. You will no longer be a slave to fear.* The light from the starfire danced across his features like the rippling of the aurora. *You will belong to me.*

Wren gulped and stared at the river. Her old fears arose and doused the hope she had felt at his first words. Belong to him? If what he was saying was true, she could be free of Boggen, but at the cost of becoming someone else's apprentice. And who knew what kind of person the Crooked Man really was? Sure, he said he cared about the Fiddlers and was their guardian or whatever, but how could she know for sure? After all, there were those legends . . . the rhythmic pounding at the back of her neck grew stronger, the pulse of fear racing through her veins. Surely there was some other way.

"Is that it, then?" Wren said wearily, exhausted by the battle within. "I either belong to him or to you. I *must* belong to someone? Will I never be free?" She was beginning to wish Coeur hadn't rescued her from the animachine. It had only prolonged the inevitable. Being captive to someone until the end.

*And why is it that you think freedom comes from not belonging?* The Crooked Man held out a beckoning hand, and it seemed as though the starfire in his palms had somehow spread, a current of fire running over his whole form, pulsing with life and energy. *I am offering you freedom, Little Bird, if you would open your hand to receive it.*

Wren felt something within her respond. Something from before Boggen's mark, from before her failure at the gateway, from before Jack almost died, from before she was even a Fiddler. Something that was a part of her very nature, her Wren-ness, knew that what he was saying was true. The starfire *was* the only way to be free of Boggen and his fear forever. She rose to her feet and walked to the river's edge.

"Will it hurt very much?" she said in a small voice.

*Do your fears not hurt you? When you have a wound, you must cleanse it. With healing comes a sting that lasts but a moment.*

Wren didn't think that this was a very satisfactory answer, but she didn't think she'd get anything more from the Crooked Man. He was already in the river, the starfire in it responding to the starfire in him, sending waves of warmth toward Wren.

She hesitated for a heartbeat on the edge. She had said she'd do anything to be free of Boggen, and here was her opportunity. She took a deep breath and plunged into the river.

The world around her disappeared in a blaze of red and orange and heat. Not a heat that burned her flesh, but one that started at the crown of her head and rippled like a wave, kindling every fiber of her being all the way down to her toes. The living river tightened around her, squeezing her core until she thought her ribs might break, but after a heart-stopping moment she felt herself growing stronger, her very bones filled with the starfire. And then the pain came. The spot where Boggen had first claimed her began to spread and wrapped around her neck like it would choke the life out of her. She screamed in pain, a wrenching cry that came from the gut, and then it was over, the spell undone, the throbbing that called her to the east, the heavy weight of Boggen's hold on her, only fully recognizable now that it was gone. In its place was the most beautiful sense of peace she had ever imagined.

She opened her eyes and gasped. The river of starfire leaped around her, not only flames of red and orange but a torrent of rainbows, the essence of living stardust itself surrounding her and strengthening her. Some time later—afterward Wren never could be sure how long her unshackling took—the Crooked Man led her back to the shore.

"So am I your apprentice, then?" Wren asked, the sound of her own voice surprisingly strong in her ears. In fact everything about her felt strong and new, as though, like the fire of a phoenix, the starfire had unmade and then made her.

*I make all things new. You will not be my Apprentice. You will be my Child, Little Bird.*

He produced out of nowhere a flask of the sweetest water Wren had ever tasted. As Wren drank, all the scratches and scrapes from before, the bruises she had from her training among the Outsiders melted away.

"That is good water," she said, wiping her mouth on her sleeve and studying the flask.

*Indeed.* They sat for some moments in companionable silence, the Crooked Man with his hands folded across his stomach, Wren studying the magnificent display of color around them.

*What is it you want, Little Bird?*

Wren didn't know what to make of this. Her new-found freedom from Boggen had driven everything else out of her mind. But as her thoughts turned toward the present, she realized that there were so many things she wanted: to find Robin, to figure out how to get the Outsiders' help, to save Mary, Jack, and Cole, to set the captives free, to get back home, even to sort out her own problems with the stardust. And suddenly, Wren knew that was exactly what she wanted. Now that she had tasted freedom, she wanted even more. She wanted to be free not just from Boggen, but from her own plague of magic—the way the stardust taunted her with its fickleness, from the out-of-control spiral of emotions she'd first known as a Weather Changer to the inconstant block she now experienced. The tight box of memories and emotions stuffed deep inside her chest rattled and jumped, and this time there was no ignoring it. She began to cry.

*Do not be afraid,* the Crooked Man said as though he was aware of her very thoughts. *You fear what you are, but take courage.* The scene shifted into empty space, where a box floated in darkness. Instantly, Wren knew that the box represented her: all her fears and emotions—the

anger and worry, and joy and happiness, too—that she
had been terrified would get out of control again. *Take
courage. Open the box.*

Wren shook her head. She didn't want to open the
box. She didn't want the kind of power that came
from stardust, didn't want to keep hurting people like
that. The image of the moment when she killed the
hovercat, made even worse by the knowledge that they
didn't want to be predators, flashed through her mind.
Then came the heart-stopping second when Jack's falcon tumbled down to its death, like a movie clip on
replay. And finally, the scene she'd relived a thousand
times, when her defensive rhyme had sent Jack's magic
shooting back at him, and left her friend nearly dead
on the floor.

*I don't want it,* she thought. *I don't want the stardust.*
And then she knew. She wasn't burned out. She wasn't
losing the magic. She had simply blocked herself from
using it, and perhaps she was okay with that.

The Crooked Man showed her a pendulum, a ball
of rainbow light swinging from one side to the other,
arcing through the darkness with slivers of color. *Some
have embraced the power of the stardust with no thought for
restraint.* The pendulum swung one way, and Wren

knew the Crooked Man was speaking of Boggen and the Magicians who never limited their power. *But denying this gift out of fear chokes out the good as well as the bad.* The pendulum swung back, and Maya's face came into Wren's mind. She thought of the way the Outsiders hated stardust and lived a life-or-death existence that rejected any possible good that could come from magic.

*Neither unrestrained power nor crippling fear will serve you well.* The pendulum swung back and forth, filling the darkness with the regular rhythm of the rainbow. Wren thought she understood what he was saying, but she still felt frightened.

*Do not be afraid. Open the box.*

The box was back, sitting alone in the middle of the darkness with a thick velvety ribbon tied around it in a nearly perfect bow. Wren took a deep breath and willed the box open. The bow unraveled, and the box disappeared, leaving behind a gemstone clear as crystal and radiant with light.

*Stardust is a gift. Being a Weather Changer is a gift.* The gem pulsed with light. *You are a gift, Wren. I've freed you for a purpose. Take my starfire and wield it as only you can, that you, too, might make all things well.* As Wren began to believe it might be true, that what she was might actually be a gift she could offer to the world, she felt the tightness in her chest melt away. The place deep inside of her, the same place that had first believed the Crooked Man, stirred to life. As though it were a scene playing out before her, she saw how she could weave the starfire into a cleansing stream, how *that* was what the Ashes meant when they said the Crooked Man would show her what to do at the right time. Hot tears leaked from her closed eyelids. Life and warmth and emotion were returning to her. The fear and worry over what might go wrong was dissipating, and the deeply felt song of joy was replacing it. *Thank you. Oh, thank you.* She opened her eyes wide to look at the Crooked Man, but he was gone. The entire scene had disappeared, and she woke in the early morning light, alone by the ashes of Simon's long-dead fire.

She would have thought it had all been an invention of her overactive imagination but for the feeling in her chest. The connection to Boggen was, in truth, gone, and the fearful box she had held on to for so long had been replaced with a sense of peace. She sat up, looking over at Simon's sleeping form, wondering if she should wake him and tell him her good news. As she did, she felt something heavy in one of her pockets. She stuck a tentative hand inside and fished out a jagged, clear gemstone filled with a liquid that danced with flames of fire. It had most definitely not been an invention of her imagination.

She decided not to tell Simon about the dream. She cradled the starfire stone in both palms. She wanted to keep the treasure the Crooked Man had given her for herself. Perhaps, like her magic, she would know in time how to share it with others.

# NINETEEN

*Animals, animals, huge and gray,*
*Open your mouth and gently bray.*
*Lift your ears and blow your horn,*
*To wake the world this sleepy morn.*

The stillness of the morning was broken by the sound of contented murmurs from a nearby flock of animachines that looked like sheep more than anything else. Now, with her fresh perspective, Wren wondered how she could ever have been frightened of them at all. She rose, stretching, and left to get some water. The valley was surprisingly peaceful, with a gentle breeze ruffling her hair and the soft lowing of the sheeplike animachines as they began feeding on the spongy ground cover. Wren walked for some time, soaking up the stillness of the morning and opening her eyes to the alien beauty of Nod.

Wren wondered how different the history of Nod could have been if it had been founded on peace instead of domination. As she made her way past one of the rocky outcroppings, she stopped, frozen in place by what she saw. There, etched into the pillar on Nod as surely as it had been back in the city, was a bird in flight, the symbol of the Outsiders. What would the Outsiders have marked way out here in the middle of nowhere?

Wren bent down, running her fingers over the symbol. It didn't look old or weathered; it must have been relatively freshly cut. She traced the path of the markings, following the series of birds as they led her through the rocky spires to the other side of the valley. There, she lost track of the markings, but the ground led upward in a swell that looked out onto the next valley. Wren climbed it, seeing in the distance what must be the Outsiders' island. As she crested the hill, she gave a little cry of surprise when she saw the low building that crouched on the other side. She had seen it once before, back in the dream where Robin had brought Wren to her laboratory. There it was: Robin's hidden lab!

Inside, Robin's lab was in disarray. Wren pulled one of the matches she had pilfered from Maya's hut from her pocket and struck it against the wall to light it.

Tools were scattered across the tabletops. The ashes in the dish Robin had so conscientiously kept filled had long since gone cold. Wren righted a chair that had toppled over, bending closer to note a set of drag marks on the floor. She drew the match closer, following them. Had someone taken Robin from the room by force? The tracks led outside the small hut and to a cave hidden from sight by a large outcropping of purplevine. Wren hacked at the plant, shredding its ropy stalks until she could push her way into a cavern that pulsed with an unnatural glow.

The whole thing had been meticulously modified to house a giant apparatus hanging from the center of the roof. The semicircle hung within a frame of connected triangles, and flares of sickly stardust flashed and sparked across its surface like bolts of lightning. Beneath a glass dome, the apparatus was honeycombed with a million carved niches, but it wasn't those that drew her eye. It was the figure hanging from a harness in one of the triangles.

"Robin!" Wren cried, rushing forward to stand below the girl. Robin's form was still and motionless. "Robin?" The girl gave off a small snore. She was fast asleep. Wren scanned the room. There was nothing for it but to climb up herself. Bracing herself against one of the triangular frames, Wren saw that it would hold her weight. She pushed off with one foot, boosting herself up, and swung over to the next. The first few were easy, but the higher she climbed, the more dizzy she felt. Her breath came in quick gasps, and she felt a curious spinning sensation whenever she looked down. But with one final push, and a painful swing over to the triangle just below her sleeping friend, she was able to reach Robin's boot.

"Robin!" Wren jiggled her foot. "Wake up."

Robin's snoring cut off and she mumbled something unintelligible. Wren yanked harder on her foot. That did the trick. Robin woke, looking around bleary-eyed.

"Where am I?" she murmured, and then, catching sight of Wren: "Hurry! You must leave the dream! She'll find you!"

Wren was baffled. "I'm here in real life, Robin. You've been asleep."

"But how?" Robin's eyes were wide open now. "I just left you in the dream. We were in my lab." She looked around her, panic crossing her face as she realized things were not as she expected. "You're here on

Nod?" She began struggling then, her harness swinging wildly as she worked to get free.

"Hold. On." Wren grunted, maneuvering herself up another frame so she was nearly level with Robin. She saw that Robin's harness held her fast with buckles. She began pulling on the straps, starting with Robin's wrists, so the girl could help free herself.

"How long have I been asleep?" Robin asked, deftly loosening the bonds around her ankles.

"A week? Maybe two?" Wren guessed. She had lost track of the days since she'd arrived in Nod. "Wait. You're telling me that you've been asleep this entire time?"

"And you're telling me that you're surprised?" Robin slipped off the final bond, and moved her muscles with a groan. "By now you have to know she'd do anything to stop me."

Wren watched open-mouthed as Robin easily maneuvered her way across the triangular frames and swung down to the ground with a grunt. She rubbed her back. "All that sleep has made me weak."

Wren worked hard to imitate Robin's descent, and her questions came in short bursts. "Who's trying to stop you?" She swung from one bar to another. "And why have they imprisoned you here?" Wren slipped and dangled wildly by one hand before finding her grip. "Wherever here is."

"One of Mother Goose's secret laboratories," Robin said from the ground. "We thought they'd all been destroyed, but we were wrong."

"Mother Goose?" Wren dropped to the ground and stared around her wonderingly. "Someone found one of her old labs and stuck you in here? But why?"

"Not someone," Robin said, giving Wren a curious look. "Mother Goose herself imprisoned me."

"Mother Goose is alive?"

Robin barked a laugh. "Oh, she's alive. And well hidden, right in the middle of the Outsider camp. No wonder we all thought she was dead." Robin was attacking the purplevines with a vengeance, but it was obvious she was weakened from her captivity.

"Here. Let me," Wren said, retracing the path she had made coming in. "So Mother Goose is one of the Outsiders?" Wren wiped the sweat off her forehead. The remarkably resilient purplevines were already growing back together.

"Mother Goose is *the* Outsider. Maya herself."

Wren stopped cold. "Maya?" She gaped at Robin.

"But she *hates* stardust."

"Exactly." Robin pushed past her and stepped into the daylight. "That's why she was so upset when she found out that I'd contacted the Alchemists and other Magicians. I thought we could all work together, but Maya can't stand the thought of compromise. She's too stuck on what happened back during the plague. For her, the only solution is to destroy all the magic on Nod." She rubbed her forehead. "She's even sending nightmares to scare people out of using the magic."

"Mother Goose is the one sending the nightmares?" What Robin said made sense. It fit in with what Maya had already done in sneaking around trying to empty Boggen's wells. She told Robin what she knew.

Robin snorted. "It doesn't surprise me. For all her talk of courage and honor, I'd wager Maya's the most fearful of them all."

Wren nodded. She thought of what the Crooked Man had said, how the pendulum could swing too far toward fear and paralysis. They were back at Robin's lab now, and Robin was already talking about all she needed to do. Making contact with her supporters in the city. Finding out how things stood with Boggen.

Discovering the location of his stronghold.

"It's to the east," Wren said in a quiet voice. "Near obsidian mountains."

Robin stared at her, mouth hanging open for a second before she said, "How can you possibly know that?"

Self-consciously at first and then more confidently, Wren told her story: how Boggen had plagued her nightmares and waking dreams, how he had marked her as his apprentice and tried to summon her in such a way that she could pinpoint his location.

"I don't know for sure it's his stronghold, but it's as good a place to start as any."

Robin was eyeing her warily. "But if you know where he is, what's to say he doesn't know exactly where you are?"

Wren laughed. Of course Robin would be worried. She had heard only half the story. "I forgot the most important part!" She described how the Crooked Man had freed her, though words failed her when she tried to explain the starfire's magic.

Robin's eyes grew wider and wider with each new revelation until Wren got to the part about the river of starfire. She whistled and sat down on a wobbly stool.

"That's amazing," she breathed. "So the legends about him . . ."

"The legends are true," Wren said. Now that she had told her tale, she felt a little wobbly inside, as though she had let Robin see into her very soul. She fought the old temptation to shut down and hide away. "I think they've been misinterpreted. Starfire will destroy Nod, but only the things that need destroying."

Robin nodded. "Like refining metals. You heat them up so hot that the impurities come to the surface, where you can remove them."

"That's exactly what it was like." Wren nodded slowly.

"So where is the Crooked Man? How do we get him to come use his starfire on the tainted stardust?"

Wren paled a little and joined Robin on the stool next to her. "He sent me," she said simply, realizing how ridiculous it sounded. She, who had just admitted to once being Boggen's apprentice, was now the one Robin was supposed to trust.

To Robin's credit, she didn't even hesitate. She didn't ask Wren how she planned to do it, or whether she really thought it would work, and Robin's faith in her bolstered Wren's own faith in herself.

"Okay," Robin said, turning around and shoving papers across the tables. "There are several mountain ranges to the east. Maybe if we find the right map, you'll be able to—"

"Wait," Wren said, looking at all the Dreamopathy equipment. "Can you show me how to use this?"

Robin did not waste any time when she heard that Wren meant to contact Jack, a spy among Boggen's forces. "That's very dangerous." There was admiration in Robin's voice. She opened a hidden container of stardust and carefully weighed it out, setting the Dreamopathy compass spinning. Soon, a mirrorlike surface—much bigger than the one Wren had managed the other night—shimmered in front of them.

Jack's startled face appeared shortly afterward. It was wet, and Wren could see fresh bruises.

"We found him when he was awake," Robin said. "This will be trickier to maintain." She hurried back to the compass.

"Jack!" Wren rushed toward him. "Are you all right?"

Jack looked over his shoulder nervously. "You shouldn't be here, Wren. Boggen could come in at any moment." He leaned close. "It's bad. They've started experimenting on Cole and Mary. It's really bad, Wren."

Wren gasped. "Did you find out where the strong-hold is?"

Jack winked, and a flicker of his old liveliness crossed his face. "I sure did, but it cost me my freedom. They've brought me to it now." His mouth twisted. "Boggen wasn't happy with my snooping. I'm his prisoner, too, Wren."

"Oh, no!" Wren exclaimed. "We'll be there soon, Jack. We'll rescue you."

"Where is the stronghold?" Robin's voice was sharp, all her attention focused on Jack, who rattled off some foreign-sounding locations.

Robin snatched a map off a crowded table and began marking things. "Beyond the illuminated lakes. Near the Valley of the Shadow. Okay. Got it."

"Don't lose hope, Jack!" Wren pleaded with her friend. She was worried by the frantic look on his face, the way he reminded her of a trapped animal. "Help is coming."

Jack gave her a weary but hopeful look before the mirror shimmered and disappeared into thin air.

When he had gone, Wren was eager to get back to Simon, but Robin had other ideas.

"I've got to contact Winter," she said, hurriedly preparing the ingredients for another Dreamopathy rhyme. "Going back to the city to find her will take too much time."

Wren saw that she was right and moved close, studying the practiced way she used the equipment. Robin was clearly a skilled Fiddler, and soon Winter's surprised face appeared in front of them.

"Robin!" Winter cried. "Where have you been?"

"Time for that later," Robin said, impatiently waving away her question. "Your work in the city. Have you gathered anti-Boggen crew members?"

Winter's face was all business. "The citizens of Nod are growing tired of Boggen's tyranny. Many still don't believe us, but at last count we had nearly two hundred who stand with us, ready for your command."

Wren did a double-take at Robin. Who was this girl? Why was Winter, who had seemed so in charge back at the rally, deferring to her? And why would two hundred full Fiddlers be prepared to follow someone so young?

But, as Robin had said, there would be time for questions later. Besides, Winter wanted to know more about the location of Boggen's stronghold. Wren described what she had seen in as much detail as possible, though without the long explanation of how she knew. Winter would gather her crew and meet them at the Valley of the Shadow as soon as they could march from the city. Robin had a few other instructions for Winter as well, which Winter accepted with curious deference, and then the interview was over.

As the flame on the Dreamopathy table flickered out, Robin studied Wren. "Where are your other crew members?" She shook her head with a little smile. "I mean, the other Alchemists. Will they help us?"

"Simon will," Wren said without hesitation. "As Jack said, the others are imprisoned. But the Outsiders owe me a favor, and I think it's time to collect."

Robin looked impressed at this information, and then her mouth formed a thin line. "Yes. I owe a visit to the Outsiders as well."

Wren frowned at the Dreamopathy equipment. It would be counterproductive to use magic to contact them. "We'll have to do it in person. Come with me."

When Wren and Robin arrived at Simon's camp, they didn't find him alone.

"Vulcan!" Wren cried, waving at the figure just

arriving on Simon's falcon. "You're here!"

Vulcan dismounted easily, as though he'd been riding falcons all his life. "That never gets old," he said, unstrapping a pack of food and handing it to a newly woken Simon.

"It's great to see you, Wren," Vulcan said, and then awkwardly began rummaging through the foodstuffs. "I mean, your time with the Outsiders seems to have suited you." He knocked the pack off the stump. "I mean—"

"I know what you mean," Wren said. "I feel different, like I can take on the world, you know?" Maybe someday she would tell Vulcan about what had happened by the river of starfire.

Vulcan dropped the food he was trying to put back.

"We may have to take on the world," Robin said, looking at them both with an amused smile. They gathered together for the morning meal, making introductions all around and telling the others what the girls had learned from Jack.

"Boggen's at the stronghold now, and it's where he does all his research, too. We have to move fast, though, before he suspects anything's amiss," Robin said.

"Vulcan." Wren set the roll she was eating aside.

"What about the Scavengers? Are they willing to help?"

"Of course!" Vulcan said. "We've gathered a lot of support in the past few days. There are plenty of Magicians who would like nothing better than to dethrone Boggen. I can return to the city right away and notify them."

"Some of the animachines will want to help." Simon got to his feet. "They are quite passionate about freedom. When do we attack?"

"As soon as possible," Wren said, getting to her feet. "Today." She turned to Coeur, whose invisibility had worn off in the night and who was now preening her feathers. "But first Robin and I must visit the Outsiders. They have a bargain to keep."

Wren hurried up the path through the Outsiders' farmland, Robin struggling to keep up at her side, but hiding it very well. It seemed that days of inactivity had made her weak and breathless. They had flown Coeur directly to the Outsiders' island in order to confront Maya. Wren was counting on the Outsiders' fierce animosity toward Boggen to work to their advantage: she was nearly certain they would want to help fight

Boggen and free the captives; she wasn't so certain that they would do it side by side with the animachines.

Robin was more confident. "Mother Goose will do anything to keep her identity hidden. Believe me, she'll help."

Wren nodded, wondering if it wouldn't be better for Maya to come clean about her past once and for all. Wren herself knew the folly of keeping things shut up and hidden. But perhaps there would be time for that later. They would need to hurry in order to join Winter and the others at the valley. Boggen would not give up willingly, and things would likely come to the use of force. They needed as many allies as they could muster.

Wren raced past the Healer's hut and the outlying hovels, sparing a fleeting thought for Auspex. She hoped he was well again, but then she was in front of Maya's hovel, ringing the little bell that hung outside.

Maya's sunburned face seemed even more hardened than Wren remembered. "Wren. So you escaped the animachines," she said, and the surprise that momentarily fluttered across her face at Robin's appearance turned into what looked like displeasure. "And found another whose hands are dirty with stardust. *Traitor*," she spit at Robin.

Wren was flustered. She hadn't expected a welcome with open arms, but she hadn't thought that Maya would be so hostile.

"It's you who are the traitor," Robin said without malice. "Not because of what you were. Mistakes can be forgiven. But because of who you are now. Hiding and lying. Sending nightmares and trapping allies." Robin's cheeks flared red and her words grew hard. "Your fear of magic could have destroyed the Outsiders. Still could unless you agree to help us stop Boggen."

Maya folded her arms across her chest with a frown and a stubborn expression that Wren had come to know well. Perhaps a gentler approach was in order.

"Outsiders are defined by courage and honor," Wren said, and Maya responded with a gruff nod.

"I know you will honor your agreement to help me free my friends," Wren continued. "And I know you also want to stop his horrible experiments on other innocent people. Of course, it will take a great deal of courage."

A steely glint came into Maya's blue eyes, along with something else. Wren wondered if it could be a glimmer of fear.

"Wren?" Auspex's face popped out from behind Maya, and he had a warm smile for her. "You're all right!" He bowed deeply then, pushing past Maya and kneeling. "Courage and Honor, Wren. You saved my life when you slew that beast."

"Oh, Auspex, I'm so glad you're all right!" she said, helping him to his feet. "But it's not like that at all, about the animachines, I mean. They're not hostile, they're just frightened!" She saw Maya's cold gaze and stumbled over her words. "But I guess there'll be time to talk about that later." She was nervous, made more so by the frown that creased Maya's face, but she didn't have the box deep down inside to shove everything into anymore. So Wren let herself be nervous and get on with things anyway.

"What's this about whether or not we will rescue prisoners?" Auspex gave Maya a slight nod of deference. "The Outsiders would like nothing better. Once we know where Boggen's stronghold is, we can—"

"We know where it is," Wren said, meeting Maya's gaze. She wondered if behind all the hardness lurked a fear that drove her. Maya gave her a grudging nod, and Wren knew that she would keep her bargain.

"And today is the day we destroy it," Robin said,

and she spoke as one with authority.

Auspex bowed his head with the same deference he had shown Maya earlier. "It will be as you say. I will gather the Outsiders."

# TWENTY

*Hey diddle, diddle!*
*The fire and the fiddle,*
*The falcon flew up to the tow'r.*
*The little girl laughed to see such sport,*
*And evil was stripped of its pow'r.*

With Maya and Auspex hastening them along, nearly the whole settlement had procured weapons and set off in no time at all, leaving the few young children with the even fewer elderly Outsiders. Wren flew on Coeur's back, instructing her falcon to go slowly and keep low. Robin, whom all the Outsiders clearly held in respect, led the way to the place where the allies had all agreed to gather. The others kept a steady pace behind her, their slow trot matching the speed of Coeur's flight.

"I still can't believe what you say about the animachines," Auspex said, glancing up at Wren as he jogged across redbush-covered flatlands. "If it is true, we have wronged them greatly over these many years. There is no courage or honor in killing them when we can live peaceably together."

"*If* what the girl says is true," Maya said in a hard voice that plainly indicated she doubted the fact, "we will deal with the issue of the animachines later. Even if they are sentient, they are still products of twisted magic." Her mouth was set in a firm, thin line. "No compromise."

"Please promise not to attack them, okay? At least not today," Wren shouted down at them. That part of the plan hadn't gone so well. The Outsiders had agreed to an uneasy truce with the animachines, but only until the prisoners were freed and Boggen was defeated. For now, it would have to do.

There was little conversation on their journey. The Outsiders needed their energy to keep up their quick pace, and Wren found that, despite her newfound confidence from the encounter with the Crooked Man, she was still physically exhausted. Even with the few stops they made to rest, she was worn out when Coeur landed among the tight formation of city dwellers gathered around Vulcan, Robin, and Winter. Robin led Wren ahead a few paces to consult.

"According to your description and our map, the stronghold's entrance is through that pass there." Behind her, the foothills of two obsidian mountains loomed, shiny black in the afternoon light, providing a natural route that was narrow enough for only a few people to enter at a time. "The prisoners are kept in the stronghold when they're not being used for research." The cliffside behind was honeycombed with alcoves that reminded Wren of a warped version of the Crooked House. Instead of the familiar welcome of those balconies, however, there were bars over these apertures, and streams of sickly gray smoke trailed into the polluted sky. The whole exterior was coated in a yellow pulsing barrier that thrummed with magic. Wren recognized it as the same color she had seen behind Boggen.

"It's a shield," Vulcan said, coming up behind them. "That's how Boggen's kept the prisoners captive. Simon said it was similar to a substance from your world. *E-lectruck*"—Vulcan stumbled on the word—"*e-lectruck-city,* that's what they called it. Does that mean something to you?"

"Electricity!" Wren echoed. "An electric shield! No wonder the prisoners can't escape."

"Oh, yes!" Vulcan said. "We should warn the Outsiders. They will surely die if they touch the shield, or at least that's what Simon said."

Robin was instructing Winter, and Wren was surprised to see that the city dwellers responded to her like the Outsiders had, as though she was their leader.

Vulcan scanned the horizon uneasily. "Where is Simon?"

"We don't need this Simon. Or the animachines," Maya shouted, waving her crossbow above her head, and the Outsiders cheered behind her. "We will fight Boggen's evil magic. No compromise!" At the sound of her battle cry, the quiet facade of the stronghold transformed. Dark shapes appeared on exterior balconies and scurried down ladders, lining up into ordered rows of troops that stretched across the width of the mountain. More henchmen poured out from the pass between and began to march in tight ranks toward their foes.

Simon's voice came from Wren's shoulder. "It looks like it's not going to be peaceful after all, doesn't it?"

"Simon!" Wren exclaimed. "Am I glad to see you!"

Simon was astride a hovercat, the other animachines

following behind him in glistening silver ranks. The Outsiders nearest them gave the animachines a wide berth, with suspicious glares for their historic foe.

"Get those beasts away from my crew," Maya hissed, and Wren motioned Simon to the side.

"The Outsiders have agreed to keep the truce," Wren told him. "But it would be better if you and the animachines kept your distance." Simon didn't have a great number of animachines, but the ones he did have were formidable in their own right. Ranks of hovercats were in the front, and there were the sheep and wolf-like versions as well. A few flying ones soared overhead in menacing arcs.

"Spiders, too?" Wren whispered when she saw the awful shapes lurking near the back.

"Spiders are animals like all the others," Simon said in an unconcerned voice. He was staring hard at his animachines, and Wren wondered if they were communicating. She saw them shift, spread out in a different formation, as Boggen's henchmen drew near. It appeared that they were prepared to fight.

"Outsiders, ready!" Robin called, and they peeled off into smaller clusters of twos and threes that looked too eager to attack the forces that were headed their way. "They have starspears," Robin warned, pointing at the stardust-powered weapons strapped to their enemies' backs. "So watch for an attack from above."

Then, all of a sudden, the wall of henchmen stopped, parting down the middle to provide a long walkway back toward the pass, and coming down the center of it was Boggen himself.

"Go home," he boomed in a menacing voice magnified to carry across the entire plain. At first, Wren's body froze, instinctively waiting for the pain to bloom in her neck or the crippling fear to overtake her body.

*He has no hold on me.* Even though Wren's heart beat faster and every sense was alert to danger, Boggen couldn't control her. She belonged to the Crooked Man now, and she carried starfire. At the thought of it, strength and courage surged through her, chasing any temptation to fear away.

Now Wren could see Boggen more clearly. He was taller and stronger, his form covered with dark spiked armor and crowned with a helmet that looked like a beetle's. Boggen looked inhuman, as though he belonged more with the obsidian mountains than with the Fiddlers that surrounded him.

"Nod cannot exist without stardust," Boggen was

saying, "and we will have no stardust without my new research. The few must be sacrificed for the good of the many. It is the only way that Nod will survive, and you are foolish to try to stop me." He leered at them, his features twisted into hate. "The Outsider wench is right. There is no room for compromise." He threw back his head and laughed. "The Alchemists learned as much." He pointed to something Wren hadn't noticed before. The pass stretched up between the two mountainsides, and a glass box swayed between them at a dizzying height. Figures crouched in the glass box, figures Wren, with a sinking sensation in her stomach, recognized.

"You think to scare us with your empty threats?" Robin spit at Boggen, raising a crossbow to aim at his helmeted head. "None of us fears death. There is courage and honor in fighting you."

Wren looked back with horror at the glass prison. Jack was up there. And Mary and Cole. She was glad Robin was drawing Boggen's attention. She began to inch sideways, toward where Coeur was roosting near the back of the Outsiders' armies.

"They will have a perfect view of your destruction." Boggen laughed, too long and too loud, and Wren felt prickles of fear all up and down her spine. "Apprentice!"

Boggen's wicked gaze locked on her. "You have long eluded me. But no longer. Come to me, Apprentice. You will wield my magic against my enemies."

Sudden realization hit Wren. If she had still been under his power, she would have obeyed. She knew it as sure as she knew anything, and the horror of the future Boggen had intended for her loomed. She would have gone to him and betrayed her friends, betrayed everything they had fought for. She could see that Boggen was growing impatient. He reached out a spiked arm and beckoned imperiously, so sure was he that Wren would come cowering.

Instead, she stood still and straight. "You are wrong, Boggen," she said in a loud, clear voice. "You will not win this fight. Your evil will not overcome the good just as darkness cannot overcome the light. All *will* be well." She remembered the Crooked Man's words and drew comfort from them.

Boggen's eyes widened in amazement at her rebellion, but he quickly masked his surprise. He flicked a gauntleted hand at her as though he were flicking aside an insect. "Foolish words from a foolish child."

"You're a monster," Vulcan said, pushing his way

out in front of the others. The lifelong animosity of someone who had lived and suffered under Boggen's oppressive rule was written plain across his face. "You won't get away with this."

Boggen drew one arm up and flung it across his chest, funneling an arc of tainted stardust straight toward Vulcan. Vulcan dove to the side, and the magic hit where he had been standing, searing a smoking hole into the ground.

"You cannot defeat me," Boggen said in a deadly quiet voice. "But I will enjoy watching you try." He raised both arms, and Wren saw the glint of silver underneath his armor.

"He's transformed himself," Maya gasped, and the horror in her voice was enough to help Wren interpret what she was seeing. Where there should have been pale flesh, silver-plated skin rippled in the sun. Black horns stuck out from Boggen's back like a porcupine's spine. Boggen had made himself into an animachine.

"Abomination!" Maya shouted. "He's using twisted magic! No compromise!" The Outsider roar echoed her cry. *No compromise!* The hunting cries of the animachines joined them, and the forces behind Wren thrust forward with fury to engage the enemy.

"Vulcan!" Wren cried. She lost sight of her friend when the two armies surged together with a clash of weapons. She hoped that he would be safe, but she knew she couldn't help him now. Instead, she pushed her way to the rear of the eager Outsider army and found her falcon. "Fly hard, little Coeur," she said as she climbed up.

Wren had become so used to living a magic-free life that it took her a few moments to recognize what was happening. Boggen's henchmen were using stardust. Their starspears fired flaming missiles that hit with surprising accuracy. A hovercat cried in agony as one reached its mark, but Coeur flew on. Boggen's armies were fierce, their stardust spears flashing blue fire as they fought, but they were not prepared for the flying creatures. The animachines swooped and clawed, easily plucking henchmen two and three at a time from the ranks of fighting Magicians. Until Boggen joined the fight. Bolts of the twisted form of electricity he had created arced through the air, scattering searing missiles among her allies. Coeur climbed higher, dodging the streams of magic and the Outsiders' crossbow bolts alike. Over the battle and up past the cages that covered the mountainside. Now that Wren was closer she could see that people were inside, people whose faces were pressed up against the yellow shield. Men, women, and children, all of them trapped in Boggen's stronghold.

"Save us!" they called to Wren as she flew past.

"Take my son," one woman with a small boy hugging her knees cried. She pressed up against the barrier and then jumped back with singed palms. "Save him!"

Wren felt hot tears sting her eyes as she saw the emaciated faces. "I will come back for you," she shouted, but she didn't think the captives heard. Up and up she flew, until the cages disappeared and the fortress turned into sheer rock. Ahead of her she saw the slick glass walls of the highest cell, and inside were her friends.

She could see them mouthing her name from their walled-off prison, and she instructed Coeur to fly closer. Mary was frantically calling to her, trying to tell her something, but Wren couldn't make it out. She reached out a hand to the clear glass, and something invisible sent a jolt into her arm that seared through her body and into Coeur's. The falcon emitted a horrible shriek and began to fall.

Wren saw Mary's face crease in alarm, saw their mouths open in anguish as she and Coeur spiraled down, spinning out of control. "I'm sorry," Wren saw Mary say.

"Coeur!" she screamed. "Coeur, fly!"

Coeur gave a weak cry and a feeble flap of the wing.

"Please, Coeur!" Wren whispered. "Please don't die."

Coeur's wings beat harder, catching air and hovering in place. They were no longer falling. They were ascending, climbing, and Wren heaved a sigh of relief that was soon supplanted by panic. What was she going to do? Fly up there and get shocked again? She had been so focused on releasing the others that she hadn't thought about the fact that Boggen's spell might extend to their prison as well. How in the world was she going to save them?

And then in an instant she knew. She knew exactly how she was going to save the others. The echoes of the Crooked Man's voice reverberated inside her, and she reached for the gemstone full of starfire. That was what had destroyed the plague. That was what made all things well. *Save the others,* he had said. *Use your gift to save the others.* The legend was true. The Crooked Man's starfire would destroy Nod, and, in so doing, save it. Coeur was nearly back at the glass cage, and she heard a cry of alarm from the ground. Boggen had spotted her, and his rasping voice was issuing orders.

"Shoot the falcon down!" Boggen roared. "Stop that girl!" But Coeur flew on, higher and higher, until she was once again hovering in front of the glass box. Wren urged her on, past the glass prison and up to the very top of the mountain, where she could see the source of the yellow shield pulsing with energy. She cupped her gemstone in her palm, the brilliant heat of the amber liquid filling her with life and strength. Was she doing the right thing? Would this even work? And with the thrumming of Coeur's wings, she felt the answering thrum of her own heart. *Yes.*

She shut her eyes, remembering the feel of the river of starfire around her, drawing on the peace she felt deep inside. Once, being a Weather Changer had made her magic go awry, stirring up a storm along with her conflicting emotions. But now, the starfire was a part of her, and her identity was aflame with the magic. "Like refining metal," Robin had said, and Wren kept that image in her mind as she wove the starfire, letting it flood into and through her, whipping the air around her into a cloud of burning wind. Bronzes and oranges and golds enveloped her, circling the stone in arcs of living starfire. She wove it together, sending a pure jolt of starfire at the pulsing yellow shield, and the two energies met in a powerful clash. The tainted Magician-made electricity met living fire, and the top of the tower exploded in a brilliant flare of light. Heat from its combustion blew Coeur backward, and Wren scrambled to grip her feathers so she didn't fall off. The bird spun, cartwheeling wingtip over wingtip before regaining her balance. The yellow shield was cracking, jagged bolts of lightning creasing down the exterior, shattering the prison doors for so many. From below, Wren heard cheers as the shield began to fail at the lower levels. Captives poured forth from their cells, empowered by all the injustice they had suffered and the residue of starfire, and came upon the enemy from behind. The confused rear guard of henchmen turned to face them, but it was too little, too late. The prisoners overpowered them, grabbing the henchmen's starspears and snapping them in starfire-powered justice. Boggen's massive army was crunched between its foes—the animachines and Outsiders from the front, and the newly freed from behind.

"Wren!" Jack was calling to her from the glass tower.

"Wren, quick!" Wren coaxed Coeur near, and she felt like crying when she saw her friends. Mary's face was thin and haggard, and she could barely stand. Cole was folded into a thin heap on the floor, bruises covering his skin. Jack looked like he might not make it at all, but when she was near enough, he climbed on Coeur's back. "Take me through the pass. Hurry!"

"But what about the others!"

"Forget us!" Cole said in a hoarse voice. "Go with Jack!"

Wren didn't stop to ask questions. Even if she had tried, it wouldn't have mattered. Jack was urging Coeur on, flying straight through the narrow gap between the two mountains and into the stronghold.

"Boggen's well of power is back here," Jack shouted in Wren's ear. "The final source of all his tainted stardust." He coughed, and Wren could feel his thin frame rattle behind her. "Can you do whatever you did at the shield again there? If we destroy that, Boggen's done for."

Wren looked at the stone that still burned in her palm. There were still a few flickers of amber flame dancing there. "Maybe. But I don't know how we'll get close enough. The blast back there nearly killed me and Coeur."

"Let me worry about that," Jack said. They landed, and Jack slid off, racing toward a flight of steps that were cut into the mountainside. "It's up here," he said, taking the steps two at a time as Wren followed after him more slowly, her breath coming in exhausted gasps. The jolt of tainted stardust had sapped her strength. She bent at the waist, trying to catch her breath as Jack hurried on ahead.

Jack ran out onto a rocky balcony next to the neon pool of liquid Wren had seen in her waking dream.

"Stop!" Boggen's voice came from a hidden crevice in front of her, but it wasn't the rasping one he had used with the armies; it was the coaxing version she had heard once before, back when he had manipulated Jack. "Don't do this, Jack. Don't do this, my son." Boggen's inhuman body creaked out of its hiding spot toward Jack. He ignored Wren completely, and stood between her and Jack. Up close Boggen was even more horrible than he was from a distance. He had lost half of his face, and a metal plate covered one eye. Flesh and steel blended together in a monstrosity that chilled Wren's blood.

But that wasn't what made Wren freeze on the stairway. It was the sight of Jack, standing on the balcony, listening to Boggen with a hungry look on his face.

"My son," Boggen continued, as if he could sense that Jack was desperate to hear those very words. "Don't fight me. Join me, as you once did before."

Wren watched in horror as Jack turned away from the last well. Jack, who had betrayed the whole world once before.

"Jack!" Wren shouted. "Don't listen to him!"

Boggen howled in displeasure and turned to aim a spell at her, but it had no effect. The tainted stardust simply melted off her. Wren took advantage of Boggen's confusion and tried to dart past him. Jack might be frozen under Boggen's spell, but she was free.

Boggen was fast. One of his mechanical arms snaked out and clamped around her waist. His spells might have no effect on her, but that didn't mean she was invincible. All he had to do was not use stardust. Wren struggled against her bonds. She couldn't believe she had been so foolish.

"If you touch one drop from my well, my son," Boggen said. "The girl dies."

Jack tilted his head as though considering Boggen's words, and he leaned back against the obsidian wall behind him, his arms folded jauntily across his chest.

"And what will you give me if I help you?"

Wren's eyes bulged in horror. Jack couldn't do this. "No!" Wren screamed, until Boggen's gauntleted hand smothered her mouth.

"Now that sounds more like my son," Boggen said.

Wren bit down hard on Boggen's gauntleted hand. Fortunately, not all of him was machine yet, and he yowled with pain, flinging Wren away with violent force.

All of the breath whooshed out of her as she tumbled down the rocky staircase. The world went dark for a moment, and then her breath returned, though all she could manage was a hoarse croak. She began to silently creep back up the stairs. Boggen had reached the balcony, and all of his attention was directed at Jack.

"For starters, I'll need you to stop calling me your son," Jack was saying with a cocky grin.

"Whatever you like, Jack." Boggen worked hard to shift his expression into a fatherly smile.

"There's another problem," Jack said, his face twisted into a frown. "I can't use the magic anymore."

Wren inched forward, one painful step at a time. She knew how powerful Boggen's hold could be on someone. She believed that Jack had meant what he said back at the airship, that he really wanted to make things right. But without starfire, what could he really do against a powerful Magician like Boggen?

"A pity," Boggen said, "but not an insurmountable problem. I will make you a suit like my own. Together, we will rule Nod. We belong together, Jack; surely you see it."

*"Belong together?"* Jack barked a hoarse laugh. "The only people I belong with are my real friends, and you are not one of them." Jack, thin and weakened as he was, put up his fists as though he was going to punch Boggen to death.

Wren felt like cheering. Jack wasn't lost to Boggen! Wren knew she couldn't make it to the balcony in time. In a flash she knew what to do. Fanning the starfire into flame, she held the gemstone aloft. "Jack!" she yelled. "Here!" and she threw it with all her might.

It arced up toward the balcony, whipping the air around them into a frenzy of bronze and yellow fire.

Jack caught it with a triumphant cry. "Your heart is as dark as the magic that's given you power. Let's see how you do without it."

"Jack," Boggen said, taking a step closer, but it was to be his last. Jack threw himself into the well, the living fire of Wren's gemstone meeting Boggen's tainted magic. The whole balcony exploded in a brilliant blaze of white light.

The blast blew Wren back, and she fell on her shoulder with a sickening crunch. "Jack!" She scrambled past the burned-out form of Boggen's suit, past the withered frame of what must be Boggen's real body, which was moaning in pain. Up the cracked stairs to the remains of the balcony.

Her friend lay there, his body still among the ashes. Wren started sobbing. "Don't be dead, Jack, please." She felt for his pulse, her breath coming in ragged sobs. "I can't do this, Jack. Not again!" His wrist was cold and limp in her hands. She looked around frantically for the gemstone. Was there the tiniest bit of starfire left? She could hardly keep her hands still, they were shaking with her sobs, but there—she held her breath—there was a faint flicker.

"Oh, please, Jack," she begged. "Stay alive." The flicker grew stronger, his pulse beating with the rhythm of life and breath, and then Jack opened his eyes, his beautiful blue eyes.

"Wren," he said when he saw her face, and he gave her his crooked grin. "I've had the most wonderful dream. The Crooked Man was there. He said you knew him?" Tears leaked out of his eyes, and he smiled through them. "Wren, he gave me my magic back."

# TWENTY-ONE

*Ring around the starfire,*
*A pocket full of flame.*
*Ashes, ashes,*
*We'll never be the same.*

**W**ren walked through the makeshift camp in the glimmering moonlight. Despite her exhaustion, she felt a deep sense of rightness with the world. They had done it. They had destroyed Boggen's corrupted stardust and liberated the captives. With Boggen's demise, for his Magician-made body could not survive without a power source, the rest of his henchmen had quickly surrendered, handing over their now-useless starspears to stone-faced Outsiders. All Wren's allies had agreed that it would be better to camp in the valley than make the journey back to Nod overnight, but everyone was too excited to sleep.

Groups of newly freed prisoners laughed and feasted around hastily built campfires. The Outsiders had procured food from somewhere, and the smell of roasting meat filled the air. In one corner of the camp, a rotating crew of animachines guarded Boggen's henchmen. Wren recognized one face among them. William's scowl turned into scientific interest as she passed. She could imagine what he was thinking— how he'd like to study the girl who once was Boggen's apprentice, the girl who had wielded starfire. His thirst for forbidden knowledge had taken him to an evil place, and after all that had happened, it still drove him. Sometimes a person could be imprisoned by invisible bonds stronger than any made of iron. Wren passed by him filled with pity. Perhaps he, too, might choose freedom one day. Until then, he would receive justice for his crimes once the new Fiddler Council was elected.

"It's too much to have power concentrated in one person," Winter had said, and now she was hemmed in by Auspex and a mixed crowd of city dwellers and Outsiders who were arguing politics.

"What we need is someone who can be a voice for

the different groups on Nod," Auspex said, his face serious.

Winter nodded. "Perhaps it's time for the Knave of Hearts to lead us. All of the city dwellers respect the Knave."

Wren felt a tap on her shoulder and turned to find Mary and Cole behind her. Their faces looked worn and haggard but also full of joy. "Well done, Wren," Cole said solemnly, but Mary enveloped her in a hug.

"Thank you."

"You're welcome," Wren said with feeling. "But it's really the Crooked Man you should thank. Without him, I'd have betrayed you all, and Boggen would still reign here." She told Mary and Cole what had happened to her, and Cole nodded thoughtfully.

"So the Ashes were right about the Crooked Man," he said.

"How wonderful!" Mary had tears shining in her eyes. "Not just for Nod, but for the Crooked House as well! We must let Astrid know as soon as possible. Tell the others to look through the old archives for whatever they can find about starfire." Mary was all business again, listing the things they needed to do, but her words brought Wren up short. Wren had been so caught up in events on Nod that she hadn't thought about Earth in some time. Or how they were going to get back there.

"But will we be able to? Return to Earth, I mean?" Wren asked in a small voice.

Mary stopped mid-instruction to Cole about how he needed to contact the Ashes immediately, her mouth working as though she hadn't even considered the possibility of anything else.

It was Cole who answered. "The taint on the stardust is cleansed," he said. "And we live in a city of Magicians who kept excellent research logs. We should be able to create a new gateway in time. With the help of starfire."

"Which is why you must get a message to the Ashes immediately . . ." Mary picked up right where she had left off.

Wren felt relief wash over her. However much she liked Nod, she didn't want to live here forever. She would have to ask Cole later how he intended to communicate with the Ashes. She thought how nice it would be to see them and to sit by the river of starfire and find out what the Crooked Man might like for her to do next. He had been right. Belonging to the starfire wasn't like belonging to Boggen had been. Wielding the starfire was when she most felt like who she was supposed to be.

Mary and Cole were deep into their plans now, and Wren left them to it. She hoped that their guidance would help further good relationships between Magicians and Alchemists. Wren wove her way past city dwellers caught up in merrymaking. They, too, had tasted the bitterness of treachery, if only for a short while, and seemed all the more determined to celebrate their freedom.

She headed deeper into the camp, where someone handed her a mug of something frothy and tried to get her to join them for a toast, but Wren shook her head with a sigh. The only reason she couldn't fully celebrate was that despite all they had accomplished, she still hadn't found Vulcan. She was worried about him. The other Scavengers hadn't seen him since the battle, and there had been no sign of him among the Outsiders, the city dwellers, or even the prisoners. Wren should know; she had stood there while hundreds of prisoners poured out of the interior cells—some as young as five years old. She was glad to see them now with smiling faces and full bellies and a promising future.

Wren wondered if Cole might know something about using Dreamopathy to contact non-Dreamers. Perhaps with his help she could try to find Vulcan that way. Wren turned back toward them, but then she stopped. A lone figure was walking away from the camp, and Wren recognized the gaunt, upright silhouette.

"Maya!" Wren called, but the older woman didn't slow. Either she didn't hear Wren or she didn't care. The fading light nearly hid her from view, but Wren hurried to catch up. She hadn't yet thanked the woman for fulfilling her part of the bargain.

The night was still and somber farther away from the camp. Wren felt the quiet envelop her like a blanket, with only the occasional laugh carrying on the air. The smell of purplevines drifted toward her, and then Wren was among them, the fragrant plants the color of twilight itself.

"Maya!" she called again, but there was no answer. Far up ahead, where the plants grew thick, there was a flash of blue-green light that flickered and grew stronger.

*A starlamp?* Who was out here making a starlamp? Wren made her way toward the light, but some instinct inside her warned of danger. She crept quietly forward. Now that she was trying to remain unnoticed, every move sounded blaringly loud to her ears. The crackling undergrowth echoed in the silence, and Wren was sure she would be found out.

"Maya?" she whispered. If the woman was near, perhaps they could confront this new mystery together, but when Wren arrived at the source of the light, she found no sinister person, no escaped henchman. Instead, there was a pool of shimmering liquid the color of moonlight. Wren knew at once it was touched by magic, and Maya was crouched down in front of it.

"Maya?" Wren asked quietly. "Are you all right?"

Maya stood in the shadows, her arms folded across her chest, a hard look on her face. "You know who I am, child. You know what I've done."

"I know about Robin. I know you sent the nightmares." Wren met her gaze. "I know you're Mother Goose."

Maya nodded grimly. "There is nothing more I can do, I'm afraid. I'm sorry that I've failed—I've failed you all."

"What do you mean?"

Maya steeled her face for condemnation. "Because

of me, thousands died." She looked at Wren pleadingly. "You see now why I had to stop it? Why I had to keep people from using the magic? That was the only reason I touched the stardust again. To scare others away from it. I thought that if the wells were empty and the city dwellers were afraid of another plague, then they'd start over, build a magic-free colony like the Outsiders have done." She was nearly crying now. "You see what the magic has done, don't you, Wren? You saw what Boggen did with his research?" It was almost as if Maya was looking to Wren for absolution, as though if she could convince Wren, then she could convince herself. Maya dropped to her knees and began shaking her head, as if she was battling with two internal voices. "Sometimes one has to compromise; you see that, don't you?"

"Maya," Wren said gently. "I know that running from the magic will never free you from it." She knelt down by her friend. "Your magic is a gift. You are a gift. Someone very wise taught me that."

Maya shrugged her hand off. "I killed thousands of people, Wren. That isn't a gift; it's a curse."

"It doesn't have to be," Wren said. "Come with us. Back to the camp. Tell the others who you are. Ask for forgiveness."

Maya laughed a brittle laugh. "You don't know the Outsiders, Wren. Nor the city dwellers. Best for me if I stay on my own."

"Here?" Wren looked around the empty cavern. "How will you survive?"

Maya tightened her jaw and looked out into the dark forest. "There are Upas trees three miles that way."

"Maya, no!" Wren remembered what Auspex had said about the trees' deadly poison. She wouldn't let Maya throw her life away. "Come with me."

Robin's voice came from the shadows. "The Outsiders will follow you. We need everyone's help if we are going to reform Nod." Robin's words were hard, like she was working to get them out.

Wren realized that Robin had been listening the entire time. "You see?" Wren said. "Others will forgive you, but you will have to forgive yourself."

Maya didn't say anything, but silent tears streamed down her weathered cheeks. She stared in the direction of the Upas trees and then swallowed down her tears as if coming to a decision.

"I will go with you, but not for forgiveness," she said to Wren. "Running away is too easy a fate for one such as me." She set her face like stone. "Courage and Honor."

Wren looked at her sadly. Maya was choosing to punish herself, but there wasn't much Wren could do about it. She clasped her friend's arm and gave her a warm smile. "I'm glad." She was relieved that Maya wasn't going to give up. Perhaps with time, Maya, like Jack, would be able to find forgiveness.

Maya led them back to camp, and when they came in sight of it, the revelry was in full swing. Music filled the air. Wild couples dancing and children swinging each other in circles greeted their eyes. As they stepped into the firelight, a ripple of curious whispers came in their direction.

At first Wren was baffled. Surely no one else knew that Maya was Mother Goose. And then she saw that the freed prisoners weren't whispering about Maya at all, but about Robin.

"The Knave!" shouted a little girl in front of them. "The Knave of Hearts is here!" Word spread fast, and as they walked deeper into the camp, they collected an entourage. Robin had apparently spent time with every faction on Nod. Prisoners had heard about her from Boggen's people. Outsiders knelt and gave her the strange cross-like gesture of respect. Even the city dwellers cheered at her approach.

"The Knave!" The cry resounded until Winter and the others found them. Winter drew Robin over to their fire and set her up on a rough stool someone had found.

"Good people of Nod," Robin said in a clear, strong voice. "You have been very courageous, very long-suffering, very compassionate." She nodded at the Outsiders, newly freed captives, and city dwellers in turn. "We all have felt the oppression of Boggen and his twisted power, and that time is over." There was a hearty cheer for this, and Robin quieted them with her hands. "Now, we have a task in front of us. A task that will require every ounce of courage and compassion you have yet shown. The Legend of Starfire has come upon us. The old Nod has been destroyed, and we must seek the counsel of the Crooked Man in order to build anew." She paused, looking directly at Maya. "It does us no good to dwell tight-fisted and ruminating on the wrongs of the past. We have all made mistakes, and perhaps the most grievous ones are the ones we've tried to hide. But now we move forward together, working to create a better, more just world for us all." There were more cheers and whoops, and then the crowd swarmed around her. Auspex clasped hands with Robin, and Mary and Cole wanted to talk to her. Winter hovered near her shoulders and children clamored around her legs.

Wren looked past them to Simon, who was over by his animachines. She moved toward him, stopping to scratch a hovercat behind the ear, causing it to send up a machine-gun purr.

"They're amazing," she said to Simon.

"Have you seen the kits?" Simon said, launching into a lecture about how the hovercats were very protective of their young, as though they hadn't all just waged a battle to save the world.

Wren rolled her eyes and followed him over to where a bundle of shiny mini-hovercats lay curled up together in a pile.

"The adults are very brave," Simon was saying. "And fierce, too." His monologue trailed to a stop. "Like you, Wren. I'm glad we're friends."

Wren glanced up in surprise. Simon was studying the hovercats clinically and had moved on from compliments to a speech about what kind of diet the kits needed.

"Me, too, Simon," Wren said. At first she wasn't sure he heard, since he barely even paused, but the tips of his ears grew red, and he gave her a shy smile between explanations of grain types and water sources. Soon he had a new audience. Rocky and Silver came over to introduce Wren to a bedraggled couple that must be their parents, and Simon somehow roped them into helping feed the kits their evening meal.

From across the way Wren heard music, something that sounded like a fiddle, and then there was laughter and calls for more dancing. Maya was stoically approaching a cluster of Outsiders, and Wren hoped she would find the courage needed to forgive herself and escape her burden of condemnation. There was Jack, sitting up against a wagon with a plate piled high with food, laughing and making jokes with a handful of Scavengers. He looked up and caught Wren's eye. For the first time in as long as she could remember, Jack's face looked truly happy. The gauntness and cynical smile had been replaced with carefree laughter. Someday, she wanted to hear the full story, what exactly he had seen at the river of starfire and what the Crooked Man had said to him. A very pretty Scavenger girl sitting next to Jack was frowning suspiciously at Wren, especially when Jack raised his cup toward Wren with a happy wink. There would be time for stories with Jack later. For now, she was glad to see that he, too, was free.

Wren sighed contentedly and reached for a mug and plate from a jovial city dweller who was passing them out to anyone with empty hands. Now she could celebrate. All was well on Nod, and, even better, all might be made well between Nod and Earth. She wished the Crooked Man could be here to see this, to see how everything had worked out in the end. But perhaps, she thought, as she looked out on the twinkling stars in the heavens, he already was.

And then Vulcan was there, one hand extended toward her, an inviting smile on his handsome face. "Wren," he said. "Would you like to dance?"

Wren set her plate and mug down with a grin, a warm feeling replacing the space where the tightly shut up box used to be. "I'd like that very much." She took Vulcan's hand, and together they danced out into the warmth and life of the music.

# ACKNOWLEDGMENTS

My brief words of gratitude can never do justice to the appreciation I feel for all those who have made it possible for me to send yet another book out into the world. I count it a great gift to work with such wonderful people, and I am so thankful for each and every one of you.

Laura Langlie, I am beyond fortunate to call you my agent, and I am grateful for your partnership, insight, and the expertise you offer in every stage of the publishing process.

Erica Sussman and Stephanie Stein, it is such a privilege to have you invest in my books. Your editorial insights never fail to prove valuable, and I have learned a great deal from both of you in the revision process.

Jakob Eirich, once again you have created breath-taking artwork for the cover. I love it!

David Coulson and Michelle Taormina, your talents with lettering and jacket design are matchless! I so appreciate the contributions each of you has made to this project.

I imagine there are many others unknown to me whose hard work at HarperCollins Children's has helped transform my manuscript into this lovely edition. Thank you!

I also want to thank my readers! I'm so glad to be able to share story-worlds with you, and am thrilled that you joined me for another adventure. Thank you for reading!

Finally, this small space seems impossibly inadequate to express how grateful I am for the dear ones who are God's loveliest gifts to me. Griffin, Elijah, Ransom, and Beatrix, you are aflame with God's grace, and each of you makes the world that much brighter. I take great delight in you and can hardly believe that I get to be your mom. Thank you for loving me, your dad, and each other so well. Aaron, you speak life to the core of who I am and live out your love in a thousand small moments. I am heartfelt glad we get to spend our lives together—thank you for choosing life with me.

And to the Lord, who knows all things, I am undone when I think of putting words to the depth of my gratitude. Ever and always, I happily belong to you.

# THERE'S MAGIC
# IN THE WORLD—AND IT'S
# WAITING FOR HER.

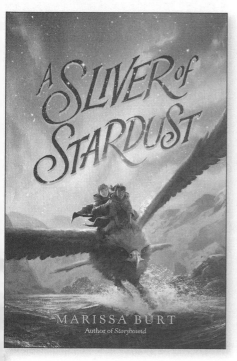

## Don't miss a single page of
## Wren's spellbinding journey!

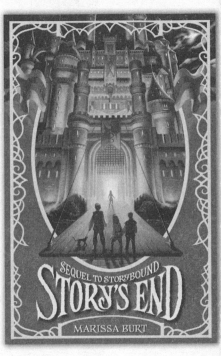